CLOSE QUARTERS

A BREED THRILLER

CAMERON CURTIS

INKUBATOR
BOOKS

Published by Inkubator Books
www.inkubatorbooks.com

ISBN (eBook): 978-1-915275-23-3
ISBN (Paperback): 978-1-915275-24-0

For Jenine

Sancte Michaele Archangele,
Defende nos in proelio;
Contra nequitiam et insidias diaboli esto praesidium.
Imperet illi Deus, supplices deprecamur:
Tuque, Princeps militae caelestis, in virtute Dei,
In infernum detrude Satanam aliosque spiritus malignos,
Qui ad perditionem animarum pervagantur in mundo.
Amen

Blessed Michael, Archangel,
Defend us in the hour of conflict.
Be our safeguard against the wickedness and snares of the
devil
May God restrain him, we humbly pray:
And do thou, O Prince of the heavenly host,
By the power of God, thrust Satan down to hell
And with him those other wicked spirits
Who wander through the world for the ruin of souls.
Amen

- The Leonine Prayer to Saint Michael Archangel

Then war broke out in heaven.
Michael and his angels waged war upon the dragon.
The dragon and his angels fought
But they had not the strength to win.

- Revelations, 12.7-8

MAPS

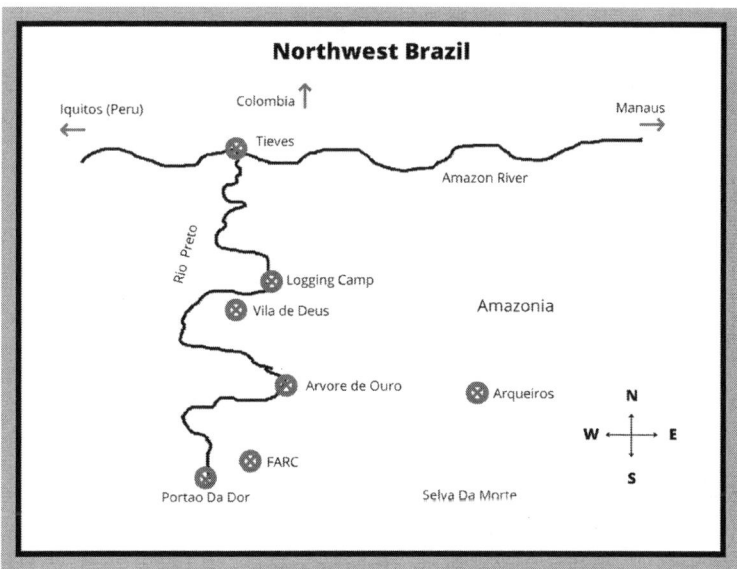

Northwest Brazil

Iquitos (Peru)

Colombia ↑

Manaus

Tieves

Amazon River

Rio Preto

Logging Camp

Vila de Deus

Amazonia

Arvore de Ouro

Arqueiros

N

FARC

W   E

Portao Da Dor

Selva Da Morte

S

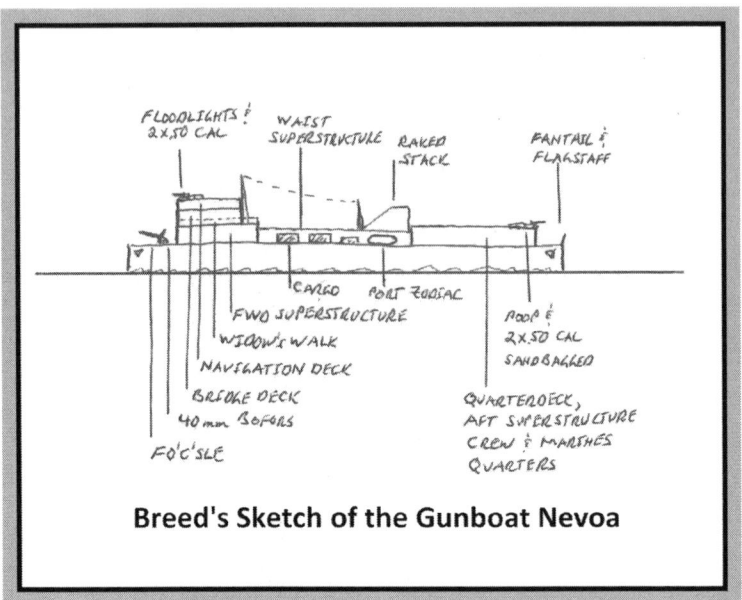

FLOODLIGHTS ÷
2X.50 CAL

WAIST
SUPERSTRUCTURE

RAKED
STACK

FANTAIL ÷
FLAGSTAFF

CARGO   PORT ZODIAC

FWD SUPERSTRUCTURE

WIDOW'S WALK

NAVIGATION DECK

BRIDGE DECK

40 mm BOFORS

FO'C'SLE

POOP ÷
2X.50 CAL
SANDBAGGED

QUARTERDECK,
AFT SUPERSTRUCTURE
CREW ÷ MARINES
QUARTERS

Breed's Sketch of the Gunboat Nevoa

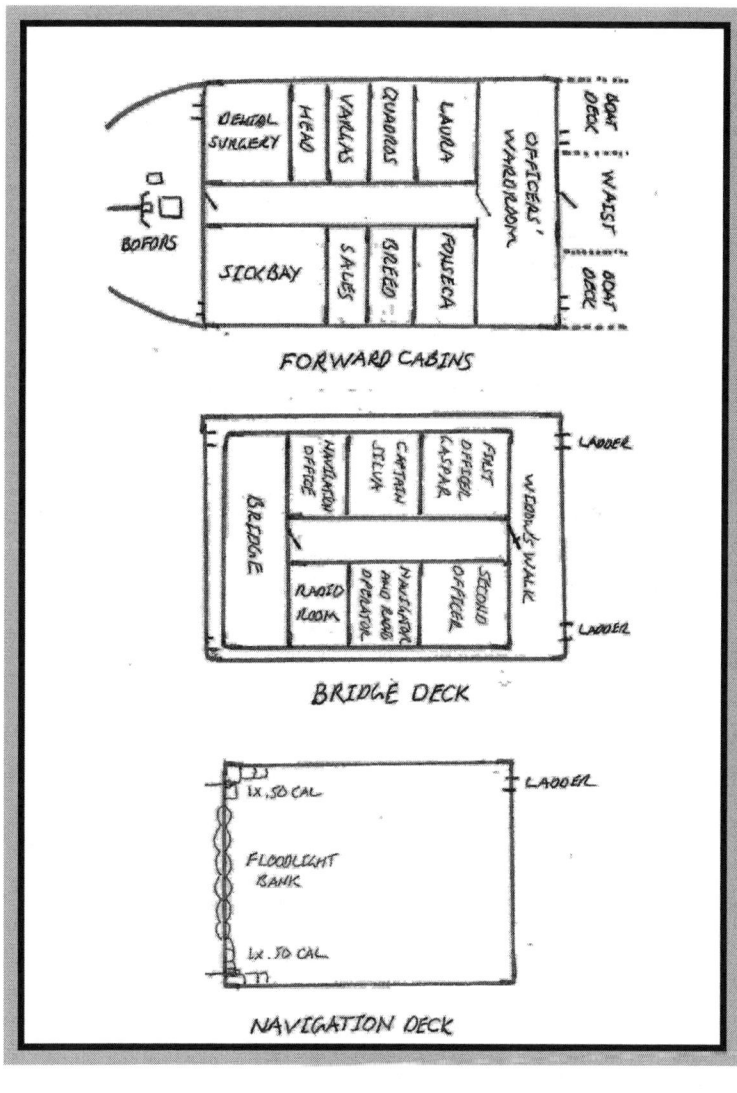

FORWARD CABINS

BRIDGE DECK

NAVIGATION DECK

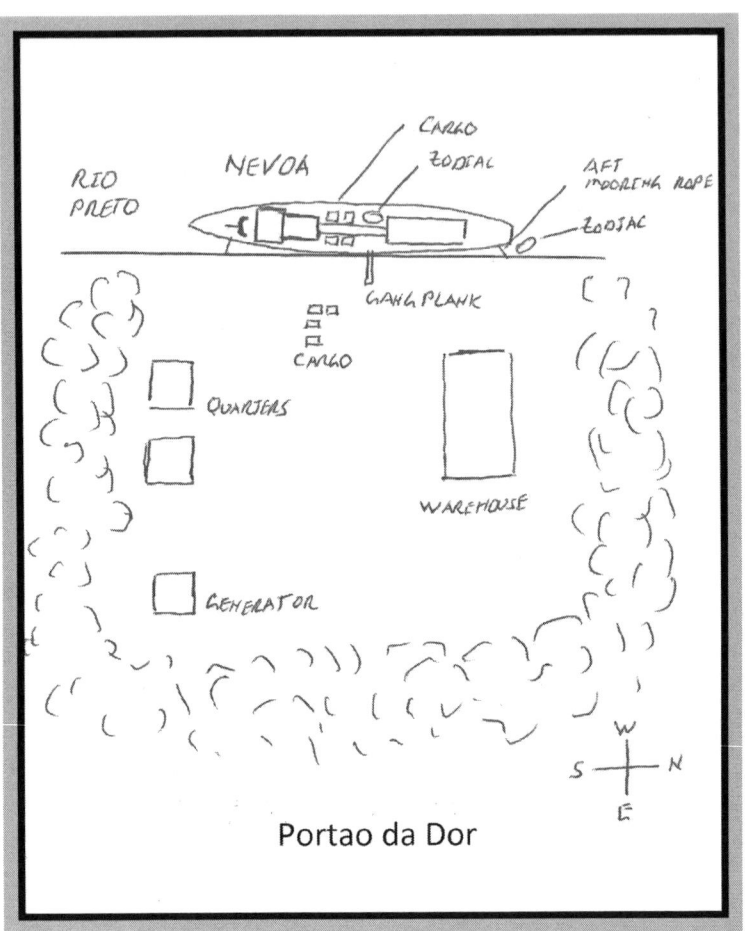

RIO PRETO

NEVOA

CARGO

ZODIAC

AFT MOORING ROPE

ZODIAC

GANG PLANK

CARGO

QUARTERS

WAREHOUSE

GENERATOR

W
S — N
E

Portao da Dor

1

KUNAR, 2005

Javelin

I focus my binoculars on Forward Operating Base Jericho.

Mortar explosions send geysers of rock and dirt skyward. The log and stone bunkers remain silent. The base is a moonscape. Troopers have gone to ground, sheltered inside the dugouts and trenches.

FOB Jericho is located at the extreme north of the Arwal valley. Its mission is to prevent the flight of Al Qaeda units to the north. It also blocks infiltration of Taliban fighters to the south.

It does neither job well. FOB Jericho is a shooting gallery. It is garrisoned by a company of the 173rd Airborne Brigade. The FOB had been located on an outcrop of a nearby mountain. Impossible to resupply, except by air. The base was moved to its present position when the garrison became isolated. Flat ground on the west bank of the Arwal river.

The Taliban don't have air resupply. On their backs, they

hump weapons and supplies over mountains. With the strength of mountain goats. They have mortars in protected positions, and snipers overlooking the FOB. The snipers act as observers and direct artillery onto the base. Sometimes, they carry PKM machine guns onto the mountain and place them outside M4 range. Drop plunging 7.62mm machine gun fire on the Americans.

"We're supposed to go in *there* for extraction?" Keller shakes his head. "Breed, I'd rather *walk* home."

My Delta team have spent the last week hiking the high mountains of the Hindu Kush. We located a major Taliban base camp and mapped a caravan trail leading east to Pakistan. Now all we want is a ride home. But helicopters will not land on an FOB blanketed with mortar fire.

We half-lie, half-sit in a ditch next to the road. Consider our options.

"Sure," Lenson says. "Let's walk over to the next bus stop."

"They'll call in air support." Hancock glances at his watch. "Get this all cleared up."

"We're supposed to own this valley," I say. "Are we going to let Hajji tell us when we can come and go?"

Keller takes a bite of a Baby Ruth. "They do all the time. Ask the boys in there."

I swing my binoculars to cover the base. From a log and corrugated tin structure, a pair of paratroopers sprint toward a bunker. With a chuffing sound and a roar, a mortar round falls from the sky. There's an explosion. A fountain of rock, dirt, and galvanized iron sheets spurts into the air. The troopers dive into the bunker.

"Damn," I say. "The Talis just blasted the outhouse."

"That settles it," Keller says. "We are *walking* to the next bus stop."

"Let me have that radio," I say to Lenson.

Lenson passes me the handset.

I lift it to my ear. "One-Four Juliet from Five-Five Actual."

"Go ahead, Five-Five Actual."

"We are a quarter click outside your north wire. Pass the word to your boys we are coming in."

Keller groans.

The radio crackles. "Five-Five Actual, we are taking fire. Maybe you want to hold off."

"Negative, One-Four Juliet. We are on the way. Pass the word."

"Roger that, Five-Five Actual."

As team leader, it's my decision. We shoulder our rucksacks. My rifle is an M24 7.62mm sniper weapon system. I'm carrying eighty pounds in a special lightweight titanium frame. An astronaut's backpack, custom-built for my loadout. Thirty pounds of spare ammunition, food, and field rations. Across the top are fifty pounds of Javelin anti-tank missile. The disposable launch tube looks like an oversized dumbbell. It's a thick tube that contains the rocket. The forward cap protects the missile's infrared seeker head. Strapped behind it is the Command Launch Unit—the CLU. It's a portable screen that provides sighting for the missile. Night and thermal imagery for operators.

I look at three unhappy faces. "Let's go."

Get to my feet, run in a low crouch toward the wire. There's four hundred meters of flat, clear ground. It ends in a concertina fence with a wooden gate. Across the top of the gate is a sign that reads:

FORT JERICHO

THIRTY YARDS behind the fence is a trench. Sandbags, and the muzzle of a tripod-mounted M240 multipurpose machine gun. The helmets of paratroopers are visible over the top.

The paratroopers in the trench call out to us. "Push it open, man. Door ain't locked."

Keller and the team on my heels, I barrel through the gate.

More chuffing sounds. Another roar. I pile into the trench. The rest of the team roll in behind me.

KABOOM!

The mortar round explodes between the trench and the main bunker complex.

"You guys get this all the time?" I ask.

"Like clockwork, dude," the paratrooper grunts. "They want to delay the sixteen hundred supply helo."

"That's the bus we want," I tell him.

"Not today, brother. We need air support to clear that mortar. *Then* the sixteen hundred bus rolls in. At eighteen hundred."

"Fuck that. Where's your CO?"

"He's at the Ponderosa. That's the main bunker twenty yards back of us."

I poke my head up, scope the terrain.

"That mortar team's on the reverse slope," I tell him.

"No shit, Warrant."

"So who's spotting him?"

Mortars are indirect-fire weapons. They lob shells over terrain features like hills, trenches, trees and rivers. When out of sight of their targets, an observer is required to spot the fall of rounds and direct their fire.

"They've got some Hajjis overlooking the valley."

The paratrooper's friend chimes in. "Yeah. Occupying the old digs we gave up for *this* hole."

I look back at the team. Under fire, everyone is a professional. Everyone is an adult. "Let's go see the CO," I say.

Pile out of the trench, run for the Ponderosa.

Mortar rounds bracket us as we run across the open ground. I hear Keller sucking wind behind me. It's not physical exertion. It's adrenaline, from knowing you can be hit by shrapnel at any second.

The Ponderosa is much better appointed than the trench. A short flight of stairs leads into a heavily sandbagged dugout. As we pile in, I see a guy sitting in a small office with a desk-mounted radio.

"One-Four Juliet?" I ask.

"You got it. Five-Five Actual?"

I nod. "Where's your CO?"

"That's Captain Harris," the radio operator says. "Back in the map room."

I push through the bunker into a lighted, sandbagged chamber fifteen feet square. A stocky paratroop captain is studying a map of the Arwal valley.

"Captain Harris." I salute. "I'm Warrant Officer Breed."

The captain returns my salute. "Warrant. We were informed you would be passing our way. Thought you might hold off until we got this shelling lifted."

"No, *sir*. We have orders to get back to Bagram A-S-A-P. We need to catch the sixteen hundred bus."

"A-S-A-Fucking-P? Warrant, today that means eighteen hundred."

"Captain, we're a sniper team. If we neutralize that Tali observer, we can lift the shelling and get the bus here... on schedule."

"Think I don't have snipers and designated marksmen in my unit, Warrant?"

"Sir, I am sure you do."

"Think they are not as mission-capable as a Delta unit, Warrant?"

"Sir, I am sure they are."

"That observer team is a click-and-a-half up that hill, behind boulders. My men have been trying to take them out for two weeks."

"Do you have Javelins on base, sir?"

Captain Harris blinks. For the first time, he notices the dumbbell strapped across my rucksack frame. How could he have missed it?

"Effective to a mile and a quarter, sir. I need a clear line of sight long enough to get a lock. That's all."

"You got authority to spend a hundred grand to get one Tali?"

"We have time-critical intel, sir. That makes this Tali a High Value Target."

"Be my guest, Warrant. Knock yourself out."

"Thank you, sir."

I ASSEMBLE THE JAVELIN, remove the missile's caps, and fire up the CLU. The thermal sight is equipped with its own built-in cooling unit. While I wait for device to make itself ready, I scan the mountainside with binoculars. Next to me, Keller has his own binoculars and a laser rangefinder.

"There they are," Keller says. "I make one, two, three Talis with a radio. Reckon it's an ICOM ICV-8 or HT. Folding antenna. Range thirteen hundred yards."

A tough ask for a .308 sniper rifle. Impossible for an M4.

Of course, the Talib is equipped with squad comms you can get off eBay. Simple, cheap, and effective.

I take a sitting position in the shallow ditch outside the wire. We'd tried to get a lock from inside the perimeter, but the Talis were hiding behind a boulder. It was impossible for me to get a direct lock on any of them.

Outside the concertina, I have a better angle. I set the CLU to maximum magnification. By default, the weapons system operates in Top Attack mode. When fired, the missile climbs to altitude. From there, it plunges onto the top of the target on which it has been locked. The top armor of a tank is invariably thinner than its frontal armor. That makes the Top Attack much more effective. Total flight time is between three and seven seconds.

It's great for taking out Taliban who hide behind rocks.

"I've got them." I lay the crosshairs of the sight on the Talib holding the ICOM. That way, if the Taliban scatter, the missile will take out the guy carrying the comms. In this business, details matter. There's enough thermal differentiation between the Talib's body and the surrounding mountainside to lock the seeker head on target. "Firing."

I launch the missile.

The Javelin is a two-stage "soft" launch system. That means the first stage of the solid fuel rocket ejects the missile from the tube. Tosses it fifteen or twenty feet downrange. Then the flight rocket ignites and sends the missile on to the target. The system minimizes backblast. It allows the Javelin to be fired from inside bunkers.

A bright flash marks the ignition of the Javelin's flight rocket. In seconds, the missile is arcing high toward the target.

I set the tube down and grab my binoculars.

Seven seconds flight time is plenty to lay your binos on target. The Taliban jabber at each other. Point at the glowing lance ascending its lethal trajectory. The missile peaks, noses over, and plunges toward them.

The Taliban duck behind the boulder. They look straight up, then cower.

KABOOM!

A bright orange and red flash erupts from the point of impact. Rock splinters, body parts, and torsos are launched into the air amidst a cloud of ugly black smoke. Debris rains on the mountainside.

"Good hit," Keller says.

Silence descends on Forward Operating Base Jericho. The mortars have stopped.

I check my watch.

"Reckon we can catch the sixteen hundred bus."

2

PRESENT DAY

Manaus – The Minister

Augusto Sales lights up a Camel and stares at me. "You will never find Fiadh Connor," he says. "I am not insensitive to her father's anguish. As one man to another, Mr Breed, I tell you she is dead. Lost somewhere in the thirty-three thousand square miles of Brazil's Selva da Morte. Cuchulain has dispatched you to find a wild goose."

We stand at the top floor windows of the Port Authority, a functional government building. The offices up here are plush. The color of a bruise, the Rio Negro stretches from the floating port to the far bank. To my left is the Encontre das Aguas, where the Negro's dark waters merge with those of the Rio Solimoes. Together, the two tributaries form the Amazon.

Ships tied up at the piers are of surprising size. Everything from large container vessels to fishing boats stop at Manaus. The streets are crowded and dusty, choked with clouds of dust particles embedded in a matrix of hot, humid air.

"I've studied the maps," I tell him. "The search area can be narrowed to within six miles of the Rio Preto."

Sales has commandeered the Harbormaster's office. A wide desktop of Amazonas Mahogany. More pedestrian wall shelves have been crammed with shipping schedules and logbooks. Charts, marked with soundings, are spread on a long table. Old watercolors of riverboats have been hung on the walls.

"The maps, the maps." Brazil's Minister of the Interior exhales a puff of smoke and waves his cigarette. "The maps are not the ground. Do you have any idea what conditions are like in that rainforest? Do you know what it means, six miles?"

Sales is fifty, of average height and build. Black hair slicked back, mustache carefully trimmed. He wears a white Panama suit, shiny Burgundy dress shoes, and a cinnamon pocket square. His tie is dark against a silk dress shirt.

"As a matter of fact, I do."

The Selva da Morte is a vast tract of virgin rainforest at the northwest edge of the Amazon River. It stretches south and east from the White Triangle. This is the Triborder between Brazil, Colombia, and Peru. The Rio Preto is a small tributary of the Amazon that cuts through the Selva. From its birth at the heights of the Andes, the larger river runs west to east. Winding through the Selva, the Rio Preto runs south to north.

"Really." Sales does not hide his skepticism. "And where did you come by this experience?"

"Triple-canopy jungle in the Philippines. Panama. Hawaii."

"In what capacity?"

"I was in the Army."

Sales turns to the third man in the Harbormaster's office. "The Army. Mr Breed has been camping in the woods."

"The Selva da Morte is a jungle like none other," Eurico Vargas says. "People die simply from entering. They die months later, *outside* the jungle. From diseases for which there is no name. As if that is not enough, the Arqueiros kill those who enter their lands."

The Arqueiros are a mysterious tribe that inhabits the Selva da Morte. These hunters rarely allow themselves to be seen, and avoid contact with outsiders. Strangers who venture too far into the jungle never return.

I study Vargas. He's a powerfully built man in his early forties. Shiny black hair, brushed smoothly to one side. The part is clean and sharp. He wears a summer suit and a dark shirt, open at the collar. His hands are heavy shovels, mounted on thick wrists. His strong jaw boasts several days of stubble. The shadow barely conceals a jutting cleft chin.

The minister has introduced Vargas as his aide. I wonder what duties Vargas performs. My opinion of Sales has been lowered by his association with this hard man. The minister is obviously a sleazy politician, and Vargas is beyond sleaze.

"Cuchulain Connor wants me to bring back his daughter." I turn from Vargas to Sales. "Failing that, I'm to find out what happened to her."

"You know what happened to her," Vargas says. His tone is ruthless. "Pedro Bernardes died, shot in the back. Before he died, he told the priest that Fiadh Connor and Anna Goulart fled into the jungle. They had been caught in a battle between Arqueiros and a band of armed men. They would not have escaped."

"I don't remember speaking to you."

Vargas's head jerks like I slapped him across the face.

Men who have taken lives recognize others who have killed. That is the off-putting quality I see in Vargas. A casual familiarity with death that treats it as a condition to be inflicted on others. I've killed for my country. Who has Vargas killed for?

Sales squirms. "Your mission has been made clear to us."

My mission—to find a billionaire's daughter, lost in the Amazon rainforest. A week ago, an isolated outpost reported it had been attacked by Arqueiros. With her friends, Pedro Bernardes and Anna Goulart, Fiadh Connor had set off on a crusade. They wasted no time, journeyed to the Selva da Morte to find evidence that the tribe had been provoked. Three days ago, one of Fiadh's friends staggered back to a Catholic mission only to die of a gunshot wound. Fiadh and another girl were missing.

Clashes between indigenous tribes and armed men were not uncommon. Illegal loggers, miners and drug runners barged into protected lands. Killed tribesmen who got in their way.

Volunteers like Fiadh worked with FUNAI, the Brazilian National Indian Foundation. They tracked the Indians, and identified threats from invaders. They reported these to the Army and Navy. If the area was accessible by road or by air, the Army would deal with the problem. If the area was only accessible from the river, the Navy and Marines would handle things.

Vargas glowers. Man-to-man, I can beat him. He thinks he can take me, but this is not the place to test ourselves.

"I have a job to do," I tell Sales. "Your president has authorized me to accompany you into the Selva."

"We have made room," the minister says. "The Nevoa leaves at dawn."

Sales and I shake hands. Vargas stands still, makes no effort at civility.

Conscious of the eyes on my back, I walk to the door.

3

DAY ONE

Manaus – FUNAI

Minister Sales's blunt assessment of Fiadh Connor's fate took me aback. It didn't matter that I agreed with him. I expected him to be more delicate. Cuchulain Connor's investments in Brazil's economy carried weight with Sales's president.

Vargas's intrusion pissed me off. As far as I'm concerned, aides are meant to be seen, not heard. Vargas is a gangster, and he's far too comfortable around Sales. The trip hasn't even started, and already, red lights are flashing.

The heat outside the Port Authority is stifling. It's a typical government office, not at as beautiful as the old Alfandega. I walk past the stately example of 19th century Portuguese architecture. The rubber barons who built Manaus wanted to compete with the best of Europe. They spared no expense.

Eighty-eight degrees. My cotton shirt clings to me. I can feel the sweat soaking my back and under my arms. I avoid the crowds and open-air markets. The humid air stinks of exhaust fumes, mixed with the cloying scent of fruit. The city is a riot of bright colors. A canvas painted by an inspired impressionist. The greens and yellows, oranges and reds... every color appears hyper-saturated.

I make my way to the offices of FUNAI on Avenida Macelo. Push my way through the front door, step into an air conditioned room. My sweat-soaked shirt, plastered to my skin, feels like it has been soaked in ice water.

"May I help you?" A pretty *mestiza* greets me.

"I have an appointment with Manuel Barros."

Before the girl can respond, a wiry man of average height steps out of an office. "Mister Breed," he says. "Welcome! I am Manuel Barros. Father Andrew has told me much about you."

Father Andrew Quinlan, Fiadh's friend and mentor, knows nothing about me. Only that Fiadh's billionaire Dad is paying me a whack of money to find his daughter. Since I left the Army, there has been no shortage of demand for my services.

"Father Andrew's a good man," I say.

"Yes, yes." Barros ushers me into his cluttered office. The sign over the doorway reads *Diretor*. "Please, sit down. Tell me how I can help you?"

I lower myself into the armchair. Barros's desktop is cluttered with stacks of papers and notebooks. Stained with crusty coffee rings. Behind him, a large map of Brazil and neighboring countries has been stapled to a corkboard. Pins with colored beads for heads have been stuck into the map.

"Tell me everything you can about Fiadh Connor and her expedition to the Selva da Morte."

"Of course." Barros straightens. "I have known Fiadh for six years. It is a terrible thing that has happened. Terrible."

I tilt my head. Encourage him to continue.

"At first, Fiadh worked at local missions with well-known native peoples. But one cannot work in the Amazon without hearing stories. Loggers and miners invade protected lands.

They destroy the rainforest, and harm isolated tribespeople. Many tribes have had little or no contact with their neighbors, let alone modern men. Fiadh was troubled by these stories. She sought me out."

"Why you?"

Barros shrugs. "I have spent many years working to protect the Indians. There are uncontacted tribes. To our knowledge, they have never met modern men. We have only heard stories about them from neighboring Indians, or villagers. On our treks to the bush, we have found evidence of their passage. There are other tribes with which we have had contact, but remain isolated. All are threatened by timber and mining interests. FUNAI is the Brazilian Indian Affairs Agency. It is our role to protect the indigenous population."

"How was Fiadh involved?"

"She and her friends worked at missions on the frontier of the Selva da Morte. They volunteered to scout for signs of tribespeople and interlopers."

I shake my head. "A bunch of kids have no business tramping around in there. Didn't you tell her it was dangerous?"

"Of course." Barros shifts in his chair. "I threw her out. But Fiadh has a very strong will. She led her friends into the jungle anyway and reported illegal activity to me. It was good information. I had to act on it."

"She won you over."

"I wouldn't say that." Barros frowns. "She bullied me into using her. Left me no choice. In the end, it was better for me to cooperate. I was able to give her guidance that might save her life."

Slowly, I digest the FUNAI director's words. The girl sounds like the Fiadh that Father Andrew described to me. "Tell me about the Arqueiros."

Barros spreads his hands. "We do not know much about

them. They have lived in the Selva da Morte for hundreds of years. They avoid strangers, but if you get too close, look out. They carry spears, blowguns, and longbows that shoot poisoned arrows."

"Why are they causing trouble now?"

"We think illegal loggers or miners have entered the Selva. Villagers on the fringes of the jungle have been attacked. There have been reports of gunfire. Fiadh told me she was going to find out what was going on."

Barros gets up and points to the map. A wide expanse of green covers the northwest of Brazil. "That," he says, "is the Selva da Morte. It is vast. A number of tribes occupy it. The Arqueiros dominate a large tract that borders Peru and the White Triangle. The White Triangle is the Tri-Border region. It's the junction between Brazil, Peru, and Colombia. The Rio Preto bisects the Arqueiros lands."

"How do they live?"

"They are hunter-gatherers. We have flown over the Selva, looking for signs. Other uncontacted tribes have been found that way. Not the Arqueiros."

"Did you know the boy who was killed?"

"Pedro Bernardes. No. Fiadh had her true believers, but she was the only one who worked with me directly. Most of her friends were volunteers from the Catholic mission. One or two were outright Marxists. Crusaders."

"Was Fiadh a Marxist?"

"Not at all. She was devout. Believed in God, wanted to help people. What she had was passion and the drive to make a difference. As far as I know, she cared nothing for politics."

Barros frowns, stares at his desktop.

"What's wrong?" I ask.

"I do not like speaking about Fiadh in the past."

"I know what you mean."

"I told her," Barros shakes his head. "This time I would not help her."

"What did she say?"

"What else? She said she would do it without my help. She sat where you are sitting. Got up and walked out to pack for Vila de Deus."

"Where's Vila de Deus?"

Barros takes a pen and points to a blue bead pinned to the map. "Vila de Deus is a Catholic mission. It lies on the Rio Preto, fifty miles from Tieves. After he was shot, the Bernardes boy managed to make it back to Vila de Deus. The mission priest could not save him. Reported the boy's death. Reported that Fiadh and another girl, Anna Goulart, were missing."

"Fiadh and two friends alone in the jungle."

"Yes. They had done it many times before. In groups of three to five. Fiadh told me she found it easier to move in small groups."

"Where would Fiadh run?"

Barros waves me over. I step around his desk and we examine the map. "This is the Rio Preto," he says. "It runs south-to-north, winds its way through the Selva da Morte to Tieves and the Amazon. Tieves is a border town. It lies between Brazil and Peru to the east, Colombia to the north."

I squint as Barros traces the river with the point of his pen. He follows it south from Tieves to Vila de Deus, then further. "Here," he says, "is an abandoned rubber plantation. It is called Arvore de Ouro. Rubber used to be a major industry in Brazil. It made many men wealthy. Until cuttings were stolen to plant in the far east. And a blight decimated the rubber plantations."

"You think she ran for the plantation?"

"I assume Fiadh's group became caught between the Arqueiros and a band of gunmen. The encounter would have occurred somewhere between Vila de Deus and Arvore de Ouro. Bernardes was shot and ran north to the mission. The girls... who knows? It would not have made sense for them to run east. That would only take them deeper into the Selva. No, they might run east for a while, to lose their pursuers. Then they would turn either north or south. If they turned south, they would turn for the plantation."

I point to another blue pin stuck into the worm of the Rio Preto. It sits an inch below Arvore de Ouro.

"That," Barros says, "is Portao da Dor."

"What's that?"

"A FUNAI outpost on the edge of the jungle. It is garrisoned by a group of my people, and a small number of Brazilian Marines. The outpost has reported an attack by Arqueiros."

"Brazilian Marines should be able to repel Arqueiros."

"The Arqueiros are savage hunters. We do not know how many there are. Eight Marines and half as many FUNAI workers could be overwhelmed."

"When was your last contact with them?"

"It has been one week since Portao da Dor reported the attack. There has been no contact since. That is why Augusto Sales is mounting his expedition in a gunboat full of Marines."

"Nothing to do with Fiadh."

Barros shakes his head. "Fiadh and her friends would not wait for an official expedition. They set off for the Selva the day after we received Portao's message. Three days ago, Bernardes brought news of the tragedy—and died. All while Sales was provisioning his gunboat."

"How did Fiadh and her friends get the jump on Sales and the Navy?"

"Sales was in no hurry. He took his time preparing his expedition until Fiadh's disappearance forced his hand.

Fiadh's father has influence with the president. That is why you are here. Sales is a political animal. If the Selva da Morte explodes into war between the Arqueiros and illegal loggers, it will look bad for him. Fiadh's disappearance has not been reported in the news. I am sure Cuchulain Connor has threatened to make this affair widely known if nothing is done to bring her back."

"Sales does not want me along."

"Of course not, but he has no choice."

"I met him. He was with a character by the name of Eurico Vargas. A very unpleasant man."

"Yes, there are many stories told about Vargas, but no one knows if they are true."

"What kind of stories?"

Barros and I sit back down.

"Many years ago, there was a gang war in São Paulo. Vargas was an enforcer. Gang members were found stuffed into barrels at prominent intersections. The barrels were filled with oil and set on fire while the men were alive. There were other atrocities attributed to Vargas. His employers were so disgusted that they forced him to leave."

"Does he have a police record?"

"No. There was no evidence linking him to the killings. He left São Paulo and disappeared for a number of years. There were rumors he was involved in smuggling. Then he reappeared at Sales's side."

"He looks like the minister's blunt instrument."

"Vargas shadowed Sales his entire political career. In one case, a man competing with Sales for an office disappeared. It is easy to make a man disappear in the Amazon. If a vessel sinks, the fish leave nothing to bury."

"Aren't they efficient."

"Now, Sales's opponents step aside."

"How long have Sales and Vargas been together?"

"Fifteen years. As long as I have been at FUNAI. When the two men joined forces, they hit their stride. Sales is not a man of violence. Rather, he is corrupt, and fancies himself a ladies' man. It is said not even Sales knows how many children he has. He likes young girls. Uses and discards them. It is thought Vargas picks up his scraps."

"Yet Sales circulates with respectable company at the highest levels of power."

Barros shrugs. "Sales takes money and spends it like water. One shudders to think how much he pays the families of young women he has impregnated."

"In this day and age?"

"Brazil is a Catholic country. Abortion is illegal. The penalty is three years for the pregnant woman. Four years for the person who performs the procedure."

"No one ever talks?"

"Only in whispers," Barros says. "Sales pays the money. Vargas ensures the money is accepted."

How nice. I have to spend the next week with a sleazy politician and his thug.

"You told Fiadh you wouldn't help her. How is it she managed to go anyway?"

Barros shrugs. "Fiadh and her friends have spent more time in the Selva than many guides. It would not cost much to finance a small group. Fiadh and I shared intelligence. She obtained her financial support from Our Lady's Mission of Hope. Failing that, she had enough money to finance the expedition herself."

Most spoiled brats take their father's credit card and go shopping. It takes a special kind of girl to mount a reconnaissance mission into a Forest of Death.

"I need maps," I tell him. "At a minimum, 1:50,000. If you have 1:25,000 it would be better. The whole area between Vila de Deus and Portao da Dor."

"I can help you," Barros says. "That is exactly what Fiadh asked me for."

The Director opens a metal filing cabinet, takes out a plastic zip-locked envelope. Inside are a collection of maps. He spreads them on the table and walks me through the selection. There is a 1:50,000 showing the region. Three detailed 1:25,000 maps of the area surrounding Vila de Deus, Arvore de Ouro, and Portao da Dor. The more detailed maps have been annotated with pencil.

"These marks," Barros says, "were made by Fiadh. She explored the Selva, made corrections in our maps."

"She knew how to do that?"

"Fiadh was competent. She provided us with triangulated coordinates of criminal encampments. We had technical discussions. It is not easy to navigate in the jungle. It is often impossible to register an azimuth. Fiadh was familiar with these issues. We worked around them as best as we could, assisted by GPS and her familiarity with landmarks and trails. An impressive girl."

Of course.

"How many copies of these maps are there?"

"Fiadh and I made several annotated packages. These include GPS coordinates for Vila de Deus, Arvore de Ouro, and Portao da Dor. Trails have been traced, but be aware the jungle is alive. Trails disappear, reappear somewhere else. Each year, the river floods many miles. You will see the same map twice, for different times of the year. Study the maps, study Fiadh's notes. You may borrow these."

I sigh.

"Thank you. Where can I find this Mission of Hope?"

4

DAY ONE

Manaus – The Mission of Hope

Avenida de Setembro is scorching. By the time I pass the Catedral de Manaus, I'm drenched in sweat and smelling ripe. I turn right onto a side street and head north. Our Lady's Mission of Hope occupies the ground floor of a small building, a hundred yards from the cathedral.

The outer walls are freshly painted. Bright pink, with green shutters over the windows. The roof and tin rain gutters are painted the same bright green. The structure is well-maintained and diligently scrubbed. The other buildings in the neighborhood are older and dustier. In need of a wash.

Local women line up at a side entrance. Two women stand behind a table in the doorway, rationing parcels of food. One of the women wears a simple nun's habit. The other is an attractive girl in white T-shirt and jeans.

A boy is sweeping the entrance. His broom has been made with the thin ribs of palm leaves, bound at the handle.

"Where can I find Father Aguiar?"

The boy looks up, expression blank.

"Father Aguiar." I keep my voice low.

"Pai Aguiar." The boy's eyes light up. He gestures toward the front door.

I accept the invitation, turn the metal doorknob, and step inside.

The interior is not air conditioned, but feels cool. From the windows, knives of sunlight slice the room. Everything they touch dissolves into blinding highlights. The black shadows are impenetrable.

"*Posso ajudar?*"

I squint, try to make out the speaker. A tall, thin shadow standing at the door to an interior room.

"Father Aguiar?" I ask.

"Yes." The man switches to English.

"I'm Breed," I tell him. "I am here to find Fiadh Connor."

"It's a terrible thing that has happened." The priest shakes my hand, leads me to a sitting room. He calls out, "Marcelo!"

We fold ourselves into wicker chairs with deep cushions. We sit on either side of a low coffee table, next to an open window. Outside, I watch the women wait in line for their charity. The nun and the girl must be in the next room, behind Father Aguiar.

A bolt of sunlight slashes across the table. The priest is tall and gaunt, with a long face and dark hair. He wears a long-sleeved black shirt and cleric's collar. In this heat. The rest of Father Aguiar's features are cloaked in shadow.

"*Sim pai?*" The boy who enters looks ten years old. Chocolate-skinned, he wears khaki shorts and Nike walking shoes.

"Marcelo, bring us some tea."

The boy leaves as silently as he arrived. Father Aguiar turns his attention to me.

"Fiadh Connor and her friends worked for Our Lady's

Mission of Hope," I say. "What can you tell me about her journey to the Selva da Morte?"

"We have a small mission at Vila de Deus. There were reports the Arqueiros attacked the FUNAI outpost at Portao da Dor. Later, they attacked villagers at the fringes of the Selva."

"Yes."

"Fiadh Connor, Anna Goulart, and Pedro Bernardes journeyed to Vila de Deus. There were reports that the Arqueiros were in conflict with gunmen in the Selva. Illegal loggers or miners. Fiadh wanted to obtain proof this was the case. She was convinced the Arqueiros would never attack unless they were provoked."

"I have heard there are cannibals and headhunters in the Selva," I say.

"That is true. But it is not the custom of tribes like the Arqueiros to seek out victims. Rather, they reserve cannibalism and headhunting for enemies. They absorb their enemy's strength by consuming him."

"I thought we didn't know anything about uncontacted tribes."

The priest waves a hand dismissively. "We know enough, from the tribes we *have* contacted. The people we have relationships with. Those we draw into our flock."

"I see."

"Fiadh was particularly talented. She worked closely with the Indians. Learned to speak one or two dialects."

"One or two?"

"Many of the dialects are similar. I meant she learned to speak dialects spoken by two separate tribes. I have no talent for languages. I cannot tell them apart."

Marcello returns with two cups of tea and a pot. They are balanced on a wooden service that he sets on the table before us. The priest thanks him, and the boy withdraws.

I stare at the shadowy figure, incredulous. "You allowed Fiadh and two friends to venture into the jungle. With open warfare brewing between a tribe of cannibals and a gang of criminals."

The priest sips his tea. "Mr Breed, I assure you... there was no way to stop Fiadh. She and her friends would have gone regardless of what I said."

"But you tried to stop her."

"I cautioned her to withdraw as soon as she had the evidence she sought."

"What did she hope to achieve?"

"Exactly what Fiadh had achieved many times before. She identified the criminals, reported them to FUNAI, the Army, and the Navy. The criminals were arrested or driven off. In some cases, Fiadh forged relationships with the tribes and we brought them to our flock. In other cases, it was necessary for the tribes to remain uncontacted. As you know, they have no immunity to diseases we may bring into the Selva. Something as simple as the common cold can wipe out a tribe."

What a smug sonofabitch. I'd like to wring his neck.

"Tell me about Fiadh's party. Anna Goulart and Pedro Bernardes."

"There isn't much to tell," Father Aguiar says. "Both were young, energetic soldiers of Christ. Anna and Pedro were committed to making things better for the poor of this country. Eliminating the gulf that exists between the wealthy and those less fortunate. They both came from good families. Most of Fiadh's friends did."

Barros had told me of the Marxist strain that ran through Our Lady's Mission of Hope. He also told me Fiadh had not been infected.

But she must have been sympathetic.

"How were they financed, Father?"

"Our mission provided some funds. Enough for provisions, and passage to Vila de Deus."

"Is that all?"

"When Father Camos told us the news, we reached out to the young people's families."

"Where do you think Fiadh and Anna went?"

Father Aguiar shrugs. "They had two choices. Run north to Vila de Deus, or south to Portao da Dor."

"Not that abandoned plantation? Arvore de Ouro?"

"There is nothing for them at Arvore de Ouro. At Vila de Deus, they would find Father Camos and his mission. At Portao da Dor, they would find FUNAI and military assistance."

"What would you do?"

"Father Camos would not have been able to offer them protection. Portao da Dor is further away, but the military would have been able to help."

I've learned all I can from Father Aguiar. I get up, shake his hand. The priest ushers me out, and I blink in the harsh sunlight. I turn for one last look, but he has gone back inside.

I walk back to the Avenida, conscious I never got a good look at the priest's face.

5

DAY ONE

Manaus – Backstreets

In the tropics, the sun sets early. Already its fiery disc has turned blood-red and the shadows grow long. While the broad Avenidas remain bright, shadows shroud the side streets. I make my way toward the hotel, half a mile from the port.

I stop at a street vendor and buy some fruit to take home for dinner. The ship will be leaving early tomorrow. I want a good night's sleep.

The street is crowded. I notice a thin young man fifty yards away. Curly black hair, loose white shirt, blue jeans. He looks familiar. I'm sure I saw him outside FUNAI. A glimpse on the Avenida de Setembro.

He must be following me, but I want to be sure. I carry the fruit in a brown paper bag tucked under my arm. Walk another fifty yards up the street, stop at another stall. The young man feigns interest in a table stacked with melons.

I wouldn't be surprised if Sales, Barros, or Father Aguiar

had me followed. They all have interests in the Selva da Morte. Cuchulain Connor has the greatest interest of all —Fiadh.

Turn down one side street, then another. Glance back.

The curly-haired kid has a phone in his hand. Glances down, punches a speed-dial, holds it to his ear.

Didn't expect that. Things are about to get interesting.

I walk faster, turn another corner. This street is dark and narrow. Beat-up cars have been parked along one side. The building to my right is having work done on it. Scaffolding has been erected against the wall. Lumber and building materials have been stacked underneath. A green mesh across the scaffolding keeps loose items from falling onto passers-by.

I'm almost at the end of the alley when two men step in front of me. A big black guy to my left, a sweaty Latino to my right. The black guy's bald head looks like a .45 caliber bullet. His red T-shirt is stretched tight over hardened pecs and his biceps look ready to split the sleeves. The Latino is smaller, but he looks quick and nasty.

Game on.

The Latino reaches behind his back for a pistol. He's seen too many movies... that's a cumbersome draw. I drop my bag of fruit. Before he can swing the pistol around, I drive four fingers, stiff as blades, into the hollow of his throat. Throw my shoulder behind the thrust. I feel the soft tissue and cartilage give, stab all the way to his spine. His eyes bug out and he drops like he's been shot.

A blur of movement in the corner of my eye. The black guy swings a sap at me. Hard leather, eight inches long. The kind they stuff with lead fishing weights. I block the blow with my left forearm. He swung with such force his arm skids along mine. I trap his wrist with my right hand, bend at the waist, put him down. His arm snaps at the elbow. I fix him in place, kick him twice in the temple with the toe of my boot. Bone crunches.

"Look out!"

A woman's voice.

It's the girl from the mission, the one who was handing out the charity boxes.

I hadn't forgotten the curly-haired kid. He's almost on me, a flick-knife open in one hand. I drop the black guy's arm. From the pile, I snatch a four-foot-long two-by-four. Swing it from a crouch.

The bat cracks the boy across the shins. I was aiming for his knees, but everything was moving too fast. There's a whack and the piece of lumber breaks in two. The impact transmits harmonic waves of vibration through my arms. One piece of wood remains in my hands, the other flies off to one side and bounces off the wall. With a shriek, the boy drops the knife and tumbles to the pavement.

Ten seconds, and it's over. I straighten and survey my attackers. The Latino is staring at the sky, hands clasped to his throat. His eyes are bursting from their sockets and he gasps like a fish out of water. His face is purple, the lips blue-black. Without a tracheotomy, he's done. Two more gasps and he lies still.

I reach down and pick up his pistol, a SIG P210.

The black guy is lying on his back, head tilted at an odd angle. His temple has been smashed. No bleeding—just a concave dent in the side of his head. A crushed eggshell inside a sack of flesh.

The girl is standing over the kid. Together, they make an odd sight. She's attractive. Mid-twenties, long chestnut hair, a thin face with high cheekbones. The kid is writhing on the ground, groaning through clenched teeth. Tears are streaming down his cheeks.

"Are you alright?" the girl asks.

"Yes, thank you." I squeeze the SIG into my waistband, pull my shirt down over it.

"I saw him follow you from the mission," she says. "I knew there would be trouble."

I grunt. The boy's flick-knife is lying on the pavement. I step on the blade, pull up on the haft until it snaps. Fling the pieces aside.

The bat wasn't the only thing that broke. The boy's right shin snapped in two. His jeans leg is torn, and the jagged end of his shattered tibia protrudes through the bloody cloth. White bone and shredded flesh.

Blood pounds in my temples as I look down on the weeping boy.

This was no robbery. These men intended to kill me.

"Who sent you?" I ask the boy.

The kid is squirming on the ground. He doesn't know what to do with his hands. Every movement is agony.

"*Quem te mandou?*" The girl translates for me.

The boy shakes his head. "*Eu nao sei.*"

Compound fractures are so convenient. I step on the splintered tibia. Put some weight on it. The boy's scream is subhuman. He falls back, glassy-eyed. Faints.

The girl licks her lips. I glimpse her pink tongue, imagine it doing other things.

I shake my head, roll the boy over, search his pockets. A handful of reals, a mobile phone. I put the phone in my pocket.

The boy regains consciousness. I pick up half the broken plank. Walk back to the boy, raise it over my head, take aim at his leg. He lifts his hands to ward off the blow. A stream of Portuguese spews from his lips.

"He doesn't know who sent them," the girl says. "A man paid his friend to make sure you never walked again. That is all he knows, he never met the man."

I'm tempted to smash his other leg. Instead, I drop the plank. It bounces on the pavement with a wooden clatter. The boy rolls on his side, presses his face against the pavement, and sobs.

Someone doesn't want me on that boat.

6

DAY ONE

Manaus – Laura

The girl and I walk from the alley and lose ourselves in a web of streets. Vendors at the alley mouth give us odd looks, but turn away. This will be like any large city. Nobody saw anything, nobody knows anything.

The girl looks at me. "What is your name?"

"Breed."

"I am Laura Alves."

"You work at the mission."

"I volunteer at the mission. Fiadh, Anna and Pedro are my friends. I overheard you speaking with Father Aguiar and decided to meet you. When you left, that boy followed. I smelled trouble."

Night has fallen. The shops and stalls lining the street have turned their lights on. Mosquitoes, flies and moths whirl in clouds around the naked bulbs. The night is warm and muggy. Again, I smell the rich scent of fruit hanging in the air.

"Are you hungry?" I ask. "We can have a meal in one of these places."

"Yes," Laura says. "This one looks good."

I lead her into the restaurant. It's dimly lit, but we find a private corner, away from other couples. A soft melody issues from speakers concealed in the shadows. A piano, Latin guitar and discreet drums. A simple, elegant samba.

The waiter comes with menus and I order beers. He sets a mosquito coil on the edge of the table and lights it. Rose-scented carcinogenic smoke curls into the air. I glance around, gauge the size of the room.

"How hungry are you?" Her accent is subtle, hard to place. As far as I can tell, her English is fluent.

"I could eat a horse," I tell her.

The girl gives me a strange look. After all, she has watched me kill two men and leave another crippled. She does not seem disturbed. Laura Alves is made of stern stuff.

"You shall have chargrilled picanha, then." She turns her menu to face me, points at an enormous steak. "Allow me to order."

"Please."

The waiter returns with our beers. Served so cold that chunks of ice seem glued to the glasses. Laura rattles off our orders in rapid-fire Portuguese. The waiter nods and disappears into the kitchen.

I drain my glass with one gulp.

Laura smiles. "Is killing men such thirsty work?"

"I didn't kill all of them."

"Two out of three." The girl shrugs. "Not bad."

"You don't seem too broken up about it."

"This is a rough town. Criminals like that are everywhere."

A silly musical ringtone sounds from my pocket. I take

the kid's phone out, hold it between myself and Laura, accept
the call.

Esta feito?

The voice is low, a man's. I can't prove anything, but I can
guess who it is—Eurico Vargas is officially on my shit list.

"Next time, send people who know what they are doing,"
I reply.

I disconnect the call, pocket the phone, and turn back to
Laura. "Where are you from?"

Laura picks up our conversation as though we had not been
interrupted. "São Paulo. Yes, it can be as rough. But Manaus is a
port city. People drift in and out. Commit crimes, disappear on
the next boat. In Amazonas, the river keeps many secrets."

Her eyes are brown, flecked with gold. They glitter in the
warm sodium light. She wears a loose cotton top that leaves
the hollow of her throat and one shoulder bare. My eyes are
drawn to her thin black bra strap. The expanse of soft, milky
skin. She's aware of my interest, but unconcerned. She's a
natural, used to the attention of men.

I signal the waiter for another round of beers. "You said
you wanted to meet me. Here we are."

"Yes. I was friends with Fiadh and the others. Many times,
we went together to the Selva da Morte. Fiadh wanted me to
come with them."

"You remained behind."

"I told Fiadh not to go. The FUNAI outpost at Portao da
Dor was attacked. The Arqueiros are at war with men who
have guns."

"Fiadh wasn't discouraged."

"She said that made it all the more important for us to go.
The Arqueiros needed our help. If we could identify the men
making war on the Arqueiros, we could involve the military
and drive them out. I told her I would not go."

The waiter slides a monstrous steak onto the table. For Laura, a salad with grilled chicken skewers.

"Now," I say, "Pedro is dead and the girls are missing."

"Yes."

"Father Aguiar doesn't seem to care much."

Laura sniffs. "Father Aguiar is interested in saving souls. So interested he counts the souls he saves, so he can report to his bishop."

"You don't like him."

"No, but he provides funding so we can help people."

"What about Father Camos, the priest at Vila de Deus?"

"He is a good man," Laura says. "He serves in the Selva, where there is no one but God to see."

"Do you believe in God?"

"Of course. I cannot serve Him like this my whole life, but for now, yes. Fiadh wants to serve Him all her life."

Laura Alves is the only person I have met today who speaks of Fiadh as though she is still alive. I wonder why that is. Perhaps she is the only one who cares.

We dine in silence. Comfortable with our thoughts, we listen to the music issuing from the speakers. A woman sings softly in Portuguese. The song is gentle and moody, a stark contrast to the violence we experienced such a short time ago.

"That's a beautiful song," I say.

Laura smiles. "*Saudade.*"

"What does that mean?

"It is Portuguese," Laura says. "How does one define a feeling? It is a single word that encompasses melancholic nostalgia. A longing for the unattainable, and an acute sense that this moment is slipping away. Once lost, it's gone forever."

The gold flecks in her eyes are hypnotic. I finish my steak

and wash the last bite down with cold beer. Lean back in my chair. "How did you meet Fiadh?"

"We met at a function in Brasilia. My father owns manufacturing companies, as does Fiadh's. We often circulate with the families of people in government. It is through such connections that contracts and approvals are obtained."

"Same all over."

"Yes. We were in college at the time, eighteen or nineteen years old. Her father brought her to Brazil often. She volunteered at the mission and told me about the work they were doing. She became friends with Anna and Pedro. When we graduated, she decided to stay and we worked at the mission together."

"I appreciate your story," I tell her, "but I don't know how it helps me."

"It doesn't." Laura's voice is calm and even. "You have been asked to find a needle in a thirty-three-thousand square mile haystack. How are you going to do it?"

"The Minister of the Interior is mounting a relief mission to Portao da Dor. I will go with him, and try to pick up Fiadh's trail. I doubt she would stray far from the river. The river twists on itself. The switchbacks are tight... barely navigable. This reduces the area further."

"That is true," Laura says. "I know the Selva well."

Barros told me Fiadh and her friends knew the Selva better than many guides. "Do you."

"You don't believe me?"

"I didn't say that. You may know the Selva, but it still doesn't help me."

Laura leans forward. "Take me with you."

That's a shot from the grassy knoll. "You're crazy."

"I should never have let Fiadh go in there. Had I been with them, I might have been able to do something."

"There is no point second-guessing yourself. Had you gone with Fiadh, you might be lying dead with a bullet in your back. Like Pedro."

Laura leans back, her expression contemplative. "Perhaps. But I feel responsible. I want to help."

"No," I say. "I should go alone."

"I know Minister Sales... slightly."

I lift an eyebrow. "How do you know Minister Sales?"

"Who else attended those socials in Brasilia? The president and all the cabinet ministers, including Sales. It's all part of the process for obtaining approvals for projects. Our families have been acquainted for some time."

"Interesting, but not a good enough reason to take you."

"You don't know the Selva. You don't speak Portuguese. You don't know a word of the indigenous dialects. You have no idea where to start."

I do calculations in my head. "Fiadh ran into trouble somewhere between Vila de Deus and Arvore de Ouro. Which way would you have run?"

Laura replies without hesitation. "East, into the jungle. Then dogleg south toward Portao da Dor."

"Same thing Father Aguiar suggested."

"Yes. The question is... from where should we mount our search?"

I can see Barros's map in my mind's eye. The twisty worm of the Rio Preto, the settlements marked with pins. "Either from Portao da Dor, or Vila de Deus."

Laura places her hands flat on the table. Spreads her long fingers. "To be thorough, we should start from Vila de Deus. To save time, we could start from Portao da Dor."

Father Aguiar has no problem using passionate young people to serve his needs. Am I any different? I study Laura Alves carefully. She looks like a girl who knows what she is doing. Her evaluation is right on... I don't know the land, the language, or the people. I need her help.

"Alright," I tell her. "If they let you on the boat, you can come."

7

DAY ONE

Manaus – Miracles

How many men have I killed?
Nine with my bare hands. Countless others with a range of weapons.

Well, that isn't *exactly* true. I beat one Talib to death with a rock. But it's accurate enough.

The Pentagon says I killed one hundred and twenty-seven men with a sniper rifle. The scope was so powerful I could see the color of their eyes, the stubble on their jaws, the stains on their teeth. The bright pink mist as the bullet blew their brains out.

The Army made a lot out of body count statistics. To me, killing was less than half of a sniper's trade. The real art was getting close without being seen. To sneak in, lie in wait for days, do the business, and sneak back out. *That* is where a sniper's brilliance shines. Not in the trivial act of killing, but in the *dance*. There is little art involved in killing a sentry. Few men in the trade do it well. The *true* artist gets *around* the sentry without killing him. Hits the target, escapes without being seen.

Then there were the women. Three Afghan women I shot while they were flaying our men alive. I did it calmly, at a distance of eight hundred yards. The last woman was running away when I shot her in the back. I put bullets in our men, to end their suffering.

I didn't keep track of the men I killed with pistols, hand grenades and rocket launchers. Whatever instrument of death came to hand.

I sit in the hotel bar, sipping a beer. Hold my hand up in front of me. Examine my fingers. They are rock steady. I am never sick at sea.

Except when I wake up in the middle of the night, drenched in sweat, standing on the balcony with a pistol in my hand. Not knowing how I got there.

TWO DAYS AGO, I was invited to meet Cuchulain Connor. The word was Cuchulain had made his fortune before he was twenty-seven. Trading commodity futures on the Chicago Board of Trade. He expanded his operations worldwide. Traded commodities in Asia, Eastern Europe, and Latin America.

Soybeans in Brazil. Some said he was personally responsible for the Amazon's Arc of Deforestation.

I sat on an original Louis XIV chair and absorbed the opulence of Cuchulain's Chicago penthouse. It occupied four stories and the rooftop of a skyscraper with a view of Lake Michigan. Wide expanses of marble, fountains, and gilded Ionic columns dazzled my eyes.

It was a beautiful spring day. The sky and lake were watercolors, two shades of blue. There wasn't a cloud in the sky. Sailboats flecked the surface. Their sails, colorful patches, billowed in the wind.

Cuchulain was a big man. The kind who might have played football in college, had he ever gone. Short blond hair, broad shoulders. He stood in front of floor-to-ceiling windows that looked onto the lake.

"Thank you for coming on short notice, Mister Breed."

A firm, manly handshake.

One side of his office was occupied by a bar and a living room set. Easy chairs, sofas, deep comfortable cushions. A glass-topped coffee table in a polished gold frame. Cuchulain obviously had a thing for gold.

A thin man with intelligent eyes got up to greet me. Five-foot-nine, mid-fifties. A little leprechaun. He was wearing a bright red sweater and a black shirt with a white clerical collar.

"Mister Breed, this is Father Andrew Quinlan."

The priest's handshake was as firm as Connor's. "Call me Andrew."

"Andrew's been a friend of the family for years. He baptized Fiadh."

I lifted an eyebrow.

Connor motioned me to make myself comfortable. "What are you drinking, Breed?"

"Bourbon and branch, if you have it."

I usually drink Bourbon neat, but Bourbon and branch works better in polite company. I supposed a meeting with one of the wealthiest men on the planet qualified as polite company. Maybe not. People don't meet with men like me because they are concerned with delicacy.

Connor poured my drink and set it on the table. He and Father Andrew settled down with glasses of Jameson's.

"Who's Fiadh?" I asked.

"My daughter," Connor says. He took a sip of his drink.

Father Andrew and I sipped ours. "Her name is old Irish. It means 'wild' or 'untamed'. That's Fiadh. Like her mother, a green-eyed Irish beauty. But that's where the likeness ends. Fiadh is a rebel."

The commodity trader nodded to the bottles of liquor on the table.

"Case in point. We are a Jameson's family. Fiadh is the only one of us who drinks Bushmills. An affectation she acquired simply to be different. Andrew, tell Breed about Fiadh's year at Trinity. It's alright."

Uncomfortable, Father Andrew cleared his throat. "Fiadh spent her junior year at Trinity. As it happened, I was scheduled to give a lecture at the college. Invited her and her girlfriends to the talk. Went to her lodging, and her roommate let me in. Asked me to wait in the sitting room. It was eleven o'clock in the morning. Fiadh came out, dressed in a cotton shirt and nothing else, holding a bottle of Bushmills by the neck."

The priest had the good grace to color. I shifted in my chair.

"Fiadh is my only child," Connor said. "I swore to raise my daughter as I would a son. I would have encouraged a young man to sow his wild oats and develop some judgment while he was at it. I did the same with Fiadh."

Parading half-naked in front of a priest didn't strike me as good judgment. Certainly not with a bottle of Bushmills in hand.

The rich are different from you and I.

Was it F. Scott Fitzgerald who said that? I took a slug of Bourbon.

"Let me freshen that up for you, Breed." Connor splashed more Bourbon into my glass. I was conscious the branch water was still sitting on the bar. My drink was rapidly turning into straight Bourbon. Connor knew what he was doing, enjoyed my discomfort.

"Don't worry," Connor said. "Fiadh is educated in the ways of the world. I tasked Andrew to guide her."

Father Andrew smiled. "Fiadh is very devout, Mister Breed. She wanted to become a nun. But she is also possessed of a fiery spirit. An unquenchable lust for life. Growing up, she was often conflicted. I did my best to ease the way."

A black cardboard album lay on the table. Connor leaned forward and flipped open the cover.

The first photograph was an 8x10 glossy of Connor and a young girl standing in a field. In his hands, Connor carried a long-barreled over-and-under shotgun, broken at the breech. Holding him by the arm, the girl beamed. She looked nineteen or twenty. A round baby face with broad shoulders and long legs. Rosy cheeks, freckles, and a bright smile. She wore a tweed car-coat, jeans, and high boots. Her athletic frame exuded her father's strength and vitality.

"That year, we shot quail in Scotland." Connor beamed with pride. "Fiadh cooked them for us. Delicious."

God puts creatures on earth to sustain each other.

"I have interests in Brazil," Connor said. "I visited the country often, took Fiadh with me. She made friends, went on safaris. Expeditions into the jungle. She wanted to learn more about the country. Help people."

"Fiadh volunteered at the Mission of Our Lady of Hope," Father Andrew said. "She saw it as a way to serve God and do good for the country."

Connor's face darkened. "Let's not sugarcoat this, Andrew. Fiadh's work at the mission, her expeditions into the jungle, were another form of rebellion. I love my daughter with all my heart, and she loves me, but I taught her to speak her mind. She educated herself about the deforestation in the

Amazon. The illegal logging and mining activities. We argued about my commodity trading in central Brazil."

"She didn't like sacrificing the rainforest for soybeans?"

"No, she did *not*. Tried to convince me to withdraw. I told her if I didn't do it responsibly, other people would... irresponsibly."

"More internal conflict," I observed.

"Yes," Father Andrew said. "Fiadh wanted to rebel, but she didn't want to act directly against her father. Rather than challenge his operations in central Brazil, she ventured into Amazonas. The Selva da Morte."

"Let me come to the point, Breed." Connor leaned forward. "Fiadh has been working with wild tribes in the Selva. There are reports one of these tribes, the Arqueiros, is on a rampage. They attacked a military outpost last week. Killed people at the edge of the forest. Some thought the Indians were stirred up by criminals. Illegal loggers.

"Fiadh went on a crusade. She and two friends entered the Selva to find evidence the Arqueiros were provoked. They ran into trouble. One of her party was shot. Yesterday, he made it back to a mission. Before he died, he said Fiadh and the other girl were still alive."

I looked at the photo of the girl. Imagined her plunging through the jungle, chased by cannibals and gunmen. I said nothing.

"I want you to go to the Selva da Morte. Find Fiadh and bring her back."

"Why me?"

"I have extensive dealings with Jacob Stein. He owns one of the biggest private equity firms in New York. His daughter, Anya, works for the government. She has a high opinion of you. She said you were a difficult, unpleasant man. Exactly the kind to deal with difficult, unpleasant business."

"How flattering."

It was, but not the way Connor thought.

"I have influence with the president of Brazil," Connor said. "The Minister of the Interior is mounting an expedition... to relieve the outpost attacked by the Arqueiros. I can get you on that boat."

I took a deep breath. "No."

"Why not?"

"I have a little experience in jungle environments, but I fought my war in the desert and mountains."

"Are the principles not the same?"

"Yes, but specific differences can get you killed."

"For example?"

"There are a thousand examples. Bullets decelerate more quickly in cold mountain air than in hot humid lowlands. That can mean the difference between a hit and a miss."

Unfazed, Connor stared at me. Reached into the pocket of his suit jacket and took out a folded piece of paper. Pushed it across the table.

I unfolded the paper. Studied it.

"You've left the amount blank," I observed.

Connor holds my gaze. "*That* is how much I love Fiadh. Find her, and *you* fill in that number."

I SAID YES. Not because of the money. The girl in the photograph intrigued me. She was beautiful. A prize. The kind of girl nobody could buy. Yet her professed piety was at odds with the image of a hard-drinking girl who shot quail in Scotland and... what else? Say it, Breed. Didn't Fiadh Connor look like a keg of dynamite in bed?

Cuchulain Connor excused himself and went to his study. Left Father Andrew to show me to the door.

"I can't see Fiadh Connor as a nun," I said.

"By the time she was eighteen, neither could she." Father

Andrew smiled. "Her love of God is sincere. That's what you want to know, isn't it? Is she a hypocrite? Is she a self-indulgent child seeking only to convey the *impression* of virtue?"

"I didn't say that."

"No, but you wondered. Professing one's faith does not earn brownie points these days. It earned Fiadh more than her share of ridicule. Young people are cruel. But her station and strength saw her through."

Father Andrew's right. Professing faith doesn't score points. But saving the rainforest and indigenous tribes does. That's a consistency, not a contradiction. Why am I looking for fault in this girl?

The priest walked me out. The foyer was ringed by Doric columns supporting a ceiling twenty feet high. The columns were decorated with gold leaf. Lit by spotlights, the gold glittered. Father Andrew leaned forward and pressed a button for the elevator.

"I can't tell you how tortured she was over birth control," the priest said. "Fiadh is a healthy girl with the appetite of a popular twenty-something. Her parish priest was very old school and put her through hell. Ditto the nuns she spoke with about seeking a vocation. I finally told her to use common sense, confess her sins, and be prepared to say a lot of Our Fathers and Hail Marys."

The elevator's arrival was announced by a discreet ding. We stepped in, and Father Andrew punched the button for the ground floor. As the doors sucked shut, he opened his black briefcase. Took out a thick brown package eight inches long and four or five inches wide. It was bound with heavy elastic bands. He handed the bundle to me.

"What's this?"

"Fiadh and I have been corresponding for years," Father Andrew said. "In some ways, she's very old-fashioned. In this day of mobile phones, messaging apps, and email, she prefers the post. She writes a kind of journal, often addressed to me, and posts it after several weeks."

The elevator doors open and we step into the skyscraper's lobby.

It strikes me that Fiadh may not be *that* old-fashioned. She's an intelligent girl, the daughter of one of the wealthiest and most powerful men in the world. She's wise not to trust her private thoughts to email.

"Get to know her, Breed." Father Andrew stared at me with genuine emotion. "Bring her back."

I have to speak the truth. "You know she's probably dead."

"Yes," Father Andrew said. "And so does Cuchulain. But he won't admit it. We will not give up hope."

"It'll take a miracle."

"That's God's business."

Now I sit in the hotel bar, sipping a cold beer, with two more dead men and a crippled kid behind me. Father Andrew's package of letters sits in my room safe, unopened. I want to know more about the pretty girl with the baby face, the rosy cheeks, and the pretty smile. Part of me is afraid of what I'll learn. I can't bring myself to open the letters.

My rational brain tells me Fiadh Connor does not have much chance of coming out of the Selva da Morte alive.

Once, in the Hindu Kush, my team was boarding a Black Hawk. I was the last man in line. No one else was near me. A voice in my head said, "Drop."

Without thinking, I dropped and ate rocks. In that instant, a Dragunov round slammed into the side of the helicopter, right where my head had been. The door gunner blazed away, lit up the sniper. Gave me time to crawl inside.

I believe in miracles.

8

DAY TWO

Manaus – Nevoa

Laura Alves shows up before dawn. Stands in front of my hotel, looking like she's been into the Selva da Morte before. Khaki pants, high jungle boots, long-sleeved shirt, forty-pound rucksack. I'm carrying the same. I've stuffed a two-quart camelback and the captured SIG into my ruck for good measure.

We walk in silence to the docks. Merchants are setting up their stalls. The waterfront is a beehive of activity. We hear the wet slap of fish sliding onto wooden trays. Propped on tables for display. I glance inside an open barrel—live eels slither over each other. The air smells of riverweed. Great mats of slimy tentacles undulate on the surface. Glisten in the light from streetlamps at the edge of the dock.

The sky is lightening to the east.

The shadow of a ship stares at us. It's low to the water, the gunwales only a few feet above the surface. The forward superstructure is a great metal box twenty feet high. On the fo'c'sle squats a turret sporting a long-barreled gun. The hull number has been painted in white numerals on the bow. Further aft lies the flat expanse of a helideck. A single-engine chopper has been tied down for safety. Its rotors droop toward the river.

A naval officer in a white uniform stands on the dock by a gangplank. He wears a pistol belt with a holstered 9mm Beretta flat against his thigh.

"Is this the Nevoa?" I ask.

The officer shakes his head. "No," he says. "*There* is the Nevoa."

He points to a dark shape. Another ship, twenty yards further along the dock. Equally low-slung, but long and sleek. The forward superstructure is less boxy than this one. It's like a layer cake. Three stories. The forward superstructure, a bridge deck, and a navigation bridge. This ship has a single 40mm Bofors automatic cannon mounted on its fo'c'sle. There is no turret—a metal shield protects the gun crew.

The navigation bridge is a sight. A row of floodlights is arranged across the front combing. The light from street-lamps glitters on their lenses. I can make out the distinctive shapes of two box-fed Browning 0.50 caliber machine guns, one at each corner. Two men are visible on the navigation bridge. The morning watch.

"Let's go." I walk toward the Nevoa.

The closer we get, the older the Nevoa looks. Dark stains near the anchor chains can only be rust. The hull is a hundred and fifty feet long. The forward superstructure narrows at the waist. The center of the hull supports the waist superstructure and boat deck. The latter sports two rubber Zodiacs. Directly forward of the quarterdeck is a low-silhou-ette, raked stack that looks newer than the rest of the ship.

Two deuce-and-a-half trucks have parked on the dock. About forty Brazilian Marines have formed up in front of the gangplank. Two men in navy whites are examining a Marine officer's orders.

One of the navy men, a commander, turns to me. "Who are you?"

"I'm Breed," I tell him. "I will be joining Minister Sales's expedition. This is Miss Alves."

The other officer, wearing a lieutenant commander's rank, barks a command to a sailor at the top of the gangplank. He motions to the Marine. "Board your men," he says. "They will be billeted in the crew's quarters aft."

That's the quarterdeck. The crew sleeps in a long after superstructure that extends from the Nevoa's waist to the poop.

"Mister Breed," the first man says, "I am Commander Itamar Silva, Captain of the Nevoa. No one has said anything to me about Miss Alves."

Silva extends his hand and the lieutenant commander hands him a clipboard. It must be the passenger manifest. He flips through it, shakes his head. "I am sorry. The young lady cannot board."

I watch the Marines march up the gangplank. The troops look sharp despite the heat. Their camouflage fatigues are creased and they carry their M16 rifles at sling arms. The petty officer points them to the quarterdeck. They disappear into the superstructure.

"Let me speak with Minister Sales," I say.

"It will do no good," Silva tells me. "No unauthorized individuals aboard military vessels."

"Captain Silva." The voice booms from the deck of Nevoa. "What seems to be the problem?"

Sales and Vargas have joined the sailor at the top of the gangplank. I scarcely recognize the minister. He has exchanged his Panama suit for white trousers and a loose cotton shirt. Vargas is dressed much the same, but he has rolled his sleeves halfway up his biceps. Looks like he drives iron four hours a day.

"Mr Breed is a member of your party," Silva says. "This lady is not."

The minister says something to the sailor. The man barks a command and the Marines halt at the foot of the plank. When the last Marines on the gangplank have boarded the ship, he motions for Sales to pass.

Followed by Vargas, the minister joins us on the dock. The Marines resume boarding.

"Mr Breed," Sales says.

"Minister."

Sales looks Laura up and down.

"Minister, this is Laura Alves. A friend of Fiadh Connor. She knows the Selva. She is going to accompany me."

"I know Miss Alves." The minister turns to Laura, takes her hand with exaggerated gallantry, and kisses it. "An honor and a pleasure to see you again, Miss Alves."

"She is not authorized," Silva says.

"I will decide that," Sales tells him. He turns to Laura. "Why do you want to join this expedition?"

"Fiadh and I have explored the Selva da Morte," Laura says. "I know the jungle, speak the Indian dialects."

"Do you?" Sales smiles.

Vargas's eyes lick Laura's body. I want to break his face.

"Enough to get by."

"Somehow I doubt you speak the dialects as well as Fiadh Connor," Sales says. "But I will take you at your word. You probably know more words of that gibberish than any of us."

"Thank you." Laura lowers her eyes. "I will do everything I can to help."

Laura's manner is submissive, very different from the confident image I've become used to. She acts like a girl who knows her place.

Sales turns to me. "Do you think Miss Alves can keep up with you in the Selva?"

"She's been before. Knowing the way can make a hike easier."

"She is welcome aboard," Sales says.

"Minister," Captain Silva interjects.

"The girl can come, Captain. Arrange quarters for her in the forward cabins."

Sales turns on his heel and strides up the gangplank. Pushes past the Marines. I watch him go, turn to find Vargas leering at Laura.

"*Pequena cortesa,*" Vargas says.

Laura smiles. The aide snorts and follows Sales onto the boat.

"What did Vargas say?" I ask. It certainly wasn't anything nice.

"It makes no difference, Breed."

"Well, it looks like you've got a ride."

Laura touches my arm. "Thank you."

"Don't thank me yet. This will be a miserable trip."

Silva is not a happy camper, and it shows. "This is Lieutenant Commander Gaspar, my first officer. He will show you to your cabins."

Gaspar delivers a courteous nod. "Please come with me."

We follow Gaspar up the gangplank and I assess their strength. Forty Marines, but I have not seen many sailors. A gunboat this size should have a crew of at least thirty men. From the top of the plank, I have a view of the poop. The long muzzle of another Browning 0.50 caliber juts from one corner.

The Nevoa is lightly armed. One 40mm Bofors on the fo'c'sle, two 0.50 calibers on the navigation bridge, and another two 0.50 calibers on the poop. Forty Marines with small arms. It's a reasonable force for police work on the

Amazon. The Brazilian Navy was never designed to combat the navies of state actors. Rather, it was built for internal policing and counter-piracy.

The waist of the gunboat is wider than I expected. There's a lot of space on the boat deck. The Zodiac looks well-equipped with a powerful outboard motor. We walk to the back of the forward superstructure. As we pass, I try to look inside the portholes of the narrow waist. They are all dark.

Gaspar leads us to a watertight door leading into the forward superstructure. Next to the hatch, mounted against the bulkhead, is a metal ladder that leads to the bridge deck above. I assume there is one like it on the starboard side.

The first officer steps over a knee-knocker. It's a high metal barrier at the base of a doorframe. A nemesis of drunken sailors. "Watch your step," he says. "The Captain would not mind leaving you behind with an injury."

"He seems very professional."

Gaspar lifts an eyebrow. "You did not take offense?"

"Of course not. I don't mind a by-the-book guy."

I can imagine Captain Silva's orders. *You will accept the direction of Minister Augusto Sales in all matters that do not compromise the safety of your vessel and crew.*

Silva can't be pleased.

Gaspar looks thoughtful. "You are military?"

"I was in the Army."

The first officer accepts this fact with a nod.

Inside, we find ourselves in a surprisingly wide mess. The cabin stretches thirty feet, the entire beam of the ship. There is table bolted to the deck, with seating for eight people. The portholes are wide open. There are cabinets and a pantry. We entered from the portside boat deck. There is another water-tight door starboard, and a proper wooden door in the center. The center door leads into the waist superstructure.

"Very comfortable," I observe.

"Yes," Gaspar says. "This is the officer's wardroom. The galley is through that door, in the waist. Also, our stores and frozen food lockers. The cabins are here."

Only one door leads forward from the officers' wardroom. Like the door to the galley, it is not watertight. Apparently, only the doors open to the outside can be sealed. This makes for a civilized interior.

We follow Gaspar forward through the center door. The corridor is narrow, to maximize space in the cabins. There are eight cabins, four on either side. I estimate each cabin to be ten feet wide by twelve feet deep.

"Doctor Fonseca," Gaspar calls.

The door immediately to our left is open. I was right... the cabin is narrow. Ten feet wide, with a bunk along one side and a writing desk at the end, under a porthole. A man is sitting at the desk with his back to us. He turns. "Yes?"

"Mister Breed and Miss Alves will be joining us on this expedition. This is Doctor Fonseca. He will be ship's surgeon on this trip."

Fonseca turns in his chair and flicks us a salty salute. Middle aged, with graying hair. He's not overweight, but his face sags with dissipation. He wears a tan short-sleeved shirt, black crescents of sweat under his arms. "Welcome aboard," he says. The doctor has taken his cue from Gaspar to speak English. "How long before we leave?"

"We have completed onboarding the supplies and Marines," the first officer says. "We shall cast off before dawn."

Fonseca grunts and turns back to the desk. I notice an open bottle of whiskey. It's early in the morning to be drinking. All that sweat the doctor is shedding isn't from the heat.

Gaspar opens the cabin next to Fonseca. "Mister Breed, you can sleep here. I will put Miss Alves across the corridor from the doctor."

Laura shrugs off her pack and sets it on the deck inside her cabin. I enter my cabin and shove my pack under the bunk. I'm not comfortable leaving the SIG unattended, but I'll check it when I return.

I step into the corridor and shut the door. Point to the cabin across from mine. "Who does that cabin belong to?"

"That is Lieutenant Quadros's billet."

"Do you all speak English so well?" I ask.

"Captain Silva and I speak English," Gaspar says. "Doctor Fonseca, Minister Sales, Mister Vargas, and our radio operator also. The rest of the crew, not so much. But we are making this journey with a skeleton crew. Two officers and six sailors. To make room for the Marines."

"You can run this ship with eight men?"

"Yes. The Nevoa is an old hull, but she has been fully modernized. She has been equipped with diesel engines. We have two engineers at the power plant, but everything can be operated from the bridge. The engine room also has a secondary helm, so the ship can be navigated if the bridge is knocked out. We will have the Marines man the gun positions."

Gaspar continues down the corridor. "Here on the left is Minister Sales, and Mister Vargas is on the right."

"Who are in the two cabins at the end?"

"No one," Gaspar says. "The room on the left is the sickbay. The one on the right is a dental surgery and room for medical supplies. Those cabins are equipped with small refrigerators. However, most medicines that must be kept cold are stored in the coolers at the waist of the ship."

"Pretty impressive medical facilities."

"Half of our mission is to provide medical assistance to isolated villages on the river," he says. "The other half is dealing with river pirates and narcos." Gaspar leads us forward. He gestures to a narrow compartment between the dental surgery and Vargas's cabin. "This is the head."

At the end of the corridor, between the sickbay and dental surgery, is another watertight door. It has been propped open. Beyond, I can see the fo'c'sle and the back of the 40mm Bofors mount.

The first officer steps over the knee-knocker.

I take Laura's hand and help her over. Follow them outside. The sky to the east is orange. The disc of the sun peeps over the river. The image ripples with mirage, blurred horizontal streaks rising from the water.

Gaspar speaks to a petty officer in Portuguese. It is the sailor who stood at the gangplank. Now he stands on the fo'c'sle. He raises his hand in acknowledgement.

"We are preparing to cast off," Gaspar says. "Come."

The deck is not open all the way around the superstructure. The forward and aft superstructures are flush with the side of the ship. This leaves the entire beam free to use. There are two shallow indentations, port and starboard. They make room for steep metal companionways that lead to the bridge deck above.

I tilt my chin skyward. I can see a row of windows stretching across the front of the bridge. Above that, the bank of floodlights is barely visible, along with the muzzles of the Brownings. Canvas condoms protect them from rain and insects. Insects crawl everywhere. They love little holes like the muzzles of weapons that are not cleaned and maintained.

There are four ways onto the bridge deck. Two companionways from the fo'c'sle, and two ladders from the boat deck. On the fo'c'sle, aft of the Bofors, is an open hatch leading below. "What's down there?" I ask.

"*That* is the forward magazine. A store of 40mm ammunition for the Bofors. Ready ammunition is in those boxes there. The magazine connects to the fresh water and fuel tank space. Further aft is the engine room."

"An underground."

"The engine deck," Gaspar says. "It is very cramped because of our shallow draft. Compartmentalization is limited, and it runs the length of the ship."

"Doesn't sound very safe," I tell him. "If you are holed anywhere, the ship will go down in minutes."

"There is a watertight bulkhead forward of the magazine. Should we collide with another vessel or a terrain feature, it will protect us. If we are rammed from the side, we are—how do you say? Out of luck. Nevoa was never meant to go head-to-head with surface combatants. The pumps can take care of small wounds. Hits from cannon or torpedoes would finish us."

Gaspar clambers up the companionway, his shoes ringing on the steel plates. Laura follows the first officer, and I bring up the rear. The companionway opens onto a narrow metal widow's walk that winds around the bridge. Gaspar opens a door and steps inside. There are instruments and a traditional helm.

Captain Silva is looking through the windows, checking instruments, assessing the river. A helmsman stands next to him, hands on the wheel.

Sales and Vargas stand to one side. They are staying out of the captain's way.

"Ten minutes." Silva is preoccupied with his preparations.

"Come this way," Gaspar says.

We follow the first officer through a door at the back of the bridge. It leads aft. As we step through, I feel Vargas's eyes on my back. My skin crawls.

The door to the cabin on the left is wide open. A desk is crammed with laptops, charts, and GPS equipment. "This is the navigation cabinet," Gaspar says. "There, on the right, is the radio room."

Gaspar pushes the door on our right open. A young man sits at another table stacked with radio equipment. I recognize a powerful HF desktop set. 400 Watts, a range of three thousand miles. A smaller radio, line-of-sight. I doubt it will be much good on the river. Not when we are surrounded by triple-canopy jungle.

"Any word, Max?" Gaspar asks.

"No, sir. They are not responding."

Gaspar turns to me. "We have been trying to raise Portao da Dor for days. Nothing."

"Can you be sure their equipment is functional?"

The radio operator is a helpful young man wearing petty officer's insignia. "No, sir," he says. "Portao da Dor has a 400 Watt set like ours, good to three thousand miles. They also have a 40 Watt ManPack for use in the bush, but that has a range of three hundred miles. Not enough to reach Manaus. When we get to Tieves, we will have a better chance of picking them up."

I notice an olive drab backpack sitting in a corner under the desk. "Like that one?"

"Yes, sir. That is our spare set. For emergencies, or when we dispatch patrols into the bush."

"I guess FM sets aren't much good in triple-canopy jungle."

"No, sir. We have them, as well as small-unit radios. But you are correct. They are not much use."

"Come." Gaspar leads us further along the corridor. "This is the captain's cabin, on the left. On the right, a cabin shared by our navigator and radio operator. Over here is my cabin. The second officer's is across from mine."

We walk the length of the corridor and through another watertight door.

"Surely the water doesn't reach this high? The bridge is twenty feet above the main deck."

"Nevoa was given to the Brazilian Navy by the United States," Gaspar smiles. "A gunboat of WW2 vintage, modernized to serve Amazonas. She was built to survive Atlantic storms."

"Brazil has more modern patrol craft."

"Yes, indeed," Gaspar says. "But the Nevoa has more space on its boat deck for cargo and supplies. The newer boats don't have that space. Some do, but they have to leave their helicopters behind. The Nevoa survives in a niche only she can fill."

We are standing on the widow's walk that surrounds the bridge. There are two gaps in the rail, port and starboard. They allow access to the long metal ladders that stretch to the boat deck below.

I look aft, admire the elegant symmetry of the Nevoa. The roof of the waist superstructure extends fifty feet aft to the raked stack. Behind that, the quarterdeck and roof of the crew's quarters. Then the narrow poop, and two Brownings, one at each corner. A flag flies at the stern. The bright green, yellow and blue colors of Brazil.

On either side of the waist superstructure are two Zodiacs. "Only two?" I ask.

"We are taking on cargo at Tieves," Gaspar says. "Supplies for Portao da Dor. We need space on the deck."

The first officer turns. "We must climb to the navigation bridge."

A single metal ladder extends from the starboard side of the bridge to the navigation deck. Gaspar climbs quickly, with the practiced movements of an old seaman. Warily, I watch Laura follow him. Only when they have both disappeared over the top do I follow.

I swing myself onto the navigation bridge. There is a

chest-high combing, open only to the top of the ladder. Now I have a good view of the bank of floodlights, extending across the combing. The machine guns are mounted on pintles at each corner. Heavy firepower. Unlike the Bofors, however, they are not equipped with shields.

A sailor stands at the front of the bridge, hands on the combing. Gaspar says something to him, and the man descends the ladder.

"Delfin Dutra, our second engineer," Gaspar says. "We are running short. He will be of more use in the engine room."

A squad radio on the first officer's belt crackles. I recognize Silva's voice. "Gaspar."

Gaspar picks up the radio and holds the handset to his ear. "Yes, Captain."

"Cast off fore and aft. We are getting underway."

"Casting off, fore and aft. Aye."

Gaspar yells down to the petty officer on the fo'c'sle. Goes to the back of the navigation bridge, and hollers at another man aft of the quarterdeck. I watch the petty officer undo the hemp tying Nevoa to the dock. He hurls it to a man on the shore.

The ship trembles and a vibration passes up the soles of my boots. A puff of gray smoke belches from the Nevoa's stack. Looking aft, I shield my eyes against the blood-red glare of the rising sun. It is halfway above the horizon. Already, I feel its heat on my face like I'm staring into an open furnace. The cry of birds echo across the water.

Laura leans close and grasps my arm. It's an intimate gesture, and I'm surprised by her touch. The Nevoa's bow pulls away from the dock and the ship slowly edges forward onto the Rio Negro.

Together, Laura and I watch the sun rise over the Amazon.

9

DAY TWO

Nevoa – Amazon Journey

Laura and I return to our cabins. I close my door, lock it, and lay a change of clothes on the bunk. I'm surprised how cool it is. Once underway, Silva ordered the portholes shut and hatches closed. He fired up the air conditioning, and the living spaces of the Nevoa were filled with blessed chilled air. The Brazilian Navy understands how debilitating hundred-degree heat can be.

I cast my eyes about the cabin. Examine the ceiling, the fixtures, the deck. The writing desk and washbasin are bolted to the bulkheads. The swivel chair at the desk is bolted to the deck. Sadly, we must all share the communal head.

Cold air hisses from the air conditioning vent above the bunk. I test the bunk, then climb onto it. Pry the grille off the vent. I reach down, take the SIG from my pack, and slide it into the tin duct. The thick package of Fiadh's letters disappears behind the pistol. I replace the grille, climb down, and ensure the vent appears undisturbed.

Time to check out the rest of the ship. I step into the

corridor and close my door. Pluck a hair from the back of my scalp, lick it with my tongue, and plaster it high on my door-jamb. There's usually no way to stop a determined burglar, but knowing someone has been in your room is valuable intel.

I walk to the officers' wardroom. Laura's room is quiet, as is Fonseca's. I wonder how intimate the good doctor is getting with that bottle of Scotch. I wonder how many bottles he has aboard.

To my surprise, a table to one side of the officers' ward-room has been converted into a well-stocked bar. The table is bolted to the bulkhead. A wooden rail six inches high runs the length of the table to prevent the contents from sliding off onto the deck. It's all there. Scotch whiskey, Kentucky Bour-bon, cachaca. Red and white wine, brandies and cognacs. A rack of polished glassware.

I'm sure this isn't Navy issue. Sales enjoys his luxuries.

I step outside and the violent sun sends me reeling. Sweat springs from every pore. My shirt is soaked. The metal of the boat deck is hot as a grill. I find myself hurrying along like I'm running on hot coals.

I reach the after superstructure and yank the hatch open. Fling myself over the knee-knocker into the blessedly cool interior. It's another large dining hall, the crew's mess. Marines are sitting at the table, playing cards, joking.

"Can I help you?"

A dark-haired young man of about thirty approaches. He wears Marine jungle camouflage and lieutenant's insignia.

"I'm Breed," I tell him. "I am familiarizing myself with the ship."

"I am Lieutenant Quadros," the man says. "My cabin is opposite yours. I, too, am touring our vessel."

"Let us go together," I suggest.

"Alright. I am looking in on my men. Come with me."

The crew's quarters in the after superstructure is larger than the officers' quarters. Quadros leads me through two barrack compartments, each with twenty men. The bulkheads are lined with rows of top and bottom racks. The air is cool, and the Marines are in good spirits. Their sergeants are directing them to clean their weapons and store their gear.

I've been in hundreds of barracks over the years and this one is no different. Quadros seems a capable officer. He is seeing to his men rather than hanging out with the bigwigs forward. A line officer, not a politician. I like him already.

"What is your business on this mission?" Quadros asks.

"You aren't shy, are you?"

"If your purpose affects the safety of my men, I have a right to know."

I suppose he does.

"My client's daughter is missing in the Selva da Morte. I am here to find her."

Quadros nods. "Fiadh Connor. Everyone has heard what happened. You know she has not much chance."

"I know."

"My men and I are to provide relief for the squad at Portao da Dor. We have not been in radio communication with the FUNAI outpost for over seventy-two hours."

"Their main radio might have been disabled."

"Yes. If their ManPack is operational, we might make contact from Tieves. I remain concerned."

"The Arqueiros."

"Not only the Arqueiros. Remember the Bernardes boy was shot. I cannot rule out any possibility. The Arqueiros, or a strong force of bandits, may have overwhelmed the outpost."

We exit the quarterdeck onto the poop. Marines are carrying sandbags from storage and barricading the Browning machine guns. Around each weapon, they pile the bags onto the combing and stack them on deck to form an open pillbox. Nevoa's poop begins to resemble a Victorian fortress.

"The machine guns are not equipped with shields," Quadros says. "We must be prepared to take fire from the jungle, or from pirate vessels. We shall sandbag the navigation bridge positions as well."

This is a wide, straight stretch of the Amazon, and the Nevoa is making a good fifteen knots. Close to its maximum speed. "Have you served on this ship before?" I ask.

"No, but I hear good things about Captain Silva. He will get us to Portao."

"You are still concerned."

"I do not like being placed under civilian authority."

"I guess the minister is concerned about his career."

"Yes, more so than the lives of men and women at Portao da Dor."

"Think we'll need those?" I jerk my chin at the Brownings.

"This section of the river is peaceful. The Rio Preto is full of trouble. We must be ready for anything."

"Let us go forward," I say.

"I will catch up to you," Quadros says. "I must set watches with Lieutenant Commander Gaspar. Assign men to the weapons for battle stations."

I make my way forward through the crew's quarters. Cross the crew's mess and step through the door into the waist superstructure. It's a cramped space, with only one row of compartments next to the corridor. It has to be so, to leave most of the ship's beam for the boat deck.

To my right is a narrow space with a watertight hatch cover locked open with a metal bar. I look down and see a ladder leading into the engine room. The engine spaces are tight. River gunboats need a shallow draft. If there is auxiliary steering down there, the wheel must be a lot smaller than the one on the bridge.

A clank of boots on metal, and a mop of dark hair sticks up through the hatchway. Long sinewy fingers clasp the locking mechanism of the hatch cover. Tug on it to make sure it is secure. I stand aside, and a man hauls himself up.

"I'm Breed," I tell him.

Over a hooked nose and droopy black mustache, a pair of sharp eyes stare at me. At last, he raises a fist and jabs a thumb at his chest. "Elvir Collor," he says. "First Engineer."

Before I can respond, the engineer turns away and heads for the crew's mess. Wipes his hands on greasy pants.

I decide to pass up the engine spaces. Carry on forward.

The first three waist compartments are meat lockers. The doors look like those of old-fashioned World War Two refrigerators. Storage for meat, medicines, and supplies. Forward of the stores is the ship's galley, two compartments long. It is wide open to the corridor... there is no fourth wall. I hear the sizzle of meat on a grill, smell the appetizing aroma of barbecue. The chef grins and waves.

I open the door at the end of the corridor and find myself in the officers' wardroom. I've surveyed the length of the ship.

Strident voices carry from the forward cabins. A man and a woman.

I pull the door open and go inside.

The voices are coming from Laura's compartment.

"Leave me alone," Laura says. I hear a slap. The door is ajar, and I see Vargas roll his head back with Laura's blow.

"*Puta.*"

"Don't you *ever* touch me again," Laura hisses. "Who do you think you are? You're the *help*, Vargas. Don't be confused."

Not to be outdone, Vargas raises his hand to slap her.

I push the door open, grab his wrist.

For a second, Vargas glares at me. With a jerk, he twists

his wrist toward my thumb, breaks my grip. Reverses the movement, slams the back of his fist into my mouth. I reel back into the corridor, stunned. Slam into Fonseca's door. It's ajar, swings open.

Fonseca, sitting in his swivel chair, greets me with frightened eyes. He's been sitting there, listening.

Coward.

Vargas grabs me with both hands, jerks me forward. He's going to butt, and I lower my own head to meet his. Our crowns meet with a crack. My vision blurs, but he's stunned. It's the kind of contact that can knock two guys out at once. I clasp my hands together, drive them high. Break his grip, sweep his arms apart. In one fluid motion, I chop the sides of his neck with the edges of my hands.

It's not a killing blow, but it's not meant to be. This isn't a fight to the death. Unarmed combat has to be calibrated to the situation.

Vargas shrugs off the blows, punches me in the gut. I stiffen my stomach muscles. Grab his wrist, catch him in an arm bar, slam him face-first into the corridor wall. Let go, club him in the right kidney. With a grunt, he drops to his knees, right arm raised to the wall.

Right arm under his, I ram my forearm into the back of his neck, throw my weight against him. It's a half-nelson, pinning him against the wall. He flails with his free arm. Big guy, he's a bitch to hold.

What now? He's not giving up. I need to choke him out.

Laura stands at the open door of her cabin, hands raised to her face.

From the fo'c'sle, Sales and Silva storm into the corridor. "That's enough," Sales snaps.

Vargas relaxes. I release him and step back. Eye him warily.

"Animal," Laura spits.

Vargas ignores her. His eyes are fixed on me, and for a moment I think he's going to attack again.

Silent, Vargas brushes himself off. Turns and pushes past Sales, goes to the fo'c'sle.

"What happened?" Silva demands.

Laura shivers. "He made advances. Breed interrupted him."

Silva turns to Sales. "Minister, I will not tolerate such disorder on my ship."

The two men follow Vargas forward.

Lieutenant Quadros joins us. "Are you alright?"

"Yes." I brush the back of my hand across my mouth, wipe blood from my lip.

The encounter took me by surprise. I didn't expect a fight. Not here.

Laura disappears into her cabin, returns with a handful of tissue. "Here," she says. "The bleeding will soon stop."

She brushes the hair from my eyes, examines my forehead. "You have a thick skull, Breed. You'll bruise, but you aren't hurt."

"What was he doing in your cabin?" I ask.

"The door was open. I was unpacking my things, and he came inside."

I remind myself Laura and the minister are acquaintances. Vargas accompanies Sales to Brasilia soirees, so he must have his eye on Laura. On the dock, his interest was plain.

The sensation of Laura's fingers running through my hair feels indescribably sensual. She's the kind of woman men start wars over.

10

DAY TWO

Nevoa – Warfare Disguised

"I have spoken with Vargas," Sales assures me. "It will not happen again."

Somehow I find the minister's words less than assuring. But what am I going to do about it? I say nothing.

"Come to dinner," Sales says. "We are going to be on this boat for a few days. We must get to know each other."

We step into the officers' wardroom and find the table has been set with a white cloth and silver for eight places. Captain Silva sits at the head, Doctor Fonseca at the foot. On one side of the table, Laura sits between Sales and Lieutenant Quadros. On the other side, Vargas sits at one end. I sit at the other, and First Officer Gaspar sits between us like a UN peacekeeper.

"How long before we reach Tieves, Captain?" Sales asks.

The chef arrives, carrying a plate in each hand. I recognize him as the petty officer at the gangplank, the one who cast off the stern line. The Nevoa is certainly running with a minimum of Navy personnel. He sets one before Laura, the other before Sales. Hurries back to the galley for more.

"We shall arrive by noon tomorrow," Silva says. "Our cargo is ready for collection. We will depart for Portao da Dor before nightfall."

"Excellent." Sales watches the chef bring meals for Vargas and Gaspar. "Has there been any contact with Portao?"

"No," Silva says. "We are monitoring their frequency, transmitting every half hour. No response."

"Who's driving the boat?" I ask.

Silva looks down his nose at me. "The Nevoa is a *ship*, Mister Breed. Petty Officer Collor is manning the bridge while we dine."

The first engineer.

"Is there much traffic on the river?"

"A great deal," Silva says.

"Do not fear, Mister Breed." Gaspar's tone is firm. "Elvir Collor has navigated this river since he was a child. The Nevoa is in safe hands."

"Has the Navy tried to reach Portao by helicopter?" I ask.

"Overflights have been conducted," Silva says. "There has been no contact. Understand, Breed... helicopters are of limited use in the Amazon. One of the reasons we are not using one of the more modern gunboats."

"Helicopters can't land?"

"No. The jungle is too close to the river. Often, outposts are built next to the river, under the jungle canopy. Frequently, the structures cannot be seen from the air. Personnel cannot be transported except by jungle penetrator."

A jungle penetrator is a weighted cable on which a man can be raised or lowered. It is an evolution of the McGuire Rig pioneered by Special Forces during the Vietnam war.

"Flying a helicopter in the Amazon is a hazardous profession," Gaspar says. "When you consider there is no place to land except the river, you understand why it takes a brave man. Our Navy loses helicopters and air crew to accidents and emergency landings in water."

The chef goes to the side table and selects a bottle of red wine. Opens it with a flourish and hands Sales the cork. The minister sniffs delicately. Satisfied the base is free of mold, he nods. Like spurting blood, wine splashes into his glass. He swirls the liquid, tests the nose.

"Yes." Sales beams. "Excellent."

The chef makes a round of the table, carefully pouring wine into our glasses. Sales drinks with obvious pleasure.

Vargas drains his glass with one gulp, signals the chef for more.

The meal is excellent. I cut my steak into little chewy pieces. Savor every bite.

"What about Vila de Deus?" Quadros asks. "Have they reported further contact with the Arqueiros?"

Gaspar shakes his head. "All is quiet at Vila de Deus," he says. "But I sense a great deal of tension."

I lift an eyebrow. "How so?"

"Our radio operator raised them earlier. I listened to the conversation. It was clear from their tone they are concerned about movement in the surrounding jungle."

"You can tell that?" Laura asks.

"Yes." Gaspar is firm. "Much is communicated by... how do you say? Subtext. You can hear a man trembling with fear."

"Bah." Vargas finishes his steak, throws his napkin onto the table. "These people are frightened of shadows."

"These shadows shoot bows and rifles," I observe.

Vargas slides his gaze toward me. "You have experience with bows and rifles?"

I say nothing.

"Now, now." Sales steps in to defuse the hostility. "Vargas. Breed. This is a social affair."

"You will excuse me." Vargas stands and leaves the compartment.

"Mister Vargas has been under some strain lately," Sales says. "I have high expectations of the man."

I wonder what those expectations might be. "Has he been falling short?"

"That is between myself and Vargas," Sales says. "He has been with me many years, and he has my confidence. You were fortunate, Mister Breed."

"How do you figure that?"

"Vargas has a certain facility with violence."

Really.

Social situations are but warfare in disguise. I say nothing.

Lieutenant Quadros changes the subject. "When can we expect to arrive at Vila de Deus?"

"Two or three days after Tieves," Silva says. "The journey to Tieves is easy. Once in the Rio Preto, we must slow down. There are places we cannot manage more than a handful of knots. Nevoa is longer than other gunboats. There are switch-backs in the Rio Preto she will have difficulty navigating. Some are not navigable after dark."

"You know the Rio Preto?" I ask.

"As well as any man can hope to know it." Silva smiles. "You must understand... the river is alive. It changes. Depending on the seasons, the flooding of the river can stretch miles on either side. That switchback that gave you so much difficulty last year may be gone tomorrow. Another will take its place in an unexpected location."

Fonseca leans forward. "Do you anticipate difficulty, Captain?"

"One never knows," Silva says. "My concern is the depth

of the river. At this time of year, the snows in the high Andes are beginning to melt. That will help. Nevoa has a draft of three feet under normal circumstances. With your cargo, the draft will increase to five feet or more."

"Have you not been up the Rio Preto before?" I ask Fonseca.

The doctor looks uncomfortable. His cheeks are ruddy from the wine. Despite the air conditioning, his face is shiny with sweat. "This is my first journey to Amazonas," he says. "My practice is in Brasilia."

"Your practice? Are you not an officer in the Brazilian Navy?"

Sales comes to the doctor's rescue. "Doctor Fonseca is my personal physician."

I didn't think the Brazilian Navy would tolerate a ship's doctor four-fifths booze. This makes more sense, but I don't understand why Sales is taking an alcoholic doctor on an Amazon cruise.

"How did you manage to get a private doctor aboard a Naval vessel?" I ask.

Sales spreads his hands. "I am Minister of the Interior," he says. "If I have a special requirement, the Navy is happy to grant my request. Besides, it appears we have a number of civilians aboard."

Of course, that isn't the question. The ship's doctor should be competent to carry out his duties on a military vessel on a mission to the Selva da Morte. There is no indication Fonseca is so qualified. Indeed, he's the last person one would want to take on this kind of trip.

Sales has two men aboard. Vargas and Fonseca. A thug and a gutless alcoholic. That thug hired three men to kill me. What kind of outfit is the minister running? He has no desire to have more civilians on the ship.

The minister laughs heartily.

I cover up my disgust, turn to Silva. "How is the draft a problem?"

"When we arrive at Portao da Dor, we have to tie up at their dock. If the draft is too shallow, we must stand off. We can use the Zodiacs to land troops, but transfer of cargo will be difficult."

Sales looks concerned. "Is this likely?"

"I don't know." Silva shrugs. "We shall wait and see. To keep the ship in trim, we must unload cargo from both the port and starboard sides. It is one thing to use our deck cranes when lying next to a dock, and another to lift to or from a small boat."

The minister's face darkens.

11

DAY THREE

Tieves – Close Call

"Peru is thirty miles upriver," Laura tells me. She turns and points north. "Over there... Colombia." Treetops, one-hundred-and-thirty feet high, tower over the corrugated tin roofs of Tieves. We stand on a pier, watching cranes lift heavy crates onto Nevoa's boat deck. We wear olive drab bush hats, purchased for a handful of reals in a shop. A little more money bought us a six-pack of cold beer.

"Dear God, this sun will melt the skin from our bodies." I pour a beer down my parched throat.

"They have almost finished loading."

"I hope you're right."

The jungle is lush green on both banks of the blue-black river. The sky above is blue as far as the eye can see. It's impossible to raise my eyes above the horizon. The sun is a molten disc, its glare and heat a violent physical assault.

Lieutenant Commander Gaspar stands on the dock, supervising the work. Forklifts carry crates from deuce-and-a-half trucks. Transport them to the edge of the river. They set them down on the dock, close to Nevoa. The crane on the boat deck swings out, and men fasten the hook to straps that bind the crate. The whine of a motor, and the crane takes up the slack. Dockhands grasp the straps to stabilize the load.

Marines on the deck have stripped to the waist. The men, the town and the ships bake under the merciless sun. Apart from the workers, the dockside is devoid of onlookers. None venture outdoors who don't have to. The men manhandle cargo into place. drinking from metal ladles chained to barrels of water.

The Nevoa's cranes work overtime, loading the cargo, then distributing it. The cranes swing several of the crates across the waist so they can be set on the opposite side of the ship. The cargo must be positioned, port and starboard, to prevent the ship from listing.

"You have made an enemy," Laura says.

She is gazing at the Nevoa's navigation bridge. Sales and Vargas stand together, surveying the activity. Vargas turns his head to stare at us, his face immobile.

"We'll lock horns again before this trip is over," I say. "There's a lot about this setup I don't like."

"Such as?"

"I didn't know Fonseca was the minister's personal physician." I shake my head. "That bunch makes my skin crawl."

"I wouldn't like Doctor Fonseca to treat me," Laura says. "His hands are not too steady."

"Sales brought his personal bar. I love the convenience, but with Fonseca aboard, the supply won't last."

A Delta sniper, I was trained to count everything. Snipers are observers and communicators. People think of us as highly skilled marksmen. In fact, more than half of the job is stalking and observing. We report enemy dispositions and activity.

Observation comes as naturally to me as breathing. I've evaluated Nevoa's liquor supply as closely as I am evaluating Nevoa's cargo. Fonseca likes Scotch. I have my eye on two bottles of Kentucky Bourbon that are going to disappear before this trip is over.

I have watched the crane swing twelve large crates aboard. They occupy the boat deck, forward of the Zodiacs. Six on either side.

"I don't see any more crates on the dock," Laura says.

"Thank God."

First Officer Gaspar strides up the gangplank, makes his way to the boat deck. He is met by Lieutenant Quadros. Together, they supervise the Marines. The crates are fastened to the deck with heavy duty cargo straps.

There is a blast from Nevoa's foghorn.

"Reckon we'd best get back to the ship," I say.

I lead the way back along the pier. We hop down onto the dock and make for the ship.

Behind us, a splash. A scaly form slides from the shadows under the pier. Thrashes briefly in the water, disappears. Despite the heat, I shiver.

I lend Laura my hand and help her step onto the gangplank.

"Easy part's over."

We head for the forward superstructure. Laura pulls open the heavy watertight door. "Coming?"

The blast of cold air from inside is tempting. I shake my head. "You go ahead," I say. "I'm going to watch Captain Silva take us into the Rio Preto."

"Enjoy," Laura says. "I have seen it before."

I climb the metal ladder to the bridge deck. Swing myself onto the widow's walk and enter the superstructure.

Captain Silva and the first engineer, Collor, are on the

bridge. Collor is at the helm, Silva is looking down at the dock with a squad radio to his ear.

Gaspar's voice crackles over the receiver. "Loading complete, Captain."

"Coordinate with Lieutenant Quadros. Ensure all our sailors are aboard, and all his Marines."

"Yes, sir."

Silva lowers the squad radio. Looks pleased. "Hello, Breed. We shall be casting off soon."

"That's an awful lot of cargo, Captain."

"Yes. Depending on our assessment of the threat, we want to grow the outpost at Portao da Dor."

"Weapons?"

Silva frowns. "This is a FUNAI outpost. Minister Sales tells me our cargo is medical supplies and food. Enough to sustain forty Marines for three months."

"Sounds like Lieutenant Quadros will find a new home."

"He is aware of the mission. Excuse me."

Silva raises the squad radio, turns his back on me.

I scan the dock, the river. There's more traffic. Fishing boats returning to their anchorage, other ships plying the waters.

Nevoa isn't a large vessel, but she's the biggest ship in Tieves. The other large ships are multipurpose affairs. Most carry cargo on container decks, and passengers on passenger decks. Cargo decks aft and passenger decks forward. That way, paying passengers don't choke on the smoke and fumes that belch from stacks and exhausts.

The ships all look like houses built on rafts. Low-slung, with big boxes for superstructures. Everything on this river looks like it's been built by hand in someone's backyard. The scene is dystopian. Nevoa, with its refurbished World War Two lines, fits right in. Certainly, one of the Navy's more modern gunboats would look out of place.

Silva's radio crackles. "All present and accounted for, Captain."

"Very well," Silva says. "Cast off fore and aft."

"Casting off, aye."

There is no fuss. Silva and I look down at a sailor on the fo'c'sle who casts a line to dockhands ashore.

Silva nods to Collor. "Thirty degrees port."

"Thirty degrees port, aye."

The Captain holsters the squad radio. Reaches forward and picks up an intercom handset. "Engine room, ahead one-quarter."

The deck shivers beneath my feet. There is a low thrum. Nevoa's bow swings to one side. Slowly, she creeps from the dock.

A large passenger ship is approaching from the Peruvian end of the river. Looks like it will cross in front of Nevoa.

"Her right-of-way," Collor says.

Silva speaks into the handset. "All stop."

"All stop, aye."

The vibration under my feet ceases. Nevoa drifts forward, carried by its inertia. "We will let her pass," Silva says.

Three hundred yards away, the other ship turns to port. Bow-on, it makes for Nevoa.

Collor swears. "What is she doing?"

"She wants our berth," Silva says. He leans forward, slams his palm against a plastic button on an instrument panel. Nevoa's foghorn booms a warning.

The passenger ship continues its charge. Unaware Nevoa has cut power, the other vessel is making for the dock we have abandoned.

Silva comes to a decision. He lifts the handset. "Ahead full," he says. Turns to Collor. "Hard aport."

The deck shudders and Collor spins the helm. Nevoa surges forward. The old ship cannot leap. Her heart and old bones are not capable of leaping. But her screws dig for traction in the slimy water. Nevoa's effort is heroic.

Captain Silva knows what he is doing. Without power, the water will not generate enough force against the rudder to turn the ship. By steaming full ahead, he is improving the maneuverability of the vessel.

Nevoa and the other ship charge straight at each other. The distance between the two vessels closes and I brace myself for impact. The deck tilts beneath my feet and Nevoa's bow swings away from the collision. Turbid water sloshes over the port side of the fo'c'sle. We pass the other ship on its starboard side. So close I can spit and hit her captain in the eye.

"Ahead one-third," Silva says.

The ship slows and Collor straightens the helm.

The door to the widow's walk opens and Gaspar steps onto the bridge. "A close one, Captain."

"We had several feet to spare," Silva says. "There is no accounting for the stupidity of others."

A good Captain. Silva is competent and cool under fire.

"I shall check the cargo," Gaspar says. "It might have shifted."

"Very well." Silva turns to me. "Breed, you have experienced an introduction to navigation on the Amazon. Incidents such as these happen all the time."

Nevoa forges upriver. The molten orb of the sun is setting on the western horizon, bathing the bridge in a red glow. I pull the brim of my bush hat low, but there is no shielding my eyes from the glare.

Darkness falls quickly in the tropics. In minutes, only a sliver remains of the sun's disc. Shadows crawl forward along the riverbanks, smother the waning orange light. The screeches of birds and wild animals carry across the water.

Silva flicks a switch on the instrument panel. The bank of

floodlights on the navigation bridge springs to life. The river ahead is bathed in a brilliant white glare that blasts the shadows out of existence.

"There it is, Captain." Collor points to a black stretch of jungle to the left.

"Yes. Make for it. Ahead one-quarter."

"One quarter, aye."

Collor guides Nevoa toward the shadow. As the ship turns slowly, the floodlights reveal a yawning maw half a mile wide. A tributary, opening to the Amazon.

"That," Silva says, "is the Rio Preto. We will be travelling upstream the whole way."

Nevoa slips into the mouth of the river. I look around and find myself engulfed in blackness. The only light is forward, where the shadows retreat from Nevoa's floodlights.

Half a mile wide at its mouth, the Rio Preto narrows quickly. Minutes tick by, and the walls of the jungle close around us. It's a claustrophobic sensation.

The Captain turns to me. "Welcome to the Selva da Morte."

I CLIMB down the portside ladder from the widow's walk to the boat deck. Haul open the hatch to the wardroom and step inside.

The air is cool, the lights are warm, and the makeshift bar looks fabulous. Fonseca sits at the wardroom table, a bottle of Scotch at his elbow and a glass in his hand.

"Welcome, Breed." The doctor's voice sounds steady enough. All the same, I don't like his shiny red complexion. He's well along before dinner. "Is the excitement over for the day?"

"It would seem so. We've entered the Rio Preto, and we're

crawling. I doubt anything will ram us with enough force to sink us."

"Dinner in half an hour," Fonseca says. "Join me for a drink."

I liberate a bottle of Bourbon from the bar and find myself a clean glass. Sit opposite Fonseca and pour myself four fingers straight. "This is quite the holiday from your practice."

Waving his glass, Fonseca gestures to the cabins. "Breed, my practice is on this boat."

"You mean you only have one patient?"

"You could say that, yes." Fonseca knocks back the whiskey, refills the glass. "I now work exclusively for Minister Sales."

I blink.

"The minister appears to be in perfect health," I say. "You can't be one hundred percent occupied with treating him."

"The minister is in very good health," Fonseca assures me. "He is a jealous client, however. He requires me at his beck and call."

"How long have you enjoyed this arrangement?" I sip my Bourbon and lean back.

"I can't remember, exactly. Five years, or six."

Fonseca's glass is down by half.

"You must find it rewarding." Fonseca's drunk, but still guarded. His presence on the Nevoa makes no sense at all. Perhaps he is qualified to serve as a gunboat's doctor, perhaps not. But any way you look at it, his arrangement with Sales is odd, and his presence on the Nevoa is more so.

"Oh, I do," he says. "I do, indeed. The minister pays exceptionally well for my specialist practice."

I wish the red nose would stop speaking in riddles. "Did you practice in Manaus, or Brasilia?"

"Brasilia." Fonseca drains the second glass. Tops it up. "I

had an extensive practice, Breed. Did you know my patients numbered over fifty former or serving cabinet ministers? That I was called to consult for the president himself?"

"That's very impressive. More so that Minister Sales was able to lure you away from such a high-profile practice."

The door to the cabins opens and Laura steps into the wardroom. "Hello," she says. "Am I too early for dinner?"

Fonseca looked about to say more, but falls silent at Laura's interruption.

Damn, it's nice she's joined us, but Fonseca was starting to open up to me.

"Never too early for dinner, my dear." Fonseca waves Laura to a seat. "I am sure everyone will be right along."

The door to the waist superstructure opens and Quadros steps into the room. He's wearing clean and pressed jungle camouflage. His service cap has been folded and neatly stored under his left epaulet.

Sales and Vargas arrive as though joined at the hip. Ten minutes later, Captain Silva takes his place at the head of the table. At nineteen hundred hours sharp, the chef enters to begin serving dinner.

"Tell us of our progress, Captain." Sales spreads a white cloth napkin on his lap.

"Our progress is excellent, Minister." Captain Silva holds his glass for the chef to fill with wine. "We have entered the Rio Preto and are on our way to Vila de Deus. We are proceeding on schedule."

"Excellent."

"Will First Officer Gaspar be joining us?" Lieutenant Quadros asks.

Silva looks at his watch. "I think not, Lieutenant. He is scheduled to relieve me at the helm early tomorrow morning. I suspect he is catching up on some much needed sleep."

"I'm surprised how dark it is out there," I say.

"They do not call this the Rio Preto for nothing," Silva says. "The Selva is gloomy at best, black at worst. The river, at least, is open to the sky. It is never completely black, though it may seem so. You will be surprised how much a dark-adapted eye can discern. All the same, we use our floodlights for safety's sake. One never knows what debris the rains have washed from the shore."

The chef sets the evening steak before me. I will say this about Nevoa. The drink and the food are as good as or better than any cruise ship I would want to board.

12

DAY THREE

Nevoa – Fiadh's Letters

The hair stretched across my doorjamb has not been disturbed. I go inside my cabin, a bottle of Sales's Bourbon in my hand. I set it on the desk, change into a loose, olive drab T-shirt. Pull my boots off.

Stretch out on the bunk, close my eyes. The Amazon is wild country, but the Rio Preto gives me the creeps. I wanted to see it for myself, wasn't prepared for the all-encompassing darkness.

The glass set in my porthole is a black slate. On the other side, I know snakes and caimans are slithering on the shore, gliding in the murky water. Predators stalk their prey, jungle cries cut through the night. Aboard Nevoa, the muggy odor of decomposition drifts from the forest. Decaying vegetation and other things. The Selva da Morte is raw nature. I can imagine how the region got its name. In this place, death is continuously recycled into new life.

From behind the air conditioning grille, Fiadh beckons.

I've resisted opening her letters. Father Andrew, the crafty leprechaun, knew I'd need motivation. He knew Fiadh was a captivating girl. Knew I wouldn't be able to resist getting to know her.

I stand on the bunk, reach for the pack of letters. Open the Bourbon and take a swig.

Father Andrew arranged the letters in chronological order. I'm not that organized. I flip through the pages, look for something interesting. A thick pack of letters has been collected from her Dublin period.

Father Andrew, Trinity is amazing. I'm in constant awe, walking down the same halls as Oscar Wilde. I'm studying Classics and Philosophy. It's not like I don't appreciate science and technology, but these are of man, and need to serve man.

Like Wilde, I've joined The Phil. The debates are fun, and I'm making a lot of new friends. They give me stick for my Catholic views and all, but I give as good as I get and they are fair-handed about it. After all, they didn't accept Catholics for their first two hundred years. Didn't take women for three hundred.

I read Wilde and Yeats in the Pav when I should be studying. Then friends come by. We drink and listen to music together.

We have our debates in pubs. Some grand, some not so much. All of them fun.

Bushmills sharpens me, I must say. I let a med student pull me at Copper's. He said that, for a while, Bushmills sends you up. Then it brings you down. He was right, but his timing sucked. It knocked him out long before it sent me up... what a wasted trip.

Hangovers? The Fear is my constant companion, but I have learned to tame it. If I miss prayers because of drink, I make my confession and pray twice as hard.

I love Wilde's work. What was done to him was a sin, I don't care what the Church says. Live and let live. Maybe when I get back, we

can talk about it. Or maybe you can come to visit. It would be grand if you can, because I won't be in Chicago this summer. Dad is putting together a deal in Brazil, and I'll spend the time there. Mostly in Brasilia, though I will visit Manaus with my friend Laura.
The idea of doing mission work in Amazonas excites me. It's so ironic. Wilde called missionaries "the divinely provided food for destitute and underfed cannibals." I'm sure he was a wonderful man, but it's the kind of thing a man would say who had never met a cannibal. I have, and can assure you they do not view human beings as a dietary staple. It's more of a "If I eat the heart and brain of my enemy, I'll add his strength and wisdom to my own" sort of thing. I'm sure it's done, but I've never seen it, and I have never been afraid of falling victim to the practice.

I smile to myself. Only an innocent teenager could speak so casually of cannibalism in the heart of the Amazon. It sounds like Fiadh enjoyed her time in Dublin. I did well in high school. There's enough math in the Delta sniper program to send a man to the moon, but I never went to college. It's fun to imagine, but I don't think I would have fit in.

You'll be proud of me, Father Andrew. I am being very disciplined. The boys here are a horny bunch, which is a good thing. Because I suffer from constant temptation. They are very good when I make them wear condoms.
One night we went to Café en Seine for a pre-drink. This hot guy caught my eye... He had a way about him. Oh, he had a line of blarney. But then, he was, "Oh darlin', you're not gonna make me wear a Johnny, are you?" I said, "Of course I am, darling." He wouldn't, and I walked out on him. I have learned this—It's easier to leave a guy's place than it is getting him to leave yours. Helps keep peace at home, too.

Father Andrew... I will never have unprotected sex until I meet
someone I know is right for me.

Damn you, Father Andrew. You are turning me into a
voyeur.

The next letter refers to the incident Father Andrew
described. The time he visited Dublin to give a talk.

Father Andrew, I'm sorry for the way I acted when you came to
Dublin. I showed myself to make you want me. I knew you were
made of iron, so I wasn't afraid you'd do anything. I felt cruel, and
took my pain out on you. It was a low, cheap thing to do and I'm
ashamed.
The night before, I had sex with Joseph. For the last time. It was
beautiful, the way God meant it to be. When it was over, I told him
I was going to America and wasn't coming back. My mind's made
up. When I graduate next year, I'll move to Brazil. There is much
good to be done there.
Joseph couldn't understand and we had an unholy row. The latest
in my long string of jilted lovers. After he left, I cried and drank
myself senseless. I wanted to forget, but it didn't work. I woke up
feeling a drunk and a whore. I would be a talented drunk and
whore, don't you think?
When Sarah told me you were there to see me, I wanted to show
myself, raw and unvarnished.
That's a pun. Please laugh.
I confessed to God and he forgave me. Will you forgive me too?
Please do, otherwise I'll hate myself the rest of my life.
Brazil is calling. I'll go with Dad this summer and spend three
months in the Selva. Last year, I saw signs of the Arqueiros. Felt
them watching. They could have hurt me had they wanted to, but
they let me pass. Reaching out to them is against the rules. It's
enough to know they are there, and... they know me.

I set the letter aside, ruffle through the package. There's an envelope of photographs and press clippings. Stories printed from the internet. Pictures of Fiadh as a child, riding a tricycle. Photos of her studying the catechism. Her confirmation, aged eight. A recent portrait of Fiadh, aged twenty-four, wearing a low-necked summer dress.

At her throat is a gleaming gold cross.

13

DAY FOUR

Nevoa – Missing

"**B**reed."

The pounding on the door wakes me. The light in my cabin is still on, the porthole is still black. Fiadh's letters and photographs are lying on my bunk, close to the bulkhead. I'd slept on them.

"What is it?"

I roll out of bed, check my watch. It's 0630 hours. I open my door, find Lieutenant Quadros and First Engineer Collor standing outside. The two men are carrying powerful flashlights.

"We cannot find First Officer Gaspar," Quadros says. "Have you seen him?"

"Not since yesterday, when we left Tieves." I nod to Collor. "He looked into the bridge after the near-collision."

"Yes," Collor says. "I have not seen him since then either."

"How long have you been looking for him?"

"He was due to relieve the Captain at the helm half an

hour ago. When he did not arrive, the Captain ordered the search."

"Where's the Captain?"

"He remains at the helm. Only four of our crew are qualified. Captain Silva, Lieutenant Commander Gaspar, Petty Officer Dutra, and myself."

Delfin Dutra is the second engineer. I do mental arithmetic. If Silva's watch ended half an hour ago, Collor must have been at the helm from the time we left Tieves to midnight. "Where's Petty Officer Dutra?" I ask.

"He is leading a second search party. The lieutenant and I are working our way from the bow, Petty Officer Dutra is working his way from the stern. This will not take long."

Collor's plan makes sense. Two search parties won't fall all over each other. Best to be deliberate and keep everyone else where they are.

"I'll help you look," I tell him. "Give me a minute."

I go back inside and replace Fiadh's photographs and letters in the air conditioning vent. My fingers brush the butt of the SIG. For a moment, I am tempted to take it with me, but I leave it where it lies.

Collor and Quadros had already roused Sales and Vargas before coming to me. Neither man remembered seeing Gaspar last night. I knock on Laura's door.

Laura opens the door a crack. She's dressed in a loose T-shirt and jeans, barefoot. "What's happening?"

I explain the situation and ask her if she remembers seeing Gaspar. She doesn't, and I'm not surprised.

"Stay in your cabin," I tell her.

"Are we in danger?"

"Of course not. But we don't need a lot of people tripping over each other while we conduct a search."

Quadros raps on Doctor Fonseca's door. There is no answer.

"Doctor," Collor calls. "Wake up."

Quadros raps on the door again. Still no answer.

"Oh, for heaven's sake." I step between the two men, turn the doorknob, and push into Fonseca's room.

The doctor has done a face-plant on his desktop. He made a lot more progress last night than I did. The bottle by his right hand is bone dry.

I grab him under his arms and pull him from the chair. "Help me," I say. "Quadros, get his legs."

Fonseca's shirt is black with sweat. Quadros lifts him by the ankles. Together, we lift the comatose doctor from the floor and swing him onto the bunk. His head lolls to one side and saliva drools from the corner of his mouth.

"We must continue our search," Collor says.

I look under Fonseca's bunk. "Not there."

We search the forward and waist superstructures. Meet Second Officer Dutra and a petty officer on the quarterdeck. We then exit onto the starboard boat deck and split up. Our team works its way to the bow, and back along the port side. The other team works its way to the stern and back.

"We have searched the quarterdeck and crew's quarters," Dutra says.

"And we have searched the bridge and navigation decks," Collor tells him. "That leaves..."

"The engineering deck," Dutra says, "but I have been there all night."

"Let us search it again."

Collor leads us into the waist superstructure in the direction of the quarterdeck. I remember this was where I first met him. Crawling from the hatch that led down a ladder into the engine room.

"The machinery space is cramped," Collor says. "Let us go. We know it well."

Collor explains that with its shallow draft, all but a small fraction of Nevoa sits above water. The twin diesels occupy the engine compartment beneath the stack and the quarter-deck. The rest of the narrow space beneath the main deck is occupied by fuel tanks, fresh water tanks, pumps, and bilges.

The two men disappear down the hatch, leaving Quadros and I to cool our heels.

"What do you think?" I ask the Marine.

"We have looked everywhere," Quadros says. "I doubt they will find him below decks."

"Think he fell overboard?"

Quadros shakes his head. "Unlikely. Gaspar struck me as an experienced officer. He knows the Nevoa."

Half an hour later, Collor climbs from the engine room. Wipes his greasy hands on his trousers, takes a squad radio from a holster on his belt. "Nothing," he says. "Petty Officer Dutra will remain below."

Collor keys the squad radio and speaks rapidly.

"The Captain wishes me to relieve his watch at the helm," Collor says. "He will meet you, Minister Sales, and the others in the officers' wardroom in fifteen minutes."

The first engineer leads us along the corridor and back into the dining room. He continues forward, sends Sales and Vargas back to join us. The doctor, of course, is sleeping off the minister's Scotch.

Sales goes straight to the bar. Pours himself an orange juice. "No sign of Gaspar?"

The minister does not have the good grace to offer us a drink. The first engineer must have told him about our fruit-less search. I say nothing, go to the bar, and help myself. Offer a glass to Quadros. The Marine shakes his head.

Laura steps into the wardroom.

"The man must have fallen overboard," Sales says.

The Captain strides into the room. He looks drawn. He

has been awake all night, navigating the twists and turns of the Rio Preto.

"Lieutenant Commander Gaspar did not fall overboard," Silva says.

"Then where is he, Captain?" Sales paces. "Your first engineer told me the ship has been thoroughly searched."

"I did not say he is on the ship."

Sales reaches for a pack of cigarettes. Taps one out, lights up. "Then you suspect... foul play?"

"Gaspar is an experienced seaman. He knows the Amazon, he knows the Nevoa. He would not fall overboard." Silva's eyes sweep the room. He stares at each one of us in turn. "There is a murderer among us."

Vargas straightens, hands on his hips. "It is not advisable to make accusations without proof, Captain."

The Captain stares Vargas down. His voice trembles. "I repeat, Gaspar was too experienced a seaman to fall overboard. He must have met with foul play."

"Vargas is right, Captain." Sales's tone is reasonable. On the edge of patronizing. "An accident might befall anyone. Even the most experienced."

Silva shakes his head. "Who had the opportunity? Gaspar was last seen on the bridge at dusk. We entered the Rio Preto at 1800 hours and I joined you for dinner half an hour later. We were all in the officers' wardroom until I left at 2330. I then relieved First Engineer Collor at the helm."

"Not so, Captain." Sales exhales a cloud of smoke and waves his cigarette with a languid hand. "Doctor Fonseca retired early, as did Miss Alves."

"Doctor Fonseca," I point out, "was in no condition to commit foul play. He was indisposed when we looked in on him this morning. Miss Alves is a small woman. I doubt she could have overcome Gaspar. She could not have heaved him over the safety rail that encloses the main deck."

"The rest of us," Sales says, "have *you* for an alibi, Captain. You were with us all night. Breed and Lieutenant Quadros left shortly after you. Mister Vargas and myself remained for a nightcap, retired at one o'clock. I went straight to bed, and assume Mister Vargas did the same."

Vargas shrugs acknowledgement. He turns away from Silva, steps to the bar, and pours himself a drink. Sales looks out a porthole at the jungle scenery. It is still shrouded in shadow, but the sky has lightened and the sun is beginning to creep above the treetops.

"You cannot exclude the possibility Gaspar fell overboard," Sales concludes.

"I have questioned my Marines and all who were on watch," Quadros says. "None saw Gaspar, or anything out of the ordinary."

"Your men are new to the Nevoa," I say gently. "They would not know Gaspar on sight."

Silva's shoulders sag. "We must turn around to look for him. I will give the order."

"No, Captain." Sales takes a deep drag on his cigarette. "You will not."

Silva darkens with rage. "I am captain of the Nevoa."

Sales turns to face the captain. "Yes, but I am in command of this mission."

"In all matters save those that affect the safety of the ship and crew."

The minister traces an arc with his cigarette. "Is the ship in danger? The crew? We have a missing man, Captain. However unfortunate that might be, there are Marines and FUNAI workers in danger at Portao da Dor."

"We must find him," Silva insists.

Vargas steps forward. "If the man has drowned, the piranha and catfish will have left nothing to find."

"Other ships may find him before we do." Sales's tone is

brisk. "I suggest we file a report with Tieves. Have them circulate a bulletin to all river traffic. Come, Captain. Let us see to it."

The minister escorts the captain from the wardroom. Vargas drains his glass and follows them into the corridor.

Quadros, Laura and I stare at each other. Whatever Augusto Sales's rationalizations, I agree with Captain Silva. There *is* a murderer aboard.

First Officer Gaspar is dead.

14

DAY FOUR

Nevoa – A Knock on the Door

There *is* a murderer aboard.

Quadros looks troubled. "I must see to my men," he says. With that, the Marine lieutenant leaves us.

"What do you think happened to the first officer?" Laura asks.

I pour her a glass of orange juice, top up my glass. "Someone killed him. Tossed him overboard. Food for the fishes."

"But *why*?"

"If we knew that, we'd know who killed him."

Laura stares at me.

"This is awkward," I say. "Apart from the other Marines and sailors, we all have alibis for most of the period in question. Gaspar's cabin is above us on the bridge deck. Collor was at the helm, and the captain was dining with us. That leaves Max Morais, the radio operator. He doesn't strike me as the murdering type."

"Gaspar might not have been killed in his cabin," Laura says.

"That's true. He could have been killed anywhere on the ship."

"Assuming he was killed."

"It's obvious he's been killed." I set my empty glass in the sink. "That's why this is so uncomfortable. It's hard to imagine why any of the Marines or sailors would want to kill him. For thirty minutes before dinner, and between one and six, anyone could have done it."

"What should we do?"

"There's nothing we can do. Frankly, the minister is right. It's possible Gaspar was killed to delay our arrival at Portao da Dor. If that's the case, we must press on."

I *want* the killer to be Vargas. I want it so bad I can taste it. But if Gaspar was killed to delay our journey, it would not make sense for Sales to order the captain to continue. That is suggestive of Sales's innocence. Vargas is Sales's man, so it is also suggestive of Vargas's innocence.

I reach for the door.

"Where are you going?" Laura asks.

"I'm going to take another look around the ship," I tell her.

"I'm coming with you."

We step out of the cool interior of the wardroom and onto the boat deck. Mid-morning, the heat and humidity are oppressive. The Nevoa noses along the river, gliding between jungle walls a hundred and fifty feet high.

I look forward to the bridge. Two men on the navigation deck, their backs to us. A sailor in his white uniform and a Marine in jungle camouflage. Turning slowly, I look aft, past the quarterdeck. There, on the poop, another Marine stands watch. His hand rests casually on one of the Brownings.

The helmsman and a lookout occupy the bridge.

"What are you thinking?" Laura asks.

"The attention of the lookouts is directed forward and aft," I tell her. "Gaspar could not have been thrown from the bow or stern without someone seeing."

"That means he must have been thrown from here."

"Yes. Assuming the body was disposed of after one o'clock."

Laura and I stand at the rail. Between us and the side of the waist superstructure are four massive wooden crates. They have been lashed down with canvas straps six inches wide. The crates are arranged in two rows, two crates deep. Aft of the crates squats one of the Nevoa's two Zodiacs.

"Look." I point to the ugly green water flowing past the Nevoa's hull. "Nevoa's draft is shallow. The killer could have pulled Gaspar's body from between the crates and slipped it into the river."

"Slipped it."

"Yes. He wouldn't *throw* the body in. A splash would draw attention from either the navigation bridge or the poop. No, the killer would *slide* the body into the river. Hold it by the legs, lower it into the water, then let the current sweep it away. We are traveling upstream, so the current would carry the body aft. The lookouts on the poop might have seen something drift past, but in the darkness, I doubt it."

The muggy atmosphere of the Rio Preto becomes twice as oppressive. I turn and head back to the wardroom.

"What are you going to do now?" Laura asks.

"I'm going to finish my sleep," I tell her. "There is nothing else to do. But let's keep our doors locked. We don't know who killed Gaspar, or why."

. . .

I RETURN to my cabin and shut the door. Again, I consider taking down the SIG. Again, I resist the temptation. Instead, I recover Fiadh's papers from their hiding place. I open the package, take out a handful of photographs and letters, and set them on the bed.

My shirt clings to my body. I peel it off and hang it on the chair back. Enjoy the feel of cool air against my bare shoulders and chest. I pour myself three fingers of Bourbon. I lie on my side on the bunk, prop myself on one elbow. Study Fiadh's pictures.

I pick up a sports photograph. Two rows of girls in uniform. Back row standing, front row kneeling. Center front —Fiadh, aged eighteen. Captain of her college lacrosse team.

A news story has been printed from the internet. A photo of Fiadh being escorted from the lacrosse box. Her hair is a sweaty tangle.

Fiadh Connor, daughter of Cuchulain Connor, arrested for assault in lacrosse fight. Charges dropped.

That's interesting. I set the article aside and pick up another printout. This is from Fiadh's college newspaper.

Holy Cross captain suspended for fighting.

Fiadh speared another girl with the butt of her lacrosse stick, shattered her sternum. Any girl who wasn't the daughter of Cuchulain Connor would have been expelled. I bet the son of a bitch was proud of her. The next letter is from Fiadh to Father Andrew.

Father Andrew, I want you to hear my side of it. That other team was willing to take me out to win the championship. That girl tried

*to clothesline me. She missed and hit my mouthguard. Could have
killed me.*

*I knocked the stick out of her hands. When she was wide open, I
speared her in the chest. She went down, and I raged out. I hit her
again and again until they pulled me off. Next thing I knew, I was
handcuffed in the back seat of a police car. She's still in the hospital.
Dad got the charges dropped, but Holy Cross suspended me and
kicked me off the team.*

*Do you know what the girls did? At the championship, they suited
up and wouldn't leave the changing room. Said they wouldn't play
unless I was reinstated.*

They defaulted—for me.

*The girls busted their asses for that championship. Had I been
there, I would have made them play.*

*I don't know how to feel, Father Andrew. The anger is gone, and
I'm sorry I hurt that girl. I love the girls on the team and feel
humbled by what they did. I feel... unworthy. I'm going to Brazil. I
don't know if I'll ever come back.*

Why does God always torture the best of us?

The OD-As and Delta are full of guys like Fiadh Connor.
Played hard in the paint all their lives.

I pick up a recent portrait and lean back in my bunk.
Reach for the Bourbon, take a drink, bite it back. I need to be
careful I don't turn into Fonseca.

This photograph is of Fiadh, aged twenty-four. Clean,
wholesome, and a fire in her belly. Wide green eyes, all pupil.
Long blond hair, a shade lighter than the golden cross at her
throat. I'm beginning to know the girl.

Unworthy?

Fiadh Connor is a natural leader.

. . .

A SOFT KNOCK on my door. I roll out of bed and open it a crack. Laura stands in the corridor. Her eyes meet mine, sweep over my bare chest.

"You aren't the type to sleep in the middle of the day," she says.

"No, you should get your rest whenever you can."

The girl is looking past me, at my bunk. Fiadh's papers. "She's beautiful, isn't she?"

"I suppose so."

"Can I come in?"

I swing the door open, and Laura steps into the room. The space is narrow, and she leans against me as I swing the door shut. Her hand goes to the stripe of raised white flesh that runs diagonally across my chest. Her thumb traces it gently.

"What happened here?"

"Bad guy had a knife."

"You were lucky."

"It's better to be lucky than good."

Laura flattens her hand against my chest, strokes it. Her right hand goes to my left bicep. Squeezes. "From what I saw in that alley, you're both."

Not much point talking. Why language a girl to death when she wants you to hold her?

My hand goes to the small of Laura's back, jerks her close. She tips her chin back, opens her mouth. Hot and humid like the Selva, we drink each other in. I explore her shoulder blades, her buttocks. Reach down and undo the buttons on her Levi's. Hook my thumbs inside the band of her under-wear, pull everything down.

She's barefoot. Steps out of the puddle of her jeans. I lift her, and she wraps her legs around my hips. Two steps and we're at the bunk. I lower her onto it and climb aboard. Clumsy, like first-time lovers are. I raise myself on my arms.

She reaches down, unbuckles my belt. Between us, the humid smell of sex.

We thrash together. Dimly, I sense Fiadh's letters sliding off the bunk and onto the floor. Laura opens herself to me. As I slide into her, I look over her shoulder. From her portrait on the floor, Fiadh smiles at me.

15

DAY FOUR

Nevoa – Into the Storm

I feel guilty. I should have been in the moment with Laura, but thoughts of Fiadh intruded. Damn you, Father Andrew. We're not two days into the expedition, and I feel like I know Fiadh better than I know Laura. Fiadh is probably dead in the jungle, and Laura is living and breathing.

Laura and I spent the whole afternoon in bed as Nevoa pushed further south. An hour before dinner, she left me with a long, lingering kiss. Pulled her clothes on, dashed across the corridor to her cabin.

I get dressed. Shuffle Fiadh's papers together and hide them in the duct. Then I go out to dinner. Join the others in the officers' wardroom.

Sales and Vargas are sipping wine, speaking softly. Fonseca nurses a glass of whiskey. Quadros isn't drinking.

"Welcome, Breed." Fonseca raises his glass to me. "Did you have a restful afternoon?"

We found the doctor in a drunken stupor this morning.

Could it have been an act? The walls that separate the cabins are thin. I wonder how much the old sponge heard.

Silva enters the wardroom as the chef carries in our dinners. Privileges of rank, the captain must have called ahead.

"Has there been any word from Portao da Dor, Captain?"

"No. We hoped they might use their ManPack to reach us. There is nothing but silence." Silva takes his seat at the table. Voice laced with bitterness, he asks, "Do you not wish to enquire about First Officer Gaspar?"

The minister takes a long drag from his cigarette. "Of course. Have any other boats found him?"

"No, but Tieves has relayed our request to all traffic on the river."

Laura enters the room and we rise to greet her. Silva gallantly holds her chair and seats her to his right. The attractive woman seems to provide a welcome distraction from the murder of Gaspar.

We have barely begun our dinner when we are interrupted by a crash of thunder. The sky opens up and a deluge drowns the portholes. The ship shudders with the impact of rain on the deck. It is like Nevoa is cruising under a massive waterfall.

I get up and step to the nearest porthole. Adjacent to the watertight door, it looks onto the waist of the ship. The rain does not deviate by so much as a degree from the vertical. Droplets pelt the boat deck and cargo like bullets. The ship, the jungle, and the river have baked under the sun all day. Rain instantly turns to steam. Thick clouds billow from the jungle and cloak the Nevoa in mist.

"Imagine being caught out there," I say.

"This is normal for the Amazon." Silva steeples his fingers. "It will slow our pace, particularly at night. The floodlights reflect from the mist. Visibility is limited to a matter of yards."

"Have you factored these conditions into your estimates?" Sales asks. "When will we arrive at Vila de Deus?"

"I have," Silva assures him. "We should arrive at Vila de Deus tomorrow afternoon. Portao da Dor the following night, or the morning after."

There's a sound like a sack of potatoes crashing to the deck behind me. Lieutenant Quadros, sitting opposite, shoots to his feet. Races around the table and tries to open the watertight door.

The hatch won't open. A body, crumpled on the deck, blocks the way. Quadros throws his shoulder into the door, forces it open, pushes the body aside. The rain pours down, blasting the boat deck.

I grab the fallen man's wrists and haul him inside. Water-logged, he's wearing the white uniform of a sailor.

Quadros hauls the hatch shut.

"Fonseca," I say. "Get over here."

The diners are on their feet They form a small crescent, looking down at the body. It's the radio operator. His skull has been crushed like an eggshell. His hair and the side of his head are matted with blood. Already the water on the deck is stained red.

Fonseca kneels beside the sailor.

"Help him," I tell Fonseca.

The doctor stares at the young man. "I can't."

I grab Fonseca by the collar, drag him forward. "I said, check him out."

Hands trembling, Fonseca examines the boy. "I can't do anything for him because he's dead."

I get up, open the door, and step outside. The impact of the rain is a physical blow. This is hell. The atmosphere is too humid to breathe. The air is clotted with the stench of decomposing vegetation, and it's hot. I stare up the ladder, metal rungs slippery and wet. The metal is shiny with water.

Dusk had been falling as we began dinner. The heavy cloud cover has brought darkness early.

Head bowed against the torrential downpour, I climb the ladder. I reach the top, grab a stanchion, and pull myself onto the widow's walk. I grab the rail with both hands, look back along the length of ship. The rain and mist are so thick I can't see past the stack. The river is boiling with steam. The Nevoa looks like it is cruising on a cloud.

Hot rainwater is pouring down my face. I spit and turn around, careful to keep my two-handed grip on the rail. The widow's walk is deserted. In front of me is the back of the bridge superstructure and the door leading inside. To the right is the ladder leading up to the navigation bridge. I crane my neck. There are two men up there, standing watch in the downpour. Their attention is fixed forward. Straining to see obstacles that could endanger the Nevoa.

From where I stand, I can see around the bridge super-structure. Look forward at the river. The floodlights are on, but the captain was right—the steam acts like a mirror, reflecting the brilliant glare back onto the ship. The light is diffused, like the river ahead is a massive light box. The ship is crawling forward. We are barely making six knots.

I consider climbing to the navigation deck, think better of it. The watch, a sailor and a Marine, will have seen nothing. Instead, I jerk open the door leading into the bridge super-structure and go inside.

Blessed cool air. I'm drenched.

The corridor is deserted.

There are six compartments aft of the bridge. I look in the first one on my left. Empty, nothing out of the ordinary. The one to my right is Gaspar's. I searched it this morning. Also empty. The adjacent cabin is Silva's.

I'm not shy. I push the door open. There is no one inside. The Captain is clean and tidy, a fastidious naval officer. Clean uniforms in a closet. Dress whites, uniform whites, jungle camouflage. Polished shoes and boots. A small shelf of books. Logs and charts.

I close the door. Look into the compartment across the corridor. Empty. This cabin was shared by the navigator and radio operator. The ship is operating on a skeleton crew. This trip, it carried only the radio operator. The Captain and First Officer handle navigation.

Careful inspection of Morais's cabin yields nothing. I shut the door behind me and check the navigation compartment. Nothing stands out. The radio compartment deserves careful examination. Not ten minutes ago, Max Morais was sitting at that chair, working his equipment. Doing... what?

Trying to raise Portao da Dor?

Receiving a transmission from Tieves?

Perhaps Gaspar has been found.

My eyes sweep the desk. A pad of paper and a ballpoint pen lie on top. I pick up the pad. Nothing has been written on it. I curse myself for not searching the dead man's pockets. Something caused him to rush out, in the downpour, and swing himself over that ladder. Did he want to bring us news?

In the corner of the radio compartment sits the 40 Watt ManPack. Undisturbed.

I leave the radio compartment and go to the bridge.

Collor stands at the helm, his attention fixed forward. The windows of the bridge are bathed in the bizarre light of the floodlights, reflected off the steam.

"How long before we get out of this fog?" I ask.

The engineer refuses to turn around. "It will grow thinner when the rain stops," he says.

"The radio operator has fallen to the boat deck," I tell him. "Did he say anything to you?"

"No. I did not even know he had left the compartment. I am quite occupied here. As you can see."

Too preoccupied to inquire about Morais's condition. "Of course."

I push through a side door, back into the rain. Make my way along the widow's walk to one of the forward companionways. Steep, with narrow risers covered with a synthetic slip-resistant material. I grip the railings with all my strength and climb down to the fo'c'sle.

Why didn't Morais come this way? The companionways are slippery, but they are easier to negotiate than the ladders aft.

I pass behind the Bofors mount. The muzzle of the gun has been covered with a canvas condom, cinched tight with a drawstring. Rain drums on the hatch to the 40mm magazine. The fo'c'sle has become a lake. I pull open the door to the forward superstructure. Step into the corridor.

The cabin space is deserted. I check left and right, find the dental surgery and sickbay empty. I push aft, past the other cabins, and re-enter the wardroom.

The group are where I left them. More or less.

Morais remains on the floor, dead. Someone had the decency to cover him with a blanket. Fonseca has collapsed into a chair. The doctor stares at the dead man. Sales and Vargas stand to one side. Laura stands with her arms folded over her chest, as though she is cold.

"Breed," Silva snaps. "Where have you been?"

"Morais fell from the bridge deck," I tell him. "I wanted to see why."

"Was he alone?"

"It would seem so." I kneel beside the corpse, look up at Fonseca. "Did the fall kill him?"

Fonseca looks at me stupidly. "What else?"

There's a professional medical opinion. I move the blanket to one side.

Silva stands over me. "What are you looking for?"

"Why do you think Morais rushed outside, into the rain, to climb down that ladder?" I turn the dead man's pockets inside out, pat him down. Nothing. "Did anyone search him before I got back?"

The penny drops. "You think he received a message?"

"Some news he wanted to give you. I thought he might have written it down. Apparently not."

"News of First Officer Gaspar," Silva says.

"He might have raised Portao da Dor."

The man's pockets are empty.

"Alright," I say. "Who else can operate the radio?"

Silva looks uncomfortable. "I have some knowledge. But transmission in the Selva is difficult. It is more art than science."

I'm not surprised. HF communication is a powerful, long-range technology. It depends a great deal on atmospheric conditions, the antennae deployed, and terrain features. Triple-canopy, one-hundred-and-fifty feet overhead, doesn't help.

Early in my career, I was cross-trained as a Special Forces communications sergeant. A useful skill for a sniper.

I don't think Morais fell.

Including the radio operator, two men have been killed. I'm not about to advertise that I have the same skill set as the last man murdered.

"We must preserve the man's body for burial," Quadros says.

"I cannot spare any of my men under these conditions," Silva says. "Have two of your Marines come forward. We will keep him with the frozen stores."

Laura wrinkles her nose. "With our *food?*"

"With the medicines," Silva says.

I smile to myself. At twenty-four, Laura Alves is still very much a child. I wonder how Fiadh Connor would react to the events of the last few days.

Again, I find myself comparing Fiadh to Laura. Two friends, both attractive young women. Yet one went into the Selva and the other didn't. I remind myself to learn more about Fiadh and her friends. Anna Goulart and Pedro Bernardes remain ciphers.

I rise to my feet.

Sales eyeballs me. "Where are you going now, Breed?"

"I'm going to change. Then I'll finish my dinner."

16

DAY FOUR

Nevoa – The Team

I lock my cabin door. Resolve not to let Laura interrupt me. My T-shirt is loose and comfortable. I tug it down over my jeans and stretch out on my bunk. The sheets still smell of sex.

Fiadh's letters form a neat pile on my desk. I prop her portrait next to them so it feels like she is speaking to me.

God, I must be losing it.

Father Andrew, I've been living in Brazil for almost two years and it feels like home. Best of all, I feel like my friends and I are making a difference in the Selva da Morte. Anna, Pedro and Laura are a great squad. We have each other's back and that's what counts when you are in the bush. The great explorers feared mutiny more than the harshest conditions.

Anna is from a small town in the Dordogne. She's proud to be French and not Parisian. She wants to go to medical school and work for Medecines Sans Frontieres. To experience the world, she spent a year with me at the mission. This is our second year

*together, and she's deferred her studies again. Next year I will
encourage her to get her degree and come back.*

*Pedro studied at the University of São Paulo. Like me, he hates the
poverty in Brazil. Most of all, he hates the income disparity that is
so in-your-face. Pedro, Laura and I come from well-off families.
We've taken our good fortune for granted all our lives. When you
come here and see the poor people scratching to make ends meet,
you want to do something about it. The mission sent us to the
Selva, a place called Vila de Deus. There, we feel we can make a
difference in a small way, working with the local people.*

*At Vila de Deus, I learned of the different tribes in the Selva. Some
have relationships with civilization. Others we don't know
anything about. When I learned illegal loggers and miners were
hurting them to exploit the country, I had to do something. I
started venturing into the bush, finding the crooks, and turning
them in. It wasn't long before the others came with me.*

*Laura was my friend before I volunteered at the mission. Years
ago, Dad brought me to Brazil on my holidays and his business
trips. We went to a lot of stultifying parties in Brasilia, so Dad
could build relationships in the country. Laura's father is a big-shot
manufacturer and played the same game. Courted politicians and
did deals. Those parties were horrible and it was great to have a
friend to spend time with.*

*Laura and I went to the beach and clubs in Rio. We had a grand
time. I've always been a little out of control, but Laura is something
else. She gets like two different people. Her wild side takes me
places I wouldn't go on my own.*

*Later, when I volunteered at the mission, I invited her to join us on
our trips to the Selva. She was reluctant at first. When we started
venturing into the bush, she became as passionate as I. Together,
with Anna and Pedro, we began to find traces of uncontacted tribes.
The Arqueiros are the ones who fascinate me most. We find traces
of their fires, their arrows.*

I'm learning their language. I make notes and write down words

from the tribes we meet in the area. A few verbs, but mostly nouns.
I can make myself understood with sign language. I'm sure their
dialects, while different, must be related.
I never feel threatened by the Arqueiros, or any other Indians, for
that matter. I feel like they know me. We have a subliminal bond,
like the way we move communicates our intentions. Laura and the
others are often frightened, but I tell them not to worry. So long as
they are with me, they have nothing to fear.
It is the criminals I worry about, Father Andrew. Illegal loggers,
miners, narcos. They kill the Indians. I am sure they would kill us
if they could. We have been responsible for the arrest of a few
gangs. In other cases, the criminals manage to escape, but at least
the Army and Navy chase them away.

Fiadh and her team of volunteers were making a difference. Two years in the Selva. Operations leading to the arrest
of a handful of criminal gangs. That's enough to make an
impression. Manuel Barros, at FUNAI, didn't want her out
there in the Selva, but he used her information.

FUNAI, the Army, and the Navy respected Fiadh. The
gangs must have respected her enough to make her a target.
Barros knew it. That's why he didn't approve of her team
tramping around the Selva da Morte. Fiadh was a crusader. A
Christian soldier, driven to make a difference, no matter the
risk.

Father Camos, the priest at Vila de Deus, doesn't want us in the
Selva anymore. He says there are gangs in the forest, he doesn't
know who they are, and one of these days they are going to kill us.
Manuel Barros told me the same thing. He says the Navy has
heard gold miners and loggers have put a bounty on our heads. I
told the squad, and they want to continue our work. God bless
them, our faith will protect us.
I don't like Father Aguiar, but I need him. He pays for our trips to

the Selva. I know he and Father Camos have had words about me.
Father Camos doesn't want us in the Selva, Father Aguiar does.
Father Aguiar is using us to impress the bishop. He doesn't mind
risking our lives to increase his earthly power.

He is risking our lives, Father Andrew. Don't think I'm a silly girl
who doesn't know what she's doing. I know how dangerous the
Selva is, and I've spoken with my friends. We all want to go. But
Father Camos and Manuel Barros are coming from a good place,
and Father Aguiar isn't.

I ask God to forgive me for disliking Father Aguiar so much. God
must make him as he is because he is helping me do God's work.
How strange that I should love those who want to stop me, and
dislike someone who is helping me.

Dad always tells me, do what you have to do. And I am my father's
daughter.

Life is funny like that.

Fiadh Connor led her team into the Selva da Morte.
Unarmed. Knowing there was a bounty on her head. Didn't
she understand she could just as easily be killed on the
streets of Brasilia? Criminal gangs have long arms.

To think of Fiadh as a naïve child is to underestimate her.
She's the daughter of a powerful man. She's intelligent,
worldly, and educated. She has everything to live for, yet she
acts like she's got a death wish.

I stare at the photograph.

Who are you?

17

DAY FIVE

Nevoa – Night Prowl

The Tritium dial on my watch reads 0200 hours. I lie in bed and listen. The black nights of the Hindu Kush honed my senses. I quarter the space around me using a clock face. Twelve to three, three to six, six to nine, and nine back to twelve. Everything within range of my hearing is quiet on the main deck.

I do the same thing on the vertical axis. There's more to notice there. The creaking of the hull on the lower deck. The murmur of water as the Nevoa makes her way upriver. Occasional footsteps above. The floor of the bridge deck.

Two different sets of footsteps. Not distinguishable by sound, but by pace. One man moves at a deliberate pace. Another moves more quickly. I think Silva is the thoughtful one. The other might be Collor. Only three men are qualified to navigate the ship. Silva's cabin is in the middle of the bridge deck, starboard side. The two engineers bunk together on the lower deck.

I push my door open. The corridor is empty. I walk past

Laura's cabin, then Fonseca's. The officers' wardroom is dark. I make my way aft, enter the waist superstructure.

The galley is empty. The chef sleeps aft, with the rest of the crew.

Spooky. There are three refrigerated compartments on my left. I go to the first one and grasp the long, chrome-plated handle. Pull the door open.

A cloud of cold air billows out. I grope for a light switch. When the light comes on, I look inside. Packaged meats have been stacked in long rows. They occupy the middle and lower shelves of the storage compartment. Below them, boxes of medicines.

I shut the refrigerator, move on to the next. The third compartment yields the radio operator's corpse. It's been wrapped in two shelter halves provided by the Marines. Bound at the feet and shoulders.

Max Morais seems heavier frozen than he looked alive. Damn, he's stiff as a log. I drag him into the corridor, undo the rope that binds the shelter halves. I expose the corpse and find that his head and neck are frozen immobile. I roll the body this way and that to examine the wound.

Only one wound. Morais's face is unmarked, as is the back of his head.

Above the right ear, the side of his head has caved in. There's blood, and his black hair is matted with it.

It's a myth that dead men don't bleed. When the heart stops, you don't get arterial spray, but blood gets pushed around. Bodies are wet sacks of mushy stuff, including flexible hoses full of blood. When all that mush settles, it puts pressure on hoses and bladders. All kinds of fluids leak out.

What interests me is the angle of the wound. It falls in a perfect, horizontal line. Four inches long, an inch above his ear. I wonder what Morais hit his head on as he fell.

I roll the body up and bind the shelter halves together.

Push it into the freezer and close the door. In the middle of the Amazon, I shiver in the frigid air.

Head to the galley. It's a wide-open space. They don't want men having to open and close doors while carrying food. In the light from the corridor, I look around for tools. Thank goodness South Americans love red meat. There's a heavy meat cleaver and a twelve-inch Golok machete. They both have spines a quarter of an inch thick.

The Golok is a bit shorter than the Malays and the British would have it. This one is a good, multipurpose tool. In the Philippines, it is used for fighting, jungle warfare, and as an agricultural tool. It'll do the job. I take it from its canvas scabbard, go back inside the wardroom.

Cautiously, I open the hatch to the starboard boat deck. The same one the radio operator's body blocked. There's enough light from the moon, and three lamps evenly spaced on the roof of the waist superstructure.

I step into the humid Amazon night. Shut the hatch behind me, stand with the Golok at my side, leaning against the superstructure. The boat deck is deserted. As usual, the watch is concentrated on the navigation bridge and poop. The Marines on the poop are out of sight. The men on the navigation deck can see the waist of the ship, but their attention is focused forward.

I step to the nearest cargo crate. Examine it with a careful eye. Rough-hewn boards. Splintery. The cover has been nailed on. I squeeze the point of the machete into the seam beneath the cover. It gives a little, and I work more of the blade underneath. With a bit of pressure, the nails holding down the lid give way.

A foot is all I need. Eighteen inches. I cast my eyes over the plastic tubular cases nestled inside the crate. Sturdy coffins designed to absorb the shock of accidental impact. Black in color, identification numbers stenciled in white.

I cover up the crate, careful to fit the nails back into the same holes. All it takes is firm pressure to seat the lid. It's been pried loose once. It will come free more easily the next time.

Back inside, I return the Golok to the galley.

Nevoa carries more than enough motive to kill two men. Enough to kill everyone aboard except the murderer. The only problem is, I still don't know who it is.

I go back to my cabin and lie down. Stare at the ceiling.

Shut my eyes and listen. Quarter the ship.

Two sets of footsteps on the deck above.

Maybe three.

Not the captain. I know Silva's deliberate, thoughtful pace. The footsteps stop.

Morais was killed for the radio. The only man aboard who could use it well in this neck of the woods. That's what Captain Silva said. Who's up there? Might not hurt to go for a walk and say hello.

I get up, return to the boat deck. Climb the ladder to the bridge, swing myself onto the widow's walk. I enter the superstructure from the back, find the corridor dark. The door to the bridge is shut. I look left and right. The first officer's and captain's cabins are shut and dark. The navigator and radio operator's cabin is dark.

I hear the soft murmur of a voice.

Slowly, I approach the radio compartment. The door is ajar, and a dim light issues from within. Casts a stripe across the floor. I strain to hear. The man inside speaks Portuguese in a low voice.

Creeping forward, I focus on the pace of the conversation. I should be able to hear the voice of the man on the other end of the comms link, but I can't. The man in the radio compartment must be wearing a headset. That way, he can hear the other party without disturbing others on the Nevoa.

I push the door to the radio compartment with two fingers of my right hand. The gap widens. The man's shoulder comes into view.

A floorboard creaks behind me.

Turning, I sense an object swinging toward my face. I roll with the blow and something solid glances off the side of my head. There's an explosion of pain. A flash as my vision whites out in the darkness of the corridor. I'm paralyzed, unable to break my fall.

Barely conscious, I stare at my attacker. Try to kick his knee, but my limbs won't obey my brain. The shadowy form reaches for me. With strong hands, he drags me along the corridor. Another shadow steps from the radio compartment. My attacker hauls me over the knee-knocker and onto the widow's walk.

This is it. Either I get thrown down the ladder like the radio operator, or I get tossed in the river like Gaspar. I shake my head to clear it. The effort results in little movement, and blinding pain.

Voices echo from the superstructure. My attacker releases me and flees over the widow's walk. I roll onto my back. Stare up at a field of stars and a channel of treetops.

A blurred face looks down at me. "Breed."

"Yes." My voice is a croak.

Captain Silva's face swims into focus. Arms loose at his sides, Collor stands behind him.

"Summon Fonseca," Silva says. "Sober up the fool."

"Go after him," I say.

"Who?"

Speaking is too much effort. I lift my arm, point down the widow's walk in the direction of the bridge. The direction in which my attacker disappeared.

I was able to lift my arm. *That* was impressive.

"There is no one there, Breed." Silva shakes his head. "He is gone."

Collor returns with Doctor Fonseca.

I struggle to one elbow. Try to rise.

"Why would you wake me?" Fonseca grumbles. "He's not hurt. Look, the man's indestructible."

"*You* look at him," Silva barks. "I want a thorough, professional examination. If you are still capable."

"I'm fine." I grip Collor's arm, get to my feet.

The doctor's voice sounds plaintive. "You see? He is fine."

"*Examine him.*"

"I need light."

Collor helps me into the bridge. I see there is no one at the helm.

"Who is steering us?" I ask.

"No one," Collor says. "We are drifting. It is alright for a few minutes, but I must return to the helm."

"Get us back under power," Silva says. "I will take it from here."

Fonseca examines my head under a bare bulb at the back of the bridge. "My God, you have a thick skull. A glancing blow. Something heavy and steel... a wrench."

"Now we know how the radio operator died," I say.

"What?" Fonseca does a double-take.

"Please. The impact that crushed his skull was perfectly aimed. A horizontal blow above the ear. His killer lined it up like a pool shot. There's no way he got *that* injury by accident."

"How long have you suspected this?" Silva asks.

"From the first time I looked at the body," I say. "Now I'm certain. Whoever killed Morais tried to kill me."

"Are you strong enough to descend the stairs?" Fonseca asks. "As Captain Silva requests, I must give you a proper examination. That is best conducted in the sickbay."

"I'm fine now."

"Maybe so, but you are certainly concussed. The effects of concussion are unpredictable and can be delayed." Fonseca gathers his dignity. "Breed, I *am* the doctor."

I can't help but smile. There might be hope for the old sponge yet.

"Okay. Sickbay it is. But I'm getting there under my own power."

I LIE IN BED, a damp cloth pressed to the side of my head. Not too bad. In the air conditioning, the water is cool. The skin was broken, but the bleeding has stopped. The cloth is tinged pink. Fonseca was indeed capable of a professional examination. Gave me what passed for a neurological exam. Pronounced me concussed but serviceable. Told me he would have to examine me daily.

Silva demanded to know what happened. I told him about the man in the radio compartment, but not about the cargo. The captain looked shocked.

"What the devil is happening aboard my ship?"

Silva's anger seems genuine. There were at least three men on the bridge deck when I went up there, but I wasn't a hundred percent sure. I thought Silva had gone to bed, *but—* he was the only person in the crew other than Morais who could operate the HF radio. Who else could have been using it?

When the radio operator took his dive onto the boat deck, Silva was dining with me in the wardroom. So were Sales, Vargas, Quadros, and Fonseca. That means there are at least *two* killers aboard. I'm certain Sales and Vargas are rotten, but they are obvious suspects. They can't be acting without accomplices.

"You have at least one killer aboard," I told him. "And it

has something to do with whatever is waiting for us at Portao da Dor."

I lie in the dark and tell myself to keep my eye on the ball.

The skullduggery aboard Nevoa needs to be addressed, but for me, it's a sideshow.

My mission is to find Fiadh Connor.

18

DAY FIVE

Rio Preto – Simon the Zealot

The clang of an alarm jerks me awake. I sit up in bed, pull my boots on. There's the sound of running footsteps in the corridor. A stampede.

I get to my feet and the deck tilts under my feet. I lurch to one side and put my hand against the bulkhead. The deck is steady, it's my balance that's off. The side of my head hurts from the blow. I touch the bump. The pain is from the bruised, broken skin.

Silva's voice carries from the ship's PA system. "*Aposentos gerais.*"

I open my cabin door in time to see helmeted Marines run past. They push through the forward hatch and onto the fo'c'sle. Sales and Vargas step into the corridor. Quadros emerges from his cabin, buckling his pistol belt. He pushes past Sales and Vargas, runs for the open door.

"What's happening?" Laura asks. She closes her cabin door, stands beside me.

"General Quarters," I tell her. "Battle stations."

Sales and Vargas step through the hatchway. They're careful not to bark their shins on the knee-knocker.

Marines have manned the 40mm Bofors. One of them reaches up and pulls the canvas condom from the muzzle. Three men rather than the usual two. Gun captain, loader, and gunner.

The jungle is a verdant green wall. Against it, I see what looks like a shallow clearing. Dark wooden pillars have been erected on the shore. At a range of four hundred yards, I cannot make out much detail. Gray smoke drifts skyward from fires on the shore.

I clamber up the portside companionway to the bridge. Despite the injury, I feel my usual strength and vigor. Looking up, I see the canvas condoms have been pulled from the .50 caliber Brownings. I push the door open and step onto the bridge. Hold the door for Laura.

"What's that on the shore?" I ask.

Collor is at the helm. Silva scans the shore through a pair of M22 7x50 binoculars. Lieutenant Quadros has his own binos lifted to his eyes. Sales and Vargas stand back, arms folded.

"Loggers," Silva says. "See for yourself."

The captain hands me the binoculars and I raise them to my eyes. Adjust focus, fine-tune the diopter. My heart pounds.

I built wooden frames like that on hunting trips. They're game racks. Usually constructed from poles, but there are sturdier resources in this camp. Two uprights formed with logs. Horizontal notches have been cut across their tops so a pole can be braced across them. The game is hung from the pole.

On this bloody shore, the game is human. Men, hung upside-down by their ankles.

"Illegals?" Sales asks.

"By definition," Silva replies. "Logging is not permitted in the Selva. These men planned to float their Mahogany down the Rio Preto to the Amazon. From there, on to Peru."

The captain and Quadros confer. Silva turns to Collor. "Approach slowly. We are going to send a shore party."

Quadros lifts a squad radio to his ear. Issues orders in a low voice.

I step to the lieutenant's side. "I'm coming," I tell him. "There may be some sign of Fiadh Connor."

"As you wish."

Sales looks at us with sharp eyes. "Vargas will accompany you."

I step onto the widow's walk, look back along the boat deck. The Marines unlimber the Zodiacs, prepare to swing them out. Quadros and Vargas behind me, I climb down the port ladder.

"We shall take eight men in each Zodiac," Quadros says. "We will launch from both port and starboard."

The Nevoa creeps closer to the shore. Two hundred and fifty yards out, she is almost motionless. Her engines provide enough thrust to keep her from being swept downstream. Silva nudges his ship forward. Halts her advance two hundred yards from the shore.

The Zodiacs are lowered and we board. It's been a while since I boarded a rigid inflatable boat. I slip on the polyurethane surface and brace myself.

"We must wait for the other boat," Quadros says.

Silva holds the Nevoa in place, turned into the current. I sit next to Quadros, with Vargas and a Marine behind us. Four more Marines occupy the back seats, rifles pointed skyward.

I look up at the Nevoa. Sales and Laura stand on the widow's walk, looking down on us. I can make out Silva through the windows of the bridge. The Marine gun crews have trained the Bofors and the .50 caliber Brownings on the shore. Other Marines stand on deck, rifles ready.

The starboard Zodiac approaches from astern and we form up. Sales signals the pilots to take us in. The two boats make their way side-by-side through the greenish-brown water.

I sweep the tree line for signs of danger.

"What do you think they ran into," I ask Quadros, "Arqueiros or gangs?"

"Impossible to say from here," Quadros replies. "Remember Gaspar said the people at Vila de Deus were wary of the jungle. The mission is upriver, so whoever did this has already bypassed the village and cut it off."

A flicker of movement in the corner of my eye. I turn my head, see an arrow sail through the air. Lazy, in a high arc, it gathers speed as it falls. It hits the water to our left with a soft splash.

"Arqueiros," the lieutenant cries. "We will fire over their heads."

The Marines are required to follow FUNAI guidance. The Indian protection organization's motto is "Die if you must, but never kill." I won't follow it, and I'm sure Quadros won't either. Not if he's about to be overrun.

There is a noise, something between a hiss and a whistle. A swarm of arrows rises high and arcs toward us. The arrows drop among our boats. Some hit the steel side of Nevoa. The Marines on the boat deck take cover behind the cargo.

The Marine behind me cries out. I twist in my seat. An arrow struck him in the chest. The missile—a thin shaft, fletched with leaves. The point buried itself in his flesh.

Quadros barks orders into his radio. The .50 caliber Brownings on the Nevoa open fire, raking the forest. The 40mm Bofors and the Marines on deck hold their fire.

"We have instructions not to kill indigenous, even if under attack," Quadros says. "Only if we are about to be overrun are we permitted to shoot to kill."

M2 Brownings are the ultimate macho machine guns. Their bullets, each as big as a man's thumb, shred the foliage. Another volley of arrows arcs toward us. I flinch involuntarily. There is nothing more hypnotic than enemy tracers swarming toward you. They look like clouds of fireflies. I swear, a hail of arrows is equally hypnotic.

The boats hit the shore and the Marines tumble out. Bullets from Nevoa's machine guns crack overhead. I sweep the tree line left and right, looking for more volleys of arrows. Nothing.

I turn, grab the wounded Marine under his arms, and haul him out of the boat. One of the other Marines grabs his legs and we set him on the muddy shore. I seize the arrow by its shaft and pull straight back.

The shaft breaks, leaving the point of the arrow and two inches of a wooden reed sticking out of the man's chest.

"Spread out," Quadros orders his men.

We crouch on the shore while the machine guns methodically beat the tree line. There are no further volleys. Quadros keys his radio. "*Segure fogo.*"

As quickly as they came to life, the machine guns fall silent.

Quadros turns to me. "The arrowhead is barbed," he says. "You cannot pull it out. The only way is to carve it from him."

The lieutenant pulls a utility knife from a scabbard on his belt. Uses it to cut away the wounded Marine's shirt. Grimly, he stabs the point into the flesh. The man cries out, but the lieutenant is already digging deep. The arrowhead comes out and Quadros holds it up for me to see.

Barbed metal. Crudely fashioned, and bound with a thin

strip of gut to the end of the shaft. There is something like black pitch clotted between the barbs.

"Mapepire," the lieutenant says. "Snake venom, mixed with meal. It is more deadly than curare."

He hurls the arrowhead into the river. The wounded Marine is convulsing.

Quadros snaps his fingers at a Marine sergeant. "Take one man, bring him to Doctor Fonseca. Have the doctor administer antivenom."

The sergeant and another Marine lift the wounded man into a Zodiac. Turn it around and push off for the Nevoa.

"He will not survive," Quadros tells me.

"Surely with antivenom..."

"No. He is a dead man."

Quadros and I get to our feet, survey the shore.

Without doubt, this was a logging camp. Trees have been felled in a swath that has pushed the tree line back forty yards. Chainsaws have been used to strip the trunks of branches.

The loggers were sleeping in tents. These were thrown into the campfires and burned. Other logging equipment... axes, chainsaws, crampons... has been piled in a heap. There is another pile of weapons a short distance away. Modern M16s. Load-bearing vests crammed with spare magazines. The rifles didn't do the loggers any good.

I wave a cloud of mosquitoes away from my face. Look toward the game racks. Fashioned from logs and poles, arranged in a long row. Several Marines are staring at the racks. One of them turns, lurches to the river's edge, and falls to his knees. Vomits into the water.

Vargas walks to the racks.

Eight racks, eight men. Strung up by their ankles to the cross-pieces, hands bound behind their backs. This is how you butcher game. String it up and gut it so the bowels spill out in a nice fat bolus for convenient disposal. Then, the skin is sliced at the wrists and ankles. The meat is delicately flayed. It is important not to let fur taint the meat. An unpleasant gamey taste results if the flaying is not done with care. Once skinned, the meat is carved and packed out. The best cuts are reserved for the hunter who bagged the kill. Gifts for his friends.

Of course, the Arqueiros are cannibals. If the tribesmen who killed these loggers were indeed Arqueiros. I see what is burning. I smell it. A shallow pit has been dug into the shore, and a fire has been built. Seven of the eight men have been gutted. The entrails of six have been thrown on the fire and the those of a seventh have been cut away. They lie in a fly-covered heap beneath his sightless eyes. The fire smolders and smoke curls skyward.

The approach of the Nevoa interrupted the Arqueiros. Drove them behind the tree line.

Six of the men were skinned, and cuts of meat carved from them. I had heard of similar things done in Africa. Thanked God I'd never seen it in my own deployments. Until now. The bodies look like they are moving. They are covered with rippling coats of black, electric blue, and emerald-green flies. Feasting, laying eggs in the necrotic flesh. Their buzz fills the air.

One man is still alive.

Number eight.

Vargas goes to him. Bends to the man's face. Questions the man in Portuguese.

The man does not answer. About thirty, he hangs upside-down, stark naked. In preparation for the feast, his trousers and shirt have been cut from him.

"*Responda!*"

The man says nothing.

Vargas goes to the pile of equipment. Picks up a chainsaw and advances on the hanging man. He yanks the recoil start handle. With a roar, the gas engine explodes to life. Steel teeth flashing, the cutting chain whines around the guide bar.

"*Responda!*" Vargas yells again.

The hanging man shrieks. The pleas pouring from his mouth are incomprehensible. My stomach clenches.

"What are you, a maniac?"

I start toward Vargas, but he's too far away. Before I can reach him, he slashes the whirling teeth toward the man's groin and cuts into him. Throws his weight onto the saw so the chain rips through flesh, bone and gristle. I remember paintings of the Christian martyr, Simon the Zealot, sawn in half. Upside-down, the brain is guaranteed blood for the whole experience. The victim will not lose consciousness until death intervenes.

The man's screams are those of a butchered animal. I lunge for Vargas. He steps away from the fountain of gore and points the chainsaw at me. His left fist is closed around the carrying handle. His right hand squeezes the throttle, revs it. Blood and bits of flesh spin from the chain and spatter us.

"Come, Breed." Teeth bared, Vargas's face is a savage mask.

I crouch, ready to slip either way. Vargas feints left and right. Jabs the weapon at me. The saw adds at least three feet to his reach.

Vargas slashes, and I dodge behind the nearest upright. The chain hits the side of the log. With a screech, the teeth bite and splinters fly. I trip and fall on my side. Land next to the smoking bonfire of guts. I grab a burning piece of firewood and throw it at Vargas. He bats it away with the saw. I scramble to my feet, grab a charred brand from the fire.

Vargas comes at me head-on, thrusts the saw at my midsection. With both hands, I swing the piece of wood at the chainsaw's guide rail. There's a clang. Pieces of glowing orange and black charcoal fly from the brand. The machine is deflected and the whirling chain bites into the earth. Before he can free the weapon, I club Vargas's exposed elbow.

With a cry, Vargas drops the chainsaw. I swing a third time at his head. He snarls, gets under the blow. Like a bull, he launches himself at me. Slams into my midsection with such force I'm thrown off-balance. I drop the brand. Boots sliding in the mud, we grapple. I strain against the iron strength in his arms. Our fingers slip on flesh greasy with sweat, and I choke on his body odor. He draws his head back to butt—his favorite move.

Cupping my hands, I box his ears. Vargas howls and lets go. I cock the heel of my right hand for the killing blow.

"Breed!"

Quadros throws his arms around me. Two of his Marines seize Vargas and haul him away.

I yell at Vargas. "You son of a bitch."

"*Voce esta morto,*" Vargas snarls.

"That is enough, both of you," Quadros snaps.

Breath rasping, Vargas and I struggle to free ourselves. Quadros pushes me away. I raise my arms in surrender.

The lieutenant addresses us. Me, Vargas, his Marines. "None of this happened, do you understand? *All* of you will forget it. Now—back to the ship."

Vargas works for the Minister of the Interior, and Sales is a powerful man. Quadros is a professional soldier. Competent, and nobody's fool. He knows tangling with Sales and Vargas could be a career-ending move.

The Zodiac that brought the wounded Marine back to Nevoa has returned. Quadros directs me and Vargas into separate boats. I'm drenched in sweat. My nose is filled with the stench of fire, burned entrails, and death. Blood pounds in my temples. I want to kill Vargas so bad my head feels ready to explode.

The Zodiac carrying Vargas pushes off and heads back to Nevoa. I watch Quadros go to the game racks. He examines the man Vargas assaulted with the chainsaw. Draws his pistol and shoots him once in the head.

The Zodiac churns its way back to the Nevoa. The Marines are silent. Some look ashen, despite their brown skin. My guts are shaking.

"What did Vargas want from that man?" I ask Quadros.

The lieutenant looks at me sharply. He does not want to talk about it.

"Come on, Quadros. I'm not going to make trouble. But two men have already died on Nevoa, and Vargas is a psycho."

Quadros shakes his head. "He wanted to know if there were more men in the logger's band. He wanted to know where they were."

"Don't you think he should be more interested in how many Arqueiros there are? The man would have told him *that*."

"Yes," Quadros says, "and now that butchered man cannot tell us. But I am convinced Vargas did not intend to silence him. He genuinely wanted to know if there are other loggers in that band. And he was prepared to torture that man to death to obtain the information."

"Vargas got carried away."

"Vargas is easily carried away," Quadros says. "There are stories."

"I've heard stories."

"Now you believe them. You have made an enemy of that man. Take the matter no further."

"Surely those on the ship saw?"

"No. We were too far away, and only Captain Silva was

using binoculars. He will have seen, but he will remain silent."

"What are you going to do?"

The Zodiacs approach Nevoa. Quadros shakes his head bitterly.

"What can I do?"

19

DAY FIVE

Rio Preto – The Catherine Wheel

Silva stares from the bridge. Silent, he watches us board.

Without a word, Vargas leaves us. He is going to report to Sales. I cannot figure them out. Obviously, Sales knows about the cargo, and the deaths of Gaspar and the radio operator. This *has* to be his operation, and he has accomplices aboard.

Everyone is suspect.

But—not everyone is complicit.

Otherwise, Gaspar and Morais would not be dead. Sales does *not* have full control of Nevoa.

There are a kaleidoscope of questions.

Who is involved in Sales's conspiracy and who is not? I must assume Vargas and Fonseca are on Sales's team, though the doctor is an unlikely murderer.

Why are they doing this, and what are they planning?

What is waiting for us at Portao da Dor?

I say nothing to Quadros. Once on the boat deck, we walk

together to the wardroom. Laura and Fonseca are sitting across from each other at the table.

The doctor is single-handedly demolishing Sales's supply of Scotch whiskey. He isn't bothering with a glass today. He's pounding it down, straight from the bottle.

"Your man is dead," Fonseca tells Quadros.

The doctor's face shines with sweat.

"Did you give him antivenom?"

"Yes." Fonseca stares as though shell-shocked. "I have never seen venom kill so quickly. His flesh was black when they brought him. The poison spread in a violet ring of dying tissue as I administered the medicine. When the necrosis reached his heart, he died."

Quadros gives me an *I told you so* look. "The Arqueiros concentrate the venom to make it more deadly."

"It could not have been normal Mapepire venom." Fonseca is speaking to himself. "Mapepire is hemorrhagic. Necrosis is a side effect. This venom caused extreme coagulapathy and necrosis. Antivenom did not slow it down."

"How much did you give him?" Quadros asks.

The lieutenant's words snap Fonseca out of his stupor. "How much would *you* give him, Lieutenant? Do you know the appropriate dose? Do you know what we have? I'm the doctor, he was my patient. I provided the appropriate treatment, *and* my patient died. Give me a *little* credit."

"I apologize, doctor." Quadros is genuinely embarrassed. "It was not my intention to question your treatment."

The doctor nods. Apology accepted. He reaches for the bottle and takes a deep swig. "My God," he says. "What we do not know about these people's medicines and poisons would fill a library. I belong in Brasilia, not the Amazon."

He takes another swig.

Fonseca has the right idea. I step to the bar and liberate a bottle of Bourbon. Grab it by the neck and head for my cabin.

Laura rises. "Breed."

"Later," I tell her. "I'm tired."

Can't handle any more right now. The shock of what happened on the riverbank is catching up to me. In combat, you do what you have to do. Stress and exhaustion don't matter. You function as you have been trained to function. Your mind operates in the face of fatigue. We're human. When the fighting is over, one has to process the experience.

I push past Laura, go to my cabin, lock the door. I've never seen a man butchered alive.

Beheadings and flayings in Afghanistan can't hold a candle to this. I slam the bottle of Bourbon on the desk. I'd heard of butchery and cannibalism in Africa, but thought the stories exaggerated. I sit on the edge of the bunk and stare at the wall.

Breathe.

Keep your eye on the ball, Breed.

I take out Fiadh's portrait, prop it on the desk, stare at it. *There* is my mission.

My hands are shaking. Adrenaline from the fight? Or something else? I press my palms flat against my knees. The khaki fabric is spattered with tiny dark flecks. Droplets of blood from the chainsaw. Now dried. There, stuck to the fabric, a little piece of damp tissue, half folded on itself. No larger than the nail on my little finger.

Human flesh.

I bury my face in my hands. Choke down the scream that rises, unbidden, from my throat. Scalding tears flood my eyes. They come, and I don't want to stop them.

FIADH WROTE home about her experiences with indigenous tribes and loggers.

Father Andrew, the Marines arrested a dozen loggers today. Last week, we found a hunting party of Korubo murdered. Fourteen men. The killers got them all, otherwise the Indians would have carried away their dead. The Korubo kill with four-foot long clubs called borduna. They're not as advanced as the Arqueiros, who kill with blowguns and bows.

The Korubo didn't have a chance against rifles. Fourteen men is seven percent of the Korubo population. There are only a couple hundred we know about.

The loggers killed most of them outright. Captured two men and tied them to trees. Then they poured gasoline from chainsaws onto their victims and set them on fire. We found the corpses, foraged by wild animals. The burned men were dragged into the bush. The animals left pieces of them tied to the trees. Scattered the rest all over the place.

Father Andrew, I can't describe it.

We followed the loggers' trail to their camp. I triangulated, like they taught us in Girl Scouts. Plotted the location on a map, checked against GPS. At Vila de Deus, I used Father Camos's radio to contact Tieves. A gunboat and a platoon of Marines made the arrest.

What makes men do such things? Atrocities committed for a purpose are evil, but one can understand them. What can you make of atrocities committed for no reason? These have to be beyond evil. I believe because I have seen, I have the capacity to judge. For only God and those who have seen can judge. Is it a sin to believe I have that capacity? I don't know, but I think I do.

I know about our martyrs. Terrible stories. Here, in the Selva, I see first-hand the evil men do. These things can't be unseen. Father... they play like movies in my head. I can't make them stop. Please, God. Make... them... stop...

The paper is wrinkled by Fiadh's tears.

*One day, they'll do the same to me. I'm scared, Father Andrew. But
I have to go on. You can't see what I've seen and do nothing.
I don't want to be broken on a wheel. I could go home to Chicago
and live out the rest of my life.
But—I couldn't live with myself.*

Cuchulain Connor will never get his daughter back.
Fiadh's a porcelain doll in pieces. I've never seen a girl so
broken up. She broke from his world and found herself. Alive
or dead, she's not the little girl he raised in a Chicago suburb.
Taught to ride a bike. Drove to summer camp. Sent to Trinity
to drink away her youth with Dubliners.

Father Andrew knew this, yet couldn't share these letters
with Cuchulain. They could only be shared with a man who
had seen the same things as Fiadh. Cuchulain told him about
my resume, but the priest looked into my heart. He chose me.

There's a soft knock on the door. Laura.

I want a woman, but I don't want her. Thoughts of Fiadh
fill me with warmth from the inside out. I pick up the bottle
of Bourbon and pour myself a glass. Lean back against the
bulkhead and take a slow sip.

Another soft knock.

I thought Fiadh dead, and took the mission.

Now, more than anything else, I want to find her alive.

I take a good slug of Bourbon, lean the back of my head
against the bulkhead. Listen to Laura's soft footsteps as she
goes back to her cabin.

Fiadh and I have more in common than either of us has
with Cuchulain.

I can't leave her behind.

20

DAY FIVE

Rio Preto – Vila de Deus

The switchback one click from Vila de Deus took Nevoa an hour to negotiate. On the bridge, Silva monitored the echo fathometer while Collor managed the helm. Second Engineer Dutra stood at the bow. Leaned over the side and took soundings with an old-fashioned lead plumb and line. The Rio Preto was so tight no man in his right mind would trust an echo device.

"There it is," Silva announces. "Vila de Deus."

I peer through the windows at the front of the bridge. Sure enough, a collection of twenty wooden huts with thatched roofs occupy the left bank of the Rio Preto. The huts are barely distinguishable from the surrounding jungle. They have been built squarely against the green wall. Smoke from small cooking fires curls skyward.

The proximity of the settlement to the tree line disturbs me. No open ground separates the houses from the jungle. Defenders of the village have no protective killing zone. Attackers from the forest can be upon them in seconds.

"Slow," Silva cautions.

Collor noses Nevoa toward the village. Pirogues hewn from tree trunks are lined up at the water's edge. Everything in the Amazon is made of wood. In this place, the ancient Nevoa looks modern.

"All stop," Silva commands. "Drop anchor."

"Let us see what these people have to tell us," Sales says.

The tension between myself and Vargas is palpable. We have not said a word to each other since the morning's confrontation. The goon tried to kill me twice. I'm this close to taking him out pre-emptively. If he so much as twitches in my direction, he's a dead man.

Sales never wanted me on the expedition. He doesn't bother to hide it. He and Vargas are one. Sales presents the thin veneer of civilization. Vargas is the minister's barbaric alter-ego.

"No crops," I observe.

"These people fish and hunt," Silva tells me. "The jungle and the river provide what they need. The soil in the Amazon is not fertile."

Quadros was right about the captain. Silva saw everything that happened at the logging camp and said nothing. I'll bet the whole incident never made it into the Nevoa's log. He probably regrets having stopped.

This is the Selva da Morte, *not* Brasilia. Whatever story Sales and Vargas tell will not be challenged.

"Let's go ashore," I say. "I want to speak with Father Camos."

"So do I." Sales and Vargas push past us. Hurry to the companionway.

I look at Silva. "Are you coming?"

"No. Lieutenant Quadros will go with you. On this visit, we want fewer military."

Marines are replacing the outboard on the portside Zodiac.

"What's wrong with it?" I ask.

"The motor is running rough after the action at the logging camp," Quadros says. "We will use the outboard from the starboard boat."

We go ashore in the portside Zodiac. Sales and Vargas sit in the bow, followed by myself and Quadros. Laura sits with the pilot, who guides us past putrescent mats of weed.

A group of people have gathered at the water's edge. Local men, women, and children. At the center of the group is a white man wearing a bush hat with the brim lowered against the blistering sun.

Father Camos is not what I expected. I was looking for a crusty, gaunt priest with white hair and white collar. Instead, I find a man of forty-five, with graying hair. His dark skin has been burned black by the sun.

Quadros steps forward, shakes the priest's hand, makes introductions. Camos and Laura nod to each other in recognition.

"I was surprised not to see you with Fiadh and the others," Camos tells her.

"I told her not to come," Laura says. "I knew there would be death."

"Yes," Camos says. "Poor Pedro."

"Tell us what happened." I want to hear the priest's story firsthand.

"There has been fighting between the Arqueiros and criminals in the Selva," Camos says.

Sales looks skeptical. "Has that been established? My understanding is that the Arqueiros have been attacking our people, unprovoked."

"That is not true," Camos says firmly. "Arqueiros do not carry guns. Pedro Bernardes was shot with a rifle, that is not in dispute. There are clear signs of illegal logging and mining."

"The outpost at Portao da Dor reported an attack."

"Yes," Camos says. "We heard the transmission on our radio. We have our doubts."

"Do you?" Vargas's tone is menacing.

Either Camos is tone-deaf, or he does not care. "We have been in regular contact with Portao ever since the post was established. The man who sent that message was not the man we usually talk to. Surely your headquarters noticed."

"Perhaps the regular radio operator has been wounded or killed," Quadros says.

"It is possible."

"Arqueiros and criminals are active north of Vila de Deus," Quadros says. "Your village has been cut off. You are in danger here."

"Neither Arqueiros nor gunmen come to Vila de Deus."

"You should evacuate with us."

Sales stabs Quadros with his eyes.

"No," the priest says. "God will protect us."

Famous last words. "Tell us about Fiadh," I say.

Camos shrugs. "There was the message from Portao. Further, two of our people went missing in the jungle. We found them, shot with arrows. Mapepire."

"Your people were killed by Arqueiros." There is a hint of triumph in Sales's voice.

"Yes," Camos says. "But we heard gunfire days before. I am certain there have been a series of provocations."

"Your opinion," Sales says.

"Yes. *My* opinion." There is no anger in Camos's voice. Only confidence. "Fiadh and her friends came. She said she would find evidence of the provocations."

"You let her go into the Selva." The accusation in Laura's tone is unmistakable.

"No one could have stopped her," Camos says. "I assume you tried."

"Yes, I tried."

"You know what she was like." Camos waves his arm at the green wall behind the village. "Fiadh went into the jungle. Anna and Pedro with her. Two days later Pedro came back... shot with a rifle."

I hold the priest's eyes. "Tell me. What exactly did he say?"

"They went south, toward Arvore de Ouro. They stumbled into an engagement between Arqueiros and gunmen. They were caught in the fighting. Fiadh, Anna and Pedro ran. He was shot, lost sight of them. He managed to escape north. As far as he knew, the girls were still running."

Battles are rarely static. They wash this way and that, like waves. Even the most alert can get caught if the center of gravity of a fight shifts. Fiadh and her friends might have been jungle-savvy, but they had no experience in combat.

"Where did the fighting take place?" I ask.

Laura pushes forward. "Did Pedro speak of any landmarks? We have passed that way many times."

"He mentioned nothing."

"Where was he shot?" I ask.

"Low in the back, to one side of the spine. I do not know how he managed to return."

"Did he bandage himself?"

"He tore his clothing. Stuffed it into the wounds. Also mud and leaves."

A healthy young man. Twenty-four years old, in good physical condition. Not experienced, but desperate enough to treat himself in the field. He would have died from blood loss. Slowed by emergency measures. I make a mental calculation. "How long before Pedro returned? Be as precise as you can."

"Two days."

"*More* precise. How many *hours*?"

Camos's brow furrows. "You are right," he says. "It was thirty-six hours."

I turn to Quadros. "This is where we part company."

"What do you mean?"

"*Your* business is in Portao da Dor. *Mine* is to find Fiadh Connor."

Quadros stares at me.

Amused, Sales lights a cigarette.

"I reckon Arvore de Ouro is a day's march from here," I tell Quadros. "Nevoa has to pass it to reach Portao. "

"We are *not* waiting for you," Sales says.

"Nevoa isn't making three knots on these switchbacks. I'm cutting through jungle. If I beat you to Arvore de Ouro, I'll signal. If you see nothing, keep going."

Sales exhales a cloud of tobacco smoke. "You are insane."

"I'll take my chances."

Laura clutches my arm. "I'm coming with you," she blurts.

I say nothing.

"This is why I came," she insists. "This is why you brought me."

Nevoa rides quietly at anchor. I consider the murderers aboard. Arguably, Laura is safer with me. At least we'll know whoever comes at us is trying to kill us.

"Alright," I tell her. "You can come."

FIADH STARES at me from her photo. I slip it into the package of papers Father Andrew gave me. Wrap it in a clear plastic bag, stuff it into my ruck. I make sure the camelback is full of water. Put my arms through the straps and adjust the weight on my shoulders.

I pick up the SIG. Drop the mag, rack the slide, and do a three-point check. Snap the loose round into the magazine, lock and load. I squeeze the weapon into my waistband, appendix carry. Tug my shirttail down.

Wish I had a 10mm or a .45, but this'll have to do.

Never shoot a large caliber man with a small caliber bullet. I guess that goes for jaguars and anacondas too.

Laura and Quadros are waiting for me in the wardroom. She has dressed for the Selva. Packed her own ruck.

"Where are you going?" Laura asks.

I go through the door into the galley. Root around, find the Golok. Go back inside. "Can you loan me a pistol belt?" I ask Quadros.

Quadros unclips his holster and hands me the pistol belt. I fasten the Golok's scabbard and strap it over my shirttail.

"I expect you to return the belt," Quadros says.

It's his way of telling me to bring myself back.

"Don't worry," I tell him. "We'll see you at Arvore."

21

DAY FIVE

Selva da Morte – Trail of Tears

The Zodiac makes its way back to the Nevoa. Laura and I are left standing on the shore. Father Camos studies us.

"I will tell you what I told Fiadh," the priest says. "Do not go. That boy Pedro—his wounds turned green overnight. When he arrived, he was in delirium. Maggots in the wounds cleaned the dead flesh better than a surgeon. Blood loss killed him."

The three of us walk toward the edge of the forest.

"I'll tell you what Quadros tried to tell *you*. Arqueiros slaughtered a band of illegal loggers a few miles north of here. What they did was unspeakable."

"What illegal loggers and miners do to the tribesmen is equally so."

"The point is, with attacks to the north and south, Vila de Deus is cut off."

"Why haven't they attacked the mission?"

"I don't know."

"God is protecting us."

We reach the edge of the forest. "Father Camos," I say, "two men were murdered on the Nevoa. I don't know why, but I have a good idea who two of the killers are. These men will kill anybody who gets in their way, including every man, woman and child at Vila de Deus."

"You think I would fare better aboard that gunboat?"

"No. I think you should use your radio. Ask to be taken off by the first passing boat, go to Tieves."

"I cannot do that, Breed."

The Selva's green wall towers over us... The forest is waiting to swallow me whole. I imagine a blond girl standing at the edge of the tree line. Her features are calm and composed, her posture relaxed. She doesn't carry a rifle, but she's not unarmed. In her gloved right hand is a long, Latin machete. The girl's green eyes glow in the gloom. There is nothing threatening about her expression. If anything, I sense an open invitation.

She turns and melts into the Selva. I stare at the hole she left in the brush, watch the branches and leaves close after her. That is *exactly* where Fiadh entered the jungle. Alive or dead, she is in there. I am consumed by the desire to find her. Not for Cuchulain, but for myself.

"Alright, then," I say. "Good luck."

"The same to you."

I turn and plunge into the jungle.

"ALRIGHT, BREED," Laura gasps. "What's the plan?"

"Stay close," I tell her. "You are the one who knows these trails. I'm relying on you to show me the trail Fiadh would have used."

Our shirts are black with sweat. We wear our bush hats and lightweight face nets to protect ourselves from swarms of insects. Despite the heat, we travel with our sleeves rolled down. To protect our hands from edged vegetation, we wear gloves. Thick rubber bands blouse our sleeves at the wrists... to keep insects from crawling up our arms. Ditto our pants legs at the tops of our jungle boots.

"This is the trail."

"I expect to find the location of the battle on this trail. Soon. Sometime in the next twelve hours."

"How do you arrive at that figure?"

"Pedro was gone thirty-six hours. But he was badly wounded on the way back. He would have traveled slower, stopped frequently. It's a wonder he made it at all."

"Yes, I see that."

"Okay. Allow time for him to evade pursuit. It must have taken him twice as long to get back as it took the group to reach the battle. The math says Fiadh's team was on the trail for twelve hours before they ran into trouble."

"That means they were halfway to Arvore de Ouro."

"I reckon."

WE FIND the site in nine hours.

Pedro must have been in a very bad way, because the ambush took place relatively close to Vila de Deus. In a combat zone, soldiers tend to avoid trails, because trails are frequently mined. Mines weren't an issue in the Selva da Morte, so all parties used the trails. Caution had to be exercised, to avoid falling into an ambush.

Somebody had set an ambush, and somebody had fallen into it.

That much is clear from the skeletons we find.

Bleached, disarticulated bones lie next to the trail. Others, we find in the bush. Many have been scattered by wild animals tearing at limbs, feasting on dead flesh.

The four skeletons lying next to the trail are wearing boots. Laura stares at the remains with morbid fascination. I've seen this before. When the fighting is over, there is often no time to bury the dead. The gunmen won the battle, so they took the time to stretch out the bodies in a kind of repose. They knew the jungle would devour the corpses in short order. Once the casualties were out of sight, they were out of mind.

Gunmen were following the trail, and they died on it. Arqueiros fought from the jungle. We find two skeletons in the brush beside the trail. These skeletons have *no* boots, indicating the men were barefoot.

"What do you think happened?" Laura asks.

"It's hard to say. The gunmen followed the trail. It's clear the Arqueiros were positioned in the jungle beside the trail. When the gunmen passed, the Arqueiros shot their bows. These four gunmen were hit. They were either killed outright, or died later from the Mapepire. They literally died with their boots on.

"Gunmen opened fire and killed two Arqueiros. Those fell where they were hit, where we found them. In the bush. The remaining Arqueiros figured they got the best of the exchange and faded back into the jungle."

"Why didn't they take away their dead?"

"No time," I tell her. "The Arqueiros were fleeing superior firepower. They carried or dragged along their wounded. Their dead—they left.

"The gunmen didn't think they had time either. They got caught with their pants down. Lost four men. They beat off the attack, but they didn't know how many men the Arqueiros had. They took the time to stretch out their dead. Maybe they took away their wounded. The wounded didn't last long. The Arqueiros concentrate the Mapepire they use to poison their projectiles."

Closer examination of the skeletons bears out my theory. There are no rifles to be found on the trail. The gunmen retrieved their casualties' weapons and ammunition. American-issue jungle boots and scraps of clothing adorn the remains. The dead men wore olive drab fatigues. Ants and worms have polished the bones. Not a scrap of flesh remains.

"My God," Laura breathes. "There were people *around* those bones."

"Sobers you up, doesn't it?" I turn the dead men's pockets inside-out, find nothing. Packs of cigarettes, lighters, and matches. "Once we're gone, that's all that's left of us. Except for our souls, if you're a believer."

"Fiadh believes."

I straighten. "Yes, I know. Don't you?"

"Of course."

Laura doesn't sound so sure.

The two skeletons in the bush are crumpled in awkward fetal positions. Bows and quivers of arrows lie close to them. Knives and hatchets, light hammocks and mosquito nets.

"These men died with their weapons close to hand," I tell Laura. "Their friends didn't come back to collect them."

"There is no blood."

"Everything has been exposed to the elements."

Laura straightens. Asks the sixty-four-thousand-dollar question. "What happened to Fiadh and Anna?"

"There are a few possibilities." My eyes sweep the trail. "Fiadh, Anna and Pedro blundered into this battle. It was dumb luck—a meeting engagement."

"What is that?"

"That's when two forces run head-on into each other. It's an accident. My guess is, Fiadh ran into the gunmen, who were just as shocked as she was. They stopped and opened fire on Fiadh. At the same time, the Arqueiros opened fire with their bows. All three groups were surprised."

"Alright," Laura says. "Which way did Fiadh and Anna go?"

"Fiadh, Anna and Pedro ran. Pedro being a courageous young man, he encouraged Fiadh and Anna to run ahead of him. He got shot in the back for his gallantry.

"Pedro fell, but fear flooded him with adrenaline. He kept running, away from the girls. He wanted to divert the attention of the gunmen. He ran north to Vila de Deus. The gunmen didn't chase him because they were still coping with the Arqueiros. Pedro got away."

"That leaves Fiadh and Anna."

"Yes." I lead the way back to the trail, stand over the bodies, and fix Laura with a stare. "You operated with them. What would *you* do?"

Laura's brow furrows. She stares at the denuded bones, the polished skulls, the empty eye sockets. The jungle recycles life and death with ruthless efficiency.

"I would run east," she says at last.

"Why?"

"I would be reluctant to run north to Vila de Deus. If the gunmen followed me, they might harm the people at the mission."

"That's one reason."

Laura points in the direction of the Arqueiros skeletons. "The Arqueiros attacked from the east and fled the same way. Fiadh would be running after the Arqueiros. She would think... the enemy of my enemy is my friend."

"Yes," I say. "Fiadh felt an affinity for the Arqueiros. It makes sense she would join their flight."

"Anna would follow her, because Anna followed Fiadh in everything."

"What lies to the east?"

"Tens of thousands of square miles of Selva. Fiadh would not continue in that direction. As soon as she felt comfortable, she would turn and strike south. Toward Arvore de Ouro and Portao da Dor."

"Why Portao da Dor?"

"There is nothing at Arvore de Ouro. At Portao, she would find FUNAI and Marines."

"Would she bypass Arvore de Ouro?" I ask.

"Unlikely. There are three trails leading from Vila de Deus to Arvore de Ouro, and only two from Arvore de Ouro to Portao da Dor. Travel through the jungle becomes increasingly difficult the further south one goes. I knew Fiadh would take *this* trail to Arvore because she told me she would. She thought it was the trail most likely to be taken by criminals because it is closest to the river. Loggers harvest trees where transportation is convenient."

"Why only two trails from Arvore to Portao?"

"The jungle is alive. It *reclaims* trails that are not frequently used. One day it is there, three months later it is gone."

"Alright," I say. "We'll pitch camp off the trail. Tomorrow we'll go to Arvore de Ouro."

The light is fading. I lead us away from the battleground, then step a hundred yards off the trail. I use the Golok to clear away vegetation, and we string our hammocks and mosquito nets.

I found it difficult to sleep on the Nevoa. It's impossible in the Selva. As night falls, the din of the jungle multiplies a hundredfold. Parrots screech and monkeys chatter. Animals large and small crash through the vegetation. Clouds of mosquitoes hurl themselves at our nets and gather in thick whining clots. They compete with midges for airtime. I close my eyes. Separate the high-pitched whine of the mosquitoes from the buzz of other insects.

Beneath our hammocks, scaly creatures slither. Out of habit, I hold the SIG at my side as I try to sleep. I have no confidence it can stop the most dangerous animals we're likely to encounter.

I close my eyes and construct a map of the battlefield in my mind. Then I replay the encounter. An ambush, or a meeting engagement. Arqueiros ambushing the gunmen. Or the gunmen running into Fiadh and her friends. It was one or the other. The gunmen did not run into the Arqueiros.

Does it matter?

At this point, I have more questions than answers.

Everything matters.

22

DAY SIX

Selva da Morte – Arvore de Ouro

Two graves.

Mounds of earth near the tree line, fifteen yards from the river. One could never tell there had once been a rubber plantation on this shore. Laura pushed aside vegetation to show me old cement foundations. Nothing made of wood survived. The Selva overwhelmed everything man left behind. Not even rubber trees remained. They were wiped out by a blight that decimated the rubber industry in Brazil.

"What do you think?" Laura asks.

I survey the clearing. The earth over the graves and mud on the shore is smooth. Rain has washed away footprints. There's no way to tell how many men gathered here.

"I think they carried the wounded away from the battle. These two didn't make it."

The two graves look the same size. I've seen how quickly concentrated Mapepire kills. These men must have been strong to make it all the way from the ambush to Arvore de Ouro.

I check my watch, survey the river. We've beaten Nevoa by going overland. Between Vila de Deus and Portao da Dor, the switchbacks become more treacherous.

We have time.

I unsnap the Golok from its canvas scabbard. Wish I had a trench tool, but the machete will have to do. I drop to my knees. Blade-up, I use the flat of the machete to scrape earth from the first grave.

Black hair, shoulder-length. A white T-shirt with blue stripes. The shoulder musculature is that of a male. I uncover the corpse as far as the waist... there is no visible wound in his back. This is consistent with an arrow wound in the chest.

Laura shrinks back, assaulted by the odor of decomposition. Foul gasses released from the grave.

I turn to the second grave and begin scraping. Flies and mosquitoes swarm me, buzz against my face net.

Blond hair. My stomach hollows.

It gets worse. Some of the hair has been punched into a hole in the back of the skull. The hole is small, but the indentation in the occiput is the size of a golf ball.

"*Mae de Deus,*" Laura gasps.

Keep scraping. It's a girl, shoulder-length hair tied back. Cotton work shirt. Another hole low in the back of the shirt. The shirt clotted with black pitch. I uncover blue jeans, hiking boots. The girl was laid face-down with her arms at her sides, palms up. The flesh of her palms is gray.

"Who is it?" I ask.

"I don't know," Laura says. "Fiadh and Anna were both fair. Turn her over."

I plant the Golok point-down in the earth. Seize the body by the ankles and drag the girl out of the grave. Roll her over.

Laura falls to her knees and vomits.

The girl's face is gone. I thought it might be when I saw the bullet wound in the back of her head. The center of her face is a hole the size of my fist. Filled with stinking black tar, decomposing flesh, and fragments of bone and teeth. That's an exit wound. A high-powered rifle bullet cavitated inside the skull before blowing out the front.

Once pale flesh at her throat, now a ghastly gray-green. Against it lies a gold cross.

I find the clasp, pocket the cross. I won't bring Fiadh Connor back in a closed casket. I will hand Cuchulain his daughter's cross. He should remember her as she was.

I don't want to be broken on a wheel...

I want to rend my clothes and scream. At who? What a useless death. There isn't a sensible target for vengeance. The man who shot her in the back could be lying dead on the trail. The man who shot her in the head could be dead tomorrow.

With a heavy heart, I inspect the rest of the body. The exit wound in her belly is just as ghastly as the one in her face. To their credit, they did their best to bind it. She was hit close to the ambush site. Was the bounty on Fiadh higher dead, or alive? They thought they could keep her alive. They couldn't. Carried her as far as Arvore de Ouro, with their wounded buddy.

When they got here, he died from the Mapepire. They took another look at her, decided she wasn't going to make it. They put a bullet in the back of her head and buried the bodies. Cooked a meal, rested up, went on their way.

Life is cheap in the Selva da Morte.

"I told her not to come," Laura says.

"You knew she wouldn't listen."

The words were meant to be accusatory. Like Laura should have tried harder, held Fiadh in Manaus.

Flies swarm in clouds. Like rivers, armies of ants pour

into the man's open grave. Already, they are marching on Fiadh's. I cover her body the way I found it. Pack the earth as hard as I can. The ants will try to dig. Perhaps I can delay them. I stand and step back. Check my pants and gloves for insects.

"Anna is still out there," Laura says.

"Yes."

"We should find her."

"My job is done." I throw my head back. Suck hot, humid air into my lungs. "The only question is how to get back to Manaus."

"Nevoa will come."

I gaze at the river. "I'm not sure I want to get back on that boat. Sales and Vargas are killers, and they aren't the only killers aboard."

"Surely not the minister."

"He might not do the killing himself, but Vargas works for him. So do the others."

"What others? Who?"

"I don't know. Sales is up to no good at Portao da Dor, and I have no reason to get involved."

"What choice do we have?"

"Hike back to Vila de Deus. Catch a boat to Tieves."

"Just like that?"

"Just like that."

"This stretch of the Selva is full of Arqueiros and gunmen. On the Nevoa, we have the protection of the Navy and Marines."

Do we? Has Sales corrupted Lieutenant Quadros? Both Silva and Quadros fear the minister.

I walk to the waterline. Survey the river, the clearing. The plantation didn't have a chance against the jungle. The river is rank with weed. Green, lazy slime waving in the water. The stench is overwhelming. Over there, is that dead wood, or a gator's scaly tail?

This isn't much of a clearing. Fifteen yards deep by forty yards wide, stretching along the shore. It's impossible to tell how far the rubber plantation extended. I wouldn't be surprised if it was half a mile square, right next to the river. The forest reclaimed it for nature as efficiently as the ants are reclaiming the gunman's corpse. A mat of ants covers Fiadh's grave. I shudder.

This clearing used to be the plantation's dock. There was a boardwalk, long since rotted away. A pier extending into the river. All gone. Termites consumed it all. There's nothing left of the plantation but its name. A waypoint between Vila de Deus and Portao. A crossroads where three trails turn into two.

Thinking of Fiadh, I feel a terrible sadness. I knew the chances of her survival were slim. I was prepared to find her. I was prepared to hear bad news. I wasn't prepared to find her mutilated corpse.

There are no coincidences. The conflict that brought Fiadh to the Selva da Morte relates to the skullduggery aboard Nevoa. At least indirectly, Sales is responsible for her death.

When Cuchulain Connor asks me why his daughter was killed, I must have an answer.

I *need* an answer.

My eyes sweep the jungle. I quarter the ground, listening carefully. I hear cries of birds, the chatter of monkeys. There, at the edge of the forest—a snake. Its body, the color of lead, is as thick as my thigh. Can't tell how long it is. The creature slithers into the brush.

The jungle goes quiet in the right quadrant. The direction of Portao da Dor.

Not good.

I hold my finger to my lips, motion Laura to crouch low. "Breed."

Laura is pointing to the river. I follow her finger. There, coming around a bend, is the Nevoa. I recognize her bows, the forward superstructure that looks like a set of stacked boxes. As she approaches, more detail becomes visible. The 40mm Bofors and the Browning machine guns are manned and ready. The sandbagged machine guns on the navigation bridge and poop make Nevoa look like a floating fortress.

Silva will be watching for us.

I take a smoke grenade from my ruck. Pull the pin, toss it on the riverbank. A red cloud billows from the canister, covers the clearing.

Nevoa's foghorn booms in recognition.

Silva guides the gunboat toward us, stands a hundred yards offshore. Marines scramble on the boat deck, lower a Zodiac.

The jungle has gone quiet. Both inland quadrants. I pull back my shirt, draw the SIG.

"What's wrong?" Laura asks.

I say nothing. Motion her to stay down.

The Zodiac approaches with three Marines aboard. A pilot and two men at the bow.

There is a high-pitched crack. An M16, firing from the tree line. The first shot is followed by a full volley. Fireflies twinkle from the brush.

The Marines on the Zodiac raise their rifles. Return fire. Tiny spouts leap from the water as bullets snap past the Zodiac and impact the river. Laura and I flatten ourselves on the riverbank.

One of the Marines on the Zodiac cries out and topples from the boat. The Zodiac stops dead in the water as the Marines struggle to haul their friend aboard.

The Nevoa opens fire. The portside .50 calibers rake the tree line. On the fo'c'sle, the gun crew traverse the Bofors.

"Swim for it," I tell Laura.

"What?"

"You heard me. They aren't coming any closer."

Men in jungle fatigues emerge from the tree line, run toward us. I raise the SIG, fire. Three rounds hit the first man center mass. He tumbles into the clearing. Two others scramble for cover.

Laura runs to the river. Wades into the shallows. Ten yards out, she's waist deep, struggling against the weed. She throws herself into the water and thrashes toward the Zodiac. I scan the shore, looking for the telltale splash of alligators giving chase.

The Marines haul their wounded man aboard. The pilot starts to turn the boat around, but the other Marine grabs his arm and points at Laura. Free of the weed, the girl is swimming for her life.

When I fired the SIG, the gunmen registered my position. Automatic weapons crack from the tree line.

I throw myself flat on the muddy shore. There's a whack. A bullet plows into my rucksack and rolls me over. I try to burrow into the mud as I crawl for the trees. Pop another smoke grenade and squirm under the blanket.

God, you can never have enough smoke.

The gunmen approached from the southeast quadrant and fanned north. They came from the direction of Portao da Dor, enveloped the clearing.

There can't be more than a dozen sets of muzzle flashes. The gunmen are thin on the ground.

Orange flares bloom from the muzzle of the Bofors. The cannon shells look like molten tennis balls hurtling across the water. They crash into the tree line and explode. The gunmen return fire, but their muzzle flashes diminish.

Laura reaches the Zodiac. The Marines haul her aboard like a drowned rat. I wonder how many diseases she'll pick up from that crap water.

Under cover of smoke, I reach the tree line. Get to my feet and charge into the brush.

The first gunman I meet sees me coming and panics. Stocky guy. Black beard, M16 raised to his shoulder. He swings around, points the rifle. I see terror in his eyes. I fire twice. Double-tap, two in the face. He goes down and I run over him. Dodge into the jungle, head south-by-east.

Behind me, I hear the pounding of the Bofors, the hammering of the .50 calibers, the crackle of the M16s.

My world dissolves as I run through a dark tunnel. Fill my lungs with the jungle air. It's heavy with the dank smell of vegetation and earth.

I disappear into the Selva da Morte.

23

DAY SIX

Selva da Morte – FARC

T he men who killed Fiadh weren't loggers.
The loggers were well armed, but they weren't
paramilitary. They were happy to kill Arqueiros,
but their business was harvesting trees for profit.

No, the men Fiadh encountered were from the same
group who attacked us at Arvore de Ouro. They wore
fatigues, jungle boots, and combat webbing. They carried
M16s. In Latin America, M16s are usually stolen or captured
from regular army troops.

The men at Arvore de Ouro wear uniforms, but they
aren't regular army. That makes them guerrillas. Very
different from the traditional criminals that come to the Selva
da Morte.

Laura told me there were *two* trails leading from Arvore
de Ouro to Portao da Dor. They'll be parallel, with one closer
to the river. I don't know how many guerrillas there are, but
they are well armed and well supplied. They're coming north

over the trails in organized units. I can move faster on the trails, but there's a good chance I'll run into trouble.

I squeeze the SIG into my waistband and draw the Golok. I thrash through the brush until I find what passes for a trail. It's overgrown, but it's probably the route our attackers took coming north. Pushing along the track, I watch for tripwires. Latin American guerrillas don't have a reputation for booby traps, but it pays to be careful.

As far as I know, Brazil doesn't have a guerrilla problem. Everyone I've met talks about illegal loggers, illegal miners, and narcos. *Not* guerrillas.

Gasping and sweating, I press on. Parched with thirst, I suck water from my camelback. I have two quarts of fresh water. In this heat, a man requires a quart an hour to stave off dehydration. With discipline, I can ration myself half a quart an hour. Then I will be down to water purification tablets dissolved in swamp slime.

That's what infects you with amoebas, nematodes, and the kind of animals antibiotics can't kill. Creatures that eat you alive from the inside out.

The heat is stifling, and the gnats are enough of a nuisance to drive a man mad. When one thinks of the Amazon, one thinks of snakes, alligators, electric eels, and jaguars. A single frog, of a species found in the Selva da Morte, carries enough toxin to kill a hundred men.

For all that, the most dangerous creatures are insects. Fire ants whose bites are agony. Malaria-bearing mosquitoes that swarm in clouds. Flies that punch through clothing and lay eggs. Maggots that burrow under the skin and grow inside you, wriggle around and poke their heads up like little periscopes.

Clothing is everything. I breathe through my face net. It's all that keeps clouds of gnats out of my nose and mouth. Military-issue gloves protect my hands against insects. Bloused sleeves keep invaders from crawling up my arms.

The heat is stupefying.

Exhaustion numbs your brain.

Ninety percent of Delta training forces you to think when you are too tired to take another step. Teaches you to pay attention when your senses have been dulled by fatigue.

I hear voices, and the sound of men pushing through vegetation. Dive to one side of the trail, roll deep into the brush. I snap the Golok into its scabbard, claw the SIG from my waistband, and hold my breath.

The stink of decaying vegetation clogs my nose. Small animals scurry in the brush. Beads of sweat trickle down the side of my face.

The men are passing not ten feet from me. No surprise. The trail is little more than a trampled path in an ocean of green. The vegetation is closing over it like the ocean rushes to fill a boat's wake. Laura was right. The tracks from Arvore de Ouro to Portao da Dor are not worthy of being called trails.

"*¿Cuanto tiempo mas?*"

"*Una hora.*"

"*Puto bosque. Puto calor.*"

"*Callate.*"

Spanish. These men are Peruvian or Colombian guerrillas. They're either Shining Path or FARC.

Both groups have been beaten. Shining Path in Peru, and FARC in Colombia. The remnants of Shining Path are holed up in a mountainous, cocaine-producing region. The Valley of the Three Rivers. In that jungle redoubt, Shining Path has strayed from its roots. Mutated into a gang of drug traffickers. I doubt they would venture into the Selva da Morte.

FARC is another matter. The Colombian military fought the Marxist Revolutionary Army of Colombia to a standstill.

FARC signed a peace deal in 2016 and surrendered seventeen sea containers full of weapons. In exchange, they were granted a general amnesty and representation in government.

The weapons were melted and turned into statues. One stands outside the UN in New York. The other resides in Bogota. All very symbolic, very encouraging. There was just one small problem. The country wasn't ready for peace.

Over the decades of war, atrocities were committed by both sides. The thirst for vengeance seemed impossible to quench.

Former FARC guerrillas took advantage of the amnesty and tried to pursue normal lives. They were hunted down and assassinated by right-wing vigilantes. Atrocities multiplied.

On the other hand, not all FARC guerrillas bought into the peace deal. The die-hard revolutionaries went on fighting. Short of weapons and money, they sought sanctuary south of the border. FARC had always operated in Venezuela, Brazil and Peru. After the peace deal, the FARC dissidents fled the country.

Aggressive Colombian Army patrols kept FARC south of the border. The guerrilla army settled in northern Brazil. It looks like an aggressive FARC unit has settled in the Selva da Morte.

"*Tenemos que matar dos Yanquis.*"

"*Y los madereros.*"

"*No hay mas madereros.*"

"*Esto es un perdido de tiempo.*"

They've been sent to kill two Americans. And loggers. They're after me and Anna.

But why are they being asked to kill loggers?

They don't think there are any more loggers. In fact, they think their mission is a waste of time. They don't like tramping around the Selva, looking for people to kill. The

Selva is hostile to modern men, and FARC guerrillas are modern men. I've only met a handful of Special Forces soldiers who are so at home in the jungle they *love* it.

I count the men who pass. A dozen in all. The men who attacked us at Arvore de Ouro were the point element of a serious force.

There could be more behind them. I wait five minutes, then get to my feet and head east. If FARC is sweeping north from Portao da Dor, I need to use the other trail. Now I'm moving between the trails, through the thick of the Selva. I work the Golok, hacking at endless nets of vines and lianas that bar my path.

Sales radioed ahead. If Captain Silva is not on the minister's payroll, one of the minister's henchmen has a working knowledge of HF comms. That's why Max Morais, the radio operator, was murdered. Sales wanted his man free to communicate with Portao da Dor. He warned FARC that a lone gringo was loose in the Selva. Told them to finish Breed off, along with the girl who escaped the ambush.

Now I have an explanation for Vargas's interrogation of the logger. He wanted to know if there were more men in the band, and where they were. Vargas didn't get an answer, so Sales instructed FARC to search the Selva.

There is one conclusion I cannot escape.

FARC has occupied Portao da Dor.

24

DAY SIX

Selva da Morte – Meeting Engagement

I can't find the second trail.

The first trail was thin, the second must be nonexistent. Laura warned me the Selva was alive. A trail could be there one day and gone three months later. The jungle was expert at clawing back evidence of man. I hack my way east through dense brush. For all I know, I've passed it.

I'm stunned by a hard impact on my right side. I crossed a man's path and we blundered into each other. The force of the collision throws me to the ground. I fall through the brush and land on my side. Carried forward by his momentum, the man trips and falls on top of me.

The man's weight pins me, his rifle trapped between us. Golok clenched in my fist, I free one arm. Arch my back, throw him off, wrestle him to the ground. He struggles to push me away, but I hold him down. He screams. I set the cutting edge of the machete against his throat, pound the blade with my gloved left hand.

Another scream, choked off by the guillotine slashing

through his cervical vertebrae. Blood from severed arteries floods his trachea and spurts from his nose and mouth.

I rip the blade free of the man's partially severed neck. Shouts carry from the surrounding ocean of green. The rest of his column rushes toward us. I grab his rifle with my left hand and plunge into the brush.

The FARCs had been following a barely recognizable trail. The path might have existed only in their imagination. I crash through the vegetation, hacking left and right. They won't know which way to go until they find the body and disturbed foliage.

That'll buy me time.

Automatic rifle fire splits the air. The FARCs are firing into the brush on full auto. Rock and roll, no fire discipline.

I stop, collect myself.

Slow is fast.

An ACOG optical would be nice, but iron sights will do. I give the weapon a quick physical. The front sight post isn't bent—that's a start. The base of the post is flush with the front sight housing. Rear sight aperture up and centered. The assembly is clean and lightly oiled. Elevation wheel correctly set.

The FARC had some grasp. He might have performed a battle sight zero, but I can't be sure. I'll assume it's zeroed for twenty-five and three-hundred. Verify by observing the fall of shot, compensate by eyeball approximation.

I check the weapon's breech and magazine. Thirty rounds of five-five-six. I lock and load, sling the rifle across my chest. I wish I'd taken his webbing and spare ammunition, but— there wasn't time.

Check my compass, strike east. I'm moving deeper into the Selva. This is the same situation in which Fiadh found herself. Unless you want to hike a few thousand miles to safety, you have to pivot to the north or south.

The gunfire dies away.

I stop and listen. Normal jungle sounds have faded. The Selva, aware of our alien presence, holds its breath. My plan is to run east and dogleg south. Problem is, the FARCs know my plan. There's nothing at Arvore de Ouro, so I must be heading for Portao.

Shouts from behind and to my left. Can't tell how far away.

The FARCs are following the disturbed vegetation. They've pivoted east and are coming for me in a loose skirmish line.

"*Yanqui!*"

"*Yanqui!*"

"*Vamos a matarte, Yanqui!*"

I put my head down and keep moving.

For half an hour, I lead the FARCs into the Selva. Is it my imagination or is the vegetation thinner?

Sunlight blasts my eyes. Blinded, I squint to shut out the merciless glare. I've broken out of the forest onto a river. A tributary of the Rio Preto. Fast-moving water, a function of narrow breadth and shallow depth. Relatively clear, it's refreshingly different from the greenish-brown Amazon.

High noon. I'm bludgeoned by the sun.

I gauge the open ground. A hundred yards. I'll be a sitting duck if the FARCs catch me. I snap the Golok into its scabbard and start across the river.

Movement on the far bank catches my eye.

Fuck me.

Arqueiros. I've never seen one, but who else could these Indians be?

They're taller than average and powerfully built. Their skin is the color of chocolate, and their bodies are painted with bluish-white vertical stripes. The marks seem to shine in the gloom of the Selva. Their eyes have been outlined with black paint. They look like ghastly skeletons flitting between the trees on the opposite bank.

The Arqueiros carry bows, quivers of arrows, and four-foot-long spears. All carry woven haversacks. Thin bedrolls and hammocks are slung diagonally over their backs. For close work, they carry blowguns, knives, and crude hatchets.

The skeletons have their eyes on me, and FARC are chasing me down.

"Yanqui!"

"Yanqui, te mueres!"

FARCs behind and Arqueiros ahead. Was this what Fiadh felt like when she and her friends stumbled into that battle?

I unsling the M16 and run like hell. I have to put distance between myself and my pursuers. The best place to do that is the riverbank.

A roaring sound fills my ears.

What is that noise?

The river bends to the left. I splash into the water and cut across. If I get around the bend, the FARCs will lose sight of me when they emerge from the forest.

Of course, I could be running into Arqueiros.

The water is knee deep. I make it onto the opposite bank and race around the bend.

A waterfall.

It's a two-step waterfall. White water plunges thirty feet to the first level. From there, it boils over, then cascades another forty feet into the river. Stones of black basalt line the falls on both sides.

If I can occupy an elevated position, I have a chance.

Look back. The FARCs have not yet rounded the bend. I splash across the river a second time, make for the rocks at the foot of the falls. I glance left. Black-and-white skeletons fade into the forest.

The Arqueiros hear the FARCs approaching. They know

what rifles can do. They're not about to make themselves targets.

I sling the rifle across my back and attack the basalt wall. Slippery stones, polished smooth by centuries of pounding water. I climb as quickly as I dare.

A rifle cracks, and a bullet whines off the rock above me. I look back. The FARCs have just rounded the bend, a hundred and fifty yards away. I count half a dozen, with more behind.

Water pounds the first level and sprays the side of my face. I'm surprised how cool it feels in the ninety-degree heat. I take a knee behind a boulder, unsling the M16.

Let's see if we can even things up.

The FARCs run toward me.

That's convenient. Unless passing above or below, a target moving *toward* you requires no lead. The spray boiling from the foot of the falls doesn't drift. The leaves are still. There isn't any wind.

I allow my breathing to normalize. Take aim at the first FARC approaching the falls, lay the sight picture on his belly. Assuming the previous owner battle-sight zeroed the weapon, I should hit seven or eight inches high.

Flick the safety off and slip my finger onto the trigger. At the moment of my natural respiratory pause, I break the shot.

Crack!

There's a tinkle of brass on basalt. The recoil of an M16A2 is light compared to heavier sniper rifles.

A red flower blooms on the man's chest, seven inches above my aiming point. A shining fan, droplets of blood, sprays from the exit wound. He drops his rifle and pitches face down in the water.

Damn. That zero isn't half bad.

The FARCs screech to a halt and their aggression gives way to panic. Snipers have that effect.

I lay the sight picture on the chest of the next guerrilla

and squeeze the trigger. The man's head explodes into a bright pink mist. He drops like a cowpunched steer.

One of the guerrillas makes like a leader. Stands in the middle of the river. With sweeping arm motions, he directs the guerrillas to spread out.

Way to call attention to yourself, Homes.

Crack!

The five-five-six round drills him in the chest. A surprised look on his face, he raises his hands to the wound and crumples.

Three kills in under five seconds. Not bad for iron sights on another man's rifle.

Not just another pretty face.

The FARCs cut loose on full auto, shooting uphill. Bullets whine off the rocks above me. I duck behind the boulder. The guerrillas adjust their fire and let fly another volley. This time they zero in on my cover. Dust and stone chips scatter.

I stay low, look to either side. The falls are a curtain drawn over a black stone face.

There's a cave behind the falls. I risk a quick look around the boulder. The FARCs are spread out. I take a breath, gauge the distance, and pick my way to the falls.

The distance is no more than twenty feet. I duck behind the curtain. The thunder is deafening. The water and wet rock smell clean. Did I read the shadows correctly... is it really a cave? It is. A yawning maw, twenty feet wide and fifteen feet high. I dodge inside, pull a flashlight from my rucksack.

Cautiously, I sweep the beam around the cave. Wonder what kind of snakes, bats and other animals make their homes in here. I sling the M16 across my chest and draw the SIG. Pistol in one hand, flashlight in the other, I push into the cave.

The FARCs will be climbing the sides of the falls. They

don't know where I've gone, so they'll be cautious. That's the effect a sniper has on morale. Everyone in the shooting gallery gets a little bit less courageous.

I hurry along the cave floor, looking for an exit. I brush dust from the floor into my gloved hand. Allow the particles to fall in front of the flashlight. They drift gently toward the back of the cave.

I mustn't doubt myself.

Behind me... voices. Echoing from the stone walls. How far back are they? I wish I had grenades or Claymores.

I quicken my pace. Before long, I'm jogging behind my bouncing flashlight beam.

A narrow shaft of daylight streams into the cave. An opening, partially obscured by vegetation. The waterfall must be a mile behind me. I turn off the flashlight, slip it back into my ruck. Push the leaves aside and step through.

I find myself facing a wall of black and blue-white skeletons.

The Arqueiros, a dozen or more, have their bows drawn. Deadly, Mapepire-tipped arrows are pointed at my chest.

25

DAY SIX

Selva da Morte – Arqueiros

girl's voice freezes my gun hand. "Don't."

Lifting the SIG is smart only if I want to get shot full of arrows. But more than anything, it's the voice that stuns me into immobility. Carefully modulated... so it doesn't carry past my ears.

"Give me your hand," the voice says.

Slowly, I turn my head to look at the girl. Pale hair bound back. Wide green eyes search mine through a fine, translucent mosquito net. It's a crudely stitched sack pulled over her head and draped across her shoulders. Much more practical than the GI-issue net I'm wearing. Her gloved hand is stretched out to me.

Fiadh.

She's not asking for my gun.

I reach out, take her right hand with my left. It's awkward. Slowly, like she's talking me off a ledge, she draws me aside. The Arqueiros remain focused on the cave mouth.

Fiadh and I stand at the edge of the clearing, behind the

Arqueiros. I'm conscious she hasn't released my hand. Through our gloves, the human contact feels reassuring in this barbaric place.

The Arqueiros allow two FARCs through the opening before loosing their arrows. The first man takes three in the chest, drops his rifle, and collapses. The second man is hit in his chest and throat. The first two arrows penetrate no further than his ribs and sternum. The third skewers him through the neck.

Neither man gets off a shot. The Arqueiros nock their arrows with blinding speed. A third FARC is shot in the chest, shoulder and mouth. Eyes wide with shock, he falls on his back and dies.

The fourth FARC trips over the bodies. He's shot in the chest, then through the armpit as he falls. A third arrow misses and bounces off rock behind him. Dying, he fires his M16 into the ground.

Cries issue from the inside the cave. A guerrilla looks out from the hole, then dodges back inside as the Arqueiros loose arrows at him. The men inside open fire and the Arqueiros retreat to the sides of the clearing. Fiadh and I give them room.

They understand angles. From inside the cave, rifles cannot be brought to bear on them.

The Arqueiros shout and gesture. Two of the black-and-white skeleton figures step forward. In a stone bowl, they have piled dried brush. It is hard to imagine anything dry in the Selva, but they've done it. Smoke curls from the tinder.

The skeletons run to the sides of the cave mouth and stuff it with vegetation. Gunshots ring out from inside the cave. The bullets fly harmlessly through the opening and into the jungle. The men with the fire-bowl bend to their task. In minutes, the vegetation packed into the mouth of the cave begins to smolder. The fire generates a huge amount of smoke.

With their rifle butts, FARCs try to push the burning foliage from the opening. Arms outstretched in surrender, a man tries to crawl from the cave. An Arqueiro steps forward with a four-foot spear. He raises it over his head and drives it through the FARC's back. Pins the man's body to the clearing floor. The Indians push the burning tinder back into the hole.

Fiadh turns to me. "There are more Arqueiros at the falls. None of these men will escape."

She acts like we've known each other all our lives. Uncanny... I feel the same.

"You're alive," I say.

"Is that so hard to believe?"

"We found a girl's body at Arvore de Ouro. Thought it was you."

"Anna," Fiadh says. "She was caught."

"She was shot." I want to throw my arms around her. Instead, I gesture at the Arqueiros. "What's your situation?"

"They trust me," Fiadh says. "Since those killers are after you, they've given you the benefit of the doubt. For now."

"For now?"

"I'll explain later. What you have to believe is—out here, these Indians are the only friends we have."

One of the Arqueiros approaches us. He's a big guy, naked but for a loincloth, painted from face to toe with fearsome vertical stripes. His eyes are etched with black, and slashes of red paint mar his forehead and cheeks. He carries the Arqueiros' standard weapon, a bow and quiver of arrows.

The Arqueiro looks me up and down. His eyes take in the rifle I've slung across my chest. The pistol I've stuck in my waistband, and the Golok hanging from my pistol belt. He leans forward and peers through my face net. Searches my eyes. The Arqueiros do not use insect repellant. I wonder if the paint they wear has a protective quality.

Fiadh grasps my arm, says a few words to the man in what must be a local dialect. No more than a few words. Her hand on my arm and her posture communicate volumes.

The man turns to Fiadh. He speaks tersely, slashes the air with his hand, and stalks into the jungle. The other Arqueiros, sixteen of them, follow him.

"That's Djumo Arqueiro," Fiadh says. "He's their war chief. He wants us to follow them."

"What did you say to him?"

"That you're my friend."

Together, Fiadh and I bring up the rear. The Indians know the land and set a fast pace. We move much faster than military jungle patrols. Operations are context-dependent. The Arqueiros know where the FARCs are. They use trails of which the FARCs are unaware.

"What's your name?" Fiadh asks.

"Breed."

She nods. "I'm Fiadh."

"Yes. Your father sent me to bring you back."

"I thought as much." Fiadh speaks without turning to me. Her attention is fixed on the trail. "I'm not going."

I feel no desire to argue. Father Andrew, the canny leprechaun, put the hook in me. He knew once I got to know her, Fiadh would mean more to me than Cuchulain's mission.

On her back, Fiadh carries a lightweight olive drab ruck-sack. It looks military, but isn't. It's made of an expensive synthetic material. Cuchulain Connor's daughter has the best survival equipment money can buy. She carries forty pounds, including her own camelback. Swings a long, Latin machete.

"Where are their women?" I ask. All the Arqueiros I have seen are males of military edge.

"Their village is deep in the Selva," Fiadh says. "The location is a closely held secret. The men won't return until the war is over. They won't risk being followed back to their women and children."

"War?"

"Those men who chased you came to the Selva two years ago. They coexisted with the Arqueiros. There were a few skirmishes, a few deaths on both sides. But no serious killing. A month ago, everything changed."

"How do you know this?"

"Djumo told me. I speak some of the indigenous dialect."

"You've been coming to the Selva for years."

"Since I was eighteen. My friends and I have tried to stop loggers and miners from taking advantage of these people. Those gunmen are new, and things have changed in the last month."

"Did you ever encounter them before?"

Fiadh shakes her head. "No. For years, they kept to themselves, well southeast of Portao da Dor. They left the Arqueiros alone. We were interested in the Arqueiros, so we spent our time further north."

"Pedro and Anna are dead," I tell her. "Before he died, Pedro told Father Camos you were on the run in the Selva."

"Poor Pedro," Fiadh says. "Poor Anna. I tried to save her."

"Your friend Laura is on the Nevoa."

Surprised, Fiadh looks back at me. "What's she doing there?"

"Laura feels guilty about not going with you. She insisted on helping me find you."

"Had Laura come along, she might have been killed too," Fiadh says. "I was lucky."

"I don't know if she's safer on the boat or out here. There are murderers on the boat, and those gunmen are all over the Selva."

"I came to find out who those gunmen are," Fiadh says. "Do you know?"

"FARC," I tell her. "Marxist guerrillas from Colombia. Tell me about the war."

"A month ago, those men started killing Arqueiros. They wiped out a couple of hunting parties. One near Portao da Dor, another near Vila de Deus. The Arqueiros retaliated. They attacked people who didn't belong. Miners, loggers, villagers unlucky enough to stray too far into the Selva."

"The men from Vila de Deus."

"Yes."

"The Arqueiros attacked Portao da Dor."

"No, they didn't."

"The garrison at Portao radioed Manaus and said so."

"Manaus received that message before I left. I always thought it was phony." Fiadh stops and faces me. "Assuming you're right, FARC has taken over Portao da Dor. Djumo tells me that they have been transporting loads from their base camp to the outpost."

"What is it they're moving?"

"Djumo doesn't know. Small, heavy crates. They transport them overland on handcarts. It's difficult. Arqueiro scouts says the FARCs only manage a couple of loads a day."

"That explains a lot," I tell her.

"What do you mean?"

"The Nevoa is carrying a secret cargo of weapons. The big-ticket items are Stinger anti-aircraft missiles and Javelin anti-tank missiles. They're hidden in crates we picked up at Tieves. Sales says they are supplies and building materials for Portao da Dor."

"A trade, you think?"

"Yes. Sales is bringing up a shipload full of arms. FARC will give him whatever is in those crates they have been hauling to Portao da Dor. Sales will float it back on the Nevoa."

"People will see."

"Sales probably has a cover story prepared. From what I've seen, senior officers like Silva are too intimidated to challenge him. Alternatively, Sales and Vargas might be planning not to leave any witnesses alive. Not everybody on Nevoa is part of Sales's gang. Vargas and Doctor Fonseca for sure. Certainly at least two members of the crew. Possibly one or two senior Marines... the officer and an NCO."

"Doctor Fonseca is aboard?"

"Yes. I can't figure him out. He's not a Navy doctor. Sales must have used his influence to bring him aboard."

"Sales, Vargas and Fonseca are no good for Laura."

"Is something going on between them?"

"It's a bit of a story. I'll tell you more later." Fiadh struggles with lianas in her path. Hacks at them with her machete. "Who was murdered on the Nevoa?"

Quid pro quo. Fiadh's a polished operator. I imagine her as a teenager, attending business meetings with Cuchulain. Sitting quietly. Observing. Listening. Learning.

"The first officer and radio operator. One disappeared. During a storm, the other took a dive off the bridge."

Fiadh uses her machete with the skill of a sushi chef. The traditional Latin American style is longer than my Golok. Arguably more effective, but less compact.

"Who killed them?"

"I have my suspicions, but I'm still thinking everything through."

"Will you tell me when you do?"

"Yes." I feel no desire to hide anything from Fiadh. "In the end, it doesn't matter which henchman killed them. Whoever they are, the murderers are working for Sales and Vargas. The other night, they tried to kill me."

"How did that happen?"

"I stumbled upon one of them using the radio. They killed the radio operator so they could communicate freely with Portao da Dor."

The Arqueiros lead us deeper into the Selva. They travel with an astonishing economy of effort. More surprising, Fiadh and I benefit from the Arqueiros' choice of route. They know the land, and they lead us over invisible paths that offer little resistance.

"Where are they taking us, if not their village?" I ask.

"They're going to meet the men they left at the waterfall."

The Arqueiros stop at a place that is surprisingly wide and dry. It's a natural clearing, the old trees are widely spaced. The tree trunks, fifteen feet around at the base, reach into the sky. They don't sprout branches till the last thirty feet. There, they spread into a thick canopy that blocks the light. Without light, the vegetation on the lower canopies is thin. The ground is clear but for the trunks of smaller, younger trees.

I watch the Arqueiros sit down and take dried food from their haversacks. A kind of jerky. I shudder to think where they got it. Fiadh sees the look on my face. "No," she says.

"No, what?"

"No to what you're thinking." Fiadh shrugs off her rucksack and sets it on the ground. Lifts the net from her face.

Surprise upon surprise. This clearing is relatively free of mosquitoes. I lift my own face net.

"They're not cannibals?"

"Of course they are, but not the way you think. It's not their usual diet. There's plenty of wild boar and tapir around. Roast boar beats boiled monkey any day."

"Comforting."

"For the Arqueiros," Fiadh says, "cannibalism is about

power. If you eat the flesh of your enemy, you diminish him and steal his strength."

"I suppose that's why deer hunters eat the heart of their first kill."

"Look at this place, Breed." Fiadh stretches and casts her arms to the vast cathedral of trees. "*This* is Eden."

The photographs didn't do her justice. If this is Eden, she's Eve.

I drop my ruck, sit cross-legged. Fiadh sits across from me, plants her machete, point-down, in the earth.

We can share an MRE from my ruck. I take one out and tear it open.

Fiadh pulls a bottle of Bushmills from her pack. My eyes widen, and she gives me a sly wink.

"If you've carried *that* around for two weeks," I tell her, "you're crazy."

Fiadh takes a swig, hands me the bottle. It's down by half. "God created the sun, moon and stars. The Irish created Bushmills."

I'm not about to argue. I wish I'd brought Sales's Bourbon along. I accept the bottle, raise it to her, and take a swig. It's fucking warm. Been humping it in ninety-degree heat all day.

Warm Bushmills. Think I'll have some more.

Hand it back, stare into the emerald pools of her eyes. She stares back, and we are quiet for a long time. It is hard to look away, so I force myself to speak.

"Tell me how you came to the Selva."

26

DAY SIX

Selva da Morte – Fiadh's Plan

Fiadh takes another long swig of whiskey. That bottle won't last long. I wonder how many she humped into the bush. I cast a suspicious glance at her ruck. That's a two-quart camelback she's stuffed in there.

"Tell you what," she says. "I'll make you a deal."

"What kind of deal?"

Fiadh pulls off her gloves. Wipes her lips with the back of her hand. "I'll tell you everything *you* want to know, but you have to answer *my* questions."

"Alright."

"Why did Dad hire *you* to find me?"

"He heard from a few misguided souls that I could work miracles."

Fiadh laughs. "You found me, so I guess they were right."

I shake my head. "The miracle is that *you* are alive."

"What are you? A cop? Army? One of those SEAL Team Six dudes? That's who Dad would buy."

"Nothing so dramatic. I was a warrant officer in the Army."

Fiadh nods. "Modest, too. How much is he paying you?"

Damn, she's tough. "You writing a book?"

"Blank check, right?"

"Something like that."

"Dad gives blank checks to ordinary people all the time." Fiadh helps herself to some cheese out of the MRE. "Don't worry, Breed. He's good for it. What are you going to charge him?"

"You told me you weren't coming back."

Another shot of Bushmills follows the cheese. "I'm not. He'll pay for news. What will you charge him?"

"A dollar."

The hell of it is, I mean it.

Fiadh stares at me. "You're serious."

"Yes."

The girl is silent for a long moment. Finally, she says, "I believe you. You're not the type."

"What type is that?"

"You know what type."

The next question is going to be a bitch. She'll ask why I'm willing to do it for a dollar, and she knows what the answer will be. She sees right through me, knows me better than I know myself. How does that happen? She didn't have a diabolical leprechaun to slip her my dossier.

Fiadh takes a breath to ask the question. Frowns, changes her mind. She knows I'll answer honestly. Who knows where that could lead?

"We planned it in Manaus," she says at last. "Laura, Anna, Pedro. We studied the maps I made with Manuel Barros."

"Laura didn't go."

"No. She tried everything to talk us out of going. Finally

she said she would help plan the expedition, but wouldn't go herself. That was the *most* she would do."

"You said you would tell me about Laura and Sales's bunch."

Fiadh gulps her whiskey. "I shouldn't. She told me in confidence, but out here she could be in real trouble."

I say nothing, give the girl time to collect her thoughts.

"Laura's fun," she says at last. "But she's wild. Minister Sales and Vargas are creeps. In Brasilia, Laura and I would meet them at socials our fathers attended. They hit on me and I avoided them. Sales makes my skin crawl. Vargas is plain scary. Laura—she slept with Sales. She flirted with Vargas, drove him crazy. I told her she was asking for trouble. She said she was just fooling around."

"How long ago was this?"

"A long time ago." Fiadh wrinkles her brow. "We couldn't have been more than eighteen. We had a lot of fun together in Rio and São Paulo. The kind of nights you enjoy and forget. The thing Laura had with Sales was different. It was edgy."

Fiadh takes a deep breath. "Then she came to me and said she'd gotten pregnant. She was upset. Told me Minister Sales was going to arrange for her to get rid of the baby. We stayed up all night crying together. She was terrified she was sinning against God.

"I've struggled with questions about birth control and sex. In this day and age. Don't laugh. Never the problem Laura had. But it seemed all of a piece. This is the twenty-first century. I can't believe God would condemn us for a mistake, or for doing what makes sense. Father Andrew said I should confess and do penance. I advised Laura to seek absolution. Any responsible priest would either absolve her, or advise her of a way forward."

"Let me guess... Doctor Fonseca did the procedure."

"Yes. It's a crime in Brazil. The penalties are severe. Laura went through the procedure, and we never spoke about it again. I can't imagine what it's like for her, to be with Sales, Vargas, and Fonseca on that boat."

"Vargas is still hitting on her." I tell Fiadh of the altercation I witnessed in Laura's cabin.

"He's an animal," Fiadh says. "She's a strong girl, but I'm afraid for her."

"Is Laura still involved with Sales?"

"I don't think so. She must feel awful, sitting on a boat with that vile crew. You saw Sales and Vargas. They're twisted."

"Tell me what happened to you in the Selva."

She does.

It was ten days ago.

Fiadh looked around the card table. They sat in the back room of the Mission of Our Lady of Hope, poring over maps. Laura sat at her right hand and Anna at her left. Pedro faced her over a 1:25,000 map of the Selva da Morte. It was folded to show the stretch of the Rio Preto between Vila de Deus and Portao da Dor.

"There are three trails leading to Arvore de Ouro," Laura said. "You'll find the Arqueiros close to the east trail."

Anna frowned. "Unless we split up, we can only search one trail at a time."

"Start with the easternmost trail," Laura said.

Pedro stared at the map, said nothing. He was the strong, quiet one. When Pedro weighed in, one could be sure he had thought everything through.

Fiadh leaned back in her chair, studied the marks penciled onto the map. Coordinates, distances. On the table lay her GPS device. It was difficult, sometimes impossible, to navigate by compass in the Selva. A GPS was convenient and accurate. Fiadh always used both navigation aids on her expeditions.

They would do what she wanted, in the end. Even Pedro, as studious as he was, followed her. It was a heavy responsibility to bear. Fiadh knew what she wanted to do. She didn't know if it would work.

"This won't be about searching trails," Fiadh said. "We have to keep our eye on the ball. If gunmen are provoking the Arqueiros, it's the gunmen we want."

"What are you saying?" Laura asked.

"We want to know who they are, and what they're up to. We'll watch Arvore de Ouro. When we pick up the gunmen, unseen, we'll follow them."

"*Follow* armed criminals?" Laura's knuckles were bone-white on the armrests of her chair. "You are going to be killed."

"What do you suggest?" Anna asked.

Anna was a plain girl from the Dordogne. She had the strong, vigorous frame of a healthy peasant.

"I *suggest* you stay here," Laura snapped. "It is one thing to look for Arqueiros and logging camps. Something else to follow men with guns."

Fiadh leaned forward, squinted at the map. "Outsiders like to stay near the river," she said. "It makes them feel comfortable. That's why they like Arvore de Ouro. We'll hide in the jungle and watch the clearing. They're bound to pass Arvore before they journey to find Arqueiros. Then we'll shadow them."

"What if we miss them?" Anna asked.

"We'll pick them up on their way back, follow them to their camp."

The group was silent for a long time.

"It makes sense," Pedro said.

Fiadh relaxed. If Pedro was sold, her plan was sound.

"You are crazy," Laura said. "Don't go. Those men will kill you."

"The Lord is my light and salvation, whom shall I fear?"

Laura threw up her hands. "The Twenty-Fourth Psalm. Fiadh, don't quote scripture. This is not a game."

Fiadh looked at Laura with hurt eyes. "Laura, this has never been a game. We've been together six years. Come with me now."

"No." Laura shook her head. "You will go on *this* journey without me."

I STARE AT FIADH. Her plan was perfect... for a team of snipers. With my best men, I would have been cautious. Three twenty-four-year-olds with minimal training? Suicidal.

"What was your operating cycle?" I ask.

"We planned to take supplies for ten days," Fiadh says. "Vila de Deus served as our base. If we made no contact in ten days, we would return to the mission. Rest and resupply, go out again."

Fiadh Connor would have made a great Delta.

27

DAY SIX

Selva da Morte – Contact

"Your plan centered around Arvore de Ouro," I say. "It was a good plan. What went wrong?"

Fiadh looks miserable. "What went wrong was... we never got there."

FIADH SAID goodbye to Father Camos at the edge of the forest. She led her team into the gloom, set off along the river trail.

The Selva was relatively quiet during the day. The oppressive heat pounded everything alive into a stupor. In the dark, under the triple-canopy, the air was hot, humid, and stifling. No breeze ruffled the leaves.

Fiadh forged her way through the jungle as quickly as she dared.

Trails were abstractions. They were often recognizable only as areas of disturbed vegetation. Fiadh would frequently lose the trail, consult her GPS, and relocate the path a hundred yards away.

Dense foliage trapped jungle odors in pockets. Here, the cloying sweetness of wildflowers. There, the smell of decaying vegetation. Slash through a curtain of lianas, and you could release the stench of a dead tapir. Food for legions of ants.

Midday, they stopped to eat a light meal.

"Do you think we will arrive at Arvore before dark?" Anna asked.

"I think so," Fiadh told her. "We're almost halfway."

They sat at the foot of an enormous tree trunk. As big around as a house, it was a landmark they used on the way to the plantation. Before they sat, Fiadh was careful to examine the area for signs others had used it. There were none, and she ensured she and the others left no signs of their own. They picked up their scraps, sealed them in plastic bags, and stuffed them in their rucksacks.

"Let's go," Fiadh said.

The little group got to their feet. Fiadh took one last look around. Turned and pushed onto the trail. Anna followed, and Pedro brought up the rear.

Fiadh was confident. Flooding of the river might alter the appearance of the forest floor. The tree was an immutable landmark. She stepped through the brush, correlating her memory with guidance from the GPS.

It would be good to reach Arvore de Ouro. They could find a hide near the river and bed down for the night. Find places to stretch hammocks and mosquito netting. Fiadh didn't plan to rely on visual surveillance of the plantation. In the Selva, especially at night, sound was a better indicator of movement.

During the day, the jungle lost its voice. The soporific heat muted all life. Dusk brought a violent resurgence. The Selva's vast panoply of creatures woke to the gloaming. Fiadh could lie in her hammock. Trace the movement of a jaguar by the order in which noises in the jungle faded into silence. So long as the team went to ground within earshot of Arvore de Ouro, she would know of the presence of gunmen.

The first bullet cracked past Fiadh's ear. She'd never been shot at, didn't recognize it for what it was. The round smacked into a tree next to the trail. Behind her, Anna shouted, "Look out!"

Fiadh threw herself to the forest floor. The sonic boom of the gunshot and the whack of the bullet hitting the tree arrived almost on top of each other. Anna and Pedro flattened themselves on the ground.

More gunfire shredded the foliage.

"Back!" Fiadh yelled. The din of gunfire was deafening. She twisted on her side and signaled the others to retreat. "Don't get up."

Anna and Pedro needed no urging. They turned around and crawled back the way they had come.

The gunfire ceased as quickly as it had begun. Fiadh stared as a man in olive drab jungle fatigues emerged from the brush. He approached slowly, rifle raised to his shoulder, panning left and right. From the gloom behind him, another man stepped into view.

Fiadh froze. The first man turned toward her, bringing his rifle to bear.

There was a disturbance in the air over Fiadh's head. A long arrow buried itself in the gunman's chest. Six inches of shaft emerged from his back, and he pitched onto his face. The second man fired into the jungle over Fiadh's head. Again, there was a flutter as arrows were loosed. The second man cried out, an arrow buried in his shoulder. He sank to his knees, clawing at the shaft.

More gunfire erupted from the jungle. In response,

arrows whizzed through the air. Fiadh crawled away, jinking her hips.

Arqueiros hidden in the jungle dueled with the gunmen. Muzzle flashes twinkled in the gloom. Men shouted to each other, advanced through the brush.

When she had crawled twenty yards, Fiadh got to her feet and ran. Strong hands seized her and dragged her to earth.

Pedro.

"Stay down," he said. "They are coming."

"We can't stay here," Fiadh hissed.

The vegetation concealed the group, but there was precious little cover. Bullets and arrows flew everywhere. Fiadh and her friends had no weapons with which to defend themselves. The gunmen could simply stroll over and shoot them. The only things keeping them alive were the Arqueiros' arrows.

"Run back to the big tree," Anna said.

"No." Fiadh reached out and grabbed Pedro and Anna by the straps of their rucksacks. "There is no protection there. Run or crawl *toward* the Arqueiros."

That way, the Arqueiros' arrows would give them cover.

"Alright," Pedro said. "Go."

Fiadh and Anna scrambled to their feet and dove into the brush on the side of the trail. Ran toward where they thought the Arqueiros were hiding. An arrow flashed past Fiadh's face. She was going in the right direction.

More shooting.

Behind her, a cry of pain. Fiadh turned, saw Pedro fall, the front of his shirt bloody.

"Pedro." She started back for him.

"Get out of here." Pedro struggled to his knees, waved her on. He got up, clutching his side. Started running back toward the trail.

The Arqueiros were retreating. Fiadh turned and ran in

the direction Anna and the Indians had gone. Bullets
snapped through the jungle.

Fiadh tripped over something heavy on the ground. She
stumbled, fell to her hands and knees. Looked behind her
and choked down a scream.

She'd fallen over a man. What must have been a man.
Naked, painted with long white stripes along the bones of his
arms and legs. Vertically down his face, chest and belly. He
was dark-skinned, powerfully muscled.

An Arqueiro.

Blood bubbled from his mouth and nose. More pumped
from a hole in his chest. A pulped exit wound the size of
Fiadh's fist. She took her machete and cut away his woven
haversack. She emptied the contents on the ground and cut
the bag into two large patches of cloth. Stuffed them in the
hole.

Gunmen were thrashing through the brush.

Fiadh took the Arqueiro's hand. Tugged at it. "Get up,"
she hissed. "Can you get up?"

The wounded man blinked at her. She tried other words
in dialect. Made running motions with her fingers and hands.

Men with guns are coming. We must run away.

The Arqueiro shook his head. He wasn't going anywhere
with that chest wound.

The brush rustled close by. Fiadh looked up. A figure
crouched in the gloom of the jungle. Stared at her.

A thrill of terror shot through her chest. She wanted to
scream, found no air in her lungs. The face staring at her was
that of an Arqueiro. His eyes were locked on hers. She was
fascinated by the shining white stripes that ran down his face,
his thin black raccoon mask. His right hand clutched a bow,
the arrow nocked and held by his left hand. It was pointing at
the earth. He had not drawn it.

The Arqueiro made no move to harm her.

There was nothing more she could do for the wounded man. Warily, she rose to her feet, eyes locked on the man she would come to know as Djumo Arqueiro. She turned and ran. When she looked back, Djumo was kneeling over the man she had tried to bandage.

Shadows flitted through the jungle on either side of her. Arrows whirred through the air and rifles cracked. Fiadh realized she was running amongst the Arqueiros, who were breaking contact.

She found Anna cowering under dense foliage at the base of towering trees. Anna had crawled in and tried to pull vegetation after herself. But she had neglected to cover up the tracks she had made in the muddy earth of the jungle floor.

Fiadh tore at the vegetation with her gloved hands, crawled inside. Found Anna sitting with her knees drawn up to her chest, sobbing.

"I thought they killed you," Anna said.

"No. But we can't stay here. They'll find us."

"They won't," Anna blubbered. "We'll be quiet."

"They'll see the tracks outside," Fiadh said. "We can't cover them up."

"Where's Pedro?"

Fiadh decided not to tell Anna that Pedro had been shot. The French girl was upset enough. "He's running toward Vila de Deus," she said. "We have to run to the Arqueiros. Their arrows will cover us."

"No," Anna insisted. "We have to hide."

Fiadh thought of the deep tracks Anna's knees and boots had left in the forest floor. She took Anna's hands in hers. Looked her in the eyes. "Listen to me, Anna. If we stay here, they'll find us, and they *will* kill us. Understand? Now they are chasing the Arqueiros east. Come with me."

"I can't."

Anna was going to break down.

"You have to." Fiadh undid the clasp of her gold cross. Fastened it around Anna's throat. "God will give you strength. He'll protect you. We have to go, *now*."

Fiadh gripped Anna's hand, pulled her from the jungle bower. The French girl flinched at the gunshots.

"Come on," Fiadh said.

"We have to go with Pedro," Anna cried. She broke free of Fiadh's grip. Ran in the direction of Vila de Deus.

"Damn... *Wait!*" Fiadh watched Anna disappear into the jungle.

The gunshots sounded so close it felt like the gunmen were right on top of them. Fiadh looked about herself, trying to gauge where the gunmen and the Arqueiros were. She decided she'd spent too much time with Anna. The Arqueiros were already a good distance off, and the gunmen were all around.

Shit.

The crack of rifles.

Fiadh ducked into the brush and ran toward the Arqueiros. Her world dissolved into a forest of blacks and greens. Bony claws snatched at her arms and shoulders. She thrashed against curtains of lianas, hacked her way through.

In that dark purgatory, time lost meaning.

She came to a stream. A little brook with lovely clear water. The shooting had stopped. She bent at the waist, put her hands on her knees, and watched droplets of sweat fall from the tip of her nose. Kneeling, she raised her protective net and splashed water on her face.

That's when she realized she wasn't alone.

"Arqueiros?" I ask.

Fiadh takes a long swig of Bushmills. We've taken the bottle down by another quarter, and she's done most of the drinking. She grimaces, bites down the liquor. "You know it," she says. "Helping Djumo's friend won me some brownie points. They didn't kill me."

"You might want to go easy on that whiskey."

"Relax, Breed. I was baptized in it."

28

DAY SIX

Selva da Morte – Fiadh and the Arqueiros

We share the bottle and Fiadh tells me of her escape. How she joined the Arqueiros and came to travel with them.

HANDS RAISED, Fiadh rose to her feet. She consciously slowed her movements and tried to appear non-threatening. She searched the faces that surrounded her. Dark faces, shining white vertical stripes.

She recognized the Arqueiro she had encountered while she was tending the wounded man. It was Djumo. By his posture and manner, he conveyed leadership.

Fiadh could communicate with people from other tribes. She knew enough of their dialects to get by. There was commonality between certain local dialects. With luck, and a bit of sign language, she would be able to make herself understood.

"I am a friend." She used the word common to all the local dialects.

Djumo spoke. *"You tried to help my man. You can go."*

"Do you know where my friends are?"

"The boy is running to Vila de Deus. The girl was shot. The men with guns took her."

Fiadh groaned. She was living a nightmare. In the jungle, any wound was serious. Infections spread quickly. Without immediate treatment, few wounds were survivable. Pedro might have a chance if he reached Vila de Deus. Father Camos could call for help. The Navy might find a way to evacuate him.

Anna was another matter. Fiadh had no idea how badly she had been wounded. The gunmen who took her would not have access to more than rudimentary first aid.

"Will you help my friends?" Fiadh asked.

Djumo shook his head. *"No. Too many guns."*

Fiadh stared at him, helpless.

Again, Djumo said, *"You may go."*

There were men with guns in the Selva, but there always had been. Loggers and miners were well-armed. They killed Indians they encountered, but they never engaged in organized provocation. Fiadh was sure the gunmen she had just escaped were not loggers or miners. But she still had no idea who they were, or of their motives.

"Let me come with you," she signed.

The Arqueiros laughed together. Djumo was amused, but kept a straight face. *"You do not know what you ask."*

"Let me come. I will not be a burden."

The Arqueiros looked to Djumo. For a long time, he was silent.

At last he said, *"I am Djumo."*

"I am Fiadh."

"If you fall behind," Djumo said, *"we will leave you."*

. . .

THE ARQUEIROS SET off and headed north. Fiadh checked their route with her compass and GPS. It was clear they were traveling toward Vila de Deus, but far enough east that they would pass the mission.

Fiadh was worried sick about Pedro and Anna, but she saw the logic in Djumo's words. Anna was with the gunmen. It was also possible they were still chasing Pedro. She had no idea where the Arqueiros intended to go, but she intended to stay with them and learn what she could.

The excitement of running with an Arqueiro band was overwhelming. For years, Fiadh had seen traces of the Arqueiros. Their campfires, arrowheads, mysterious marks they left on trees. She had felt their eyes as she navigated the Selva. But they remained an "uncontacted" tribe. One of the tribes FUNAI refused to let its workers approach.

Now, Fiadh had made contact with the Arqueiros. There was nothing she could have done. It had happened, and FUNAI had to accept the Arqueiros were "uncontacted" no longer. The fact was, most uncontacted tribes did not *wish* to be contacted. Djumo had given Fiadh a unique opportunity.

The Arqueiros possessed astonishing endurance. Fiadh was in excellent physical condition, but she struggled to keep up.

GPS indicated they passed Vila de Deus before nightfall. Made camp and hung their hammocks and mosquito netting. As Fiadh expected, they passed so far east of the mission they never saw it. She reasoned that Pedro was still on the trail. Wounded, there was no way he could have managed the pace the Arqueiros were traveling.

Djumo posted sentries, and the Arqueiros built small cooking fires. Rather than sitting by herself, Fiadh sought Djumo.

The Arqueiros were impressed that Fiadh had managed to keep up. She found they were as curious about her as she was about them. Their conversation focused on the gunmen she had encountered that day.

Fiadh learned that the Arqueiros had happened upon her and the gunmen by accident. They had been on their way north when they heard the shooting. Rushed forward and found gunmen trying to kill Fiadh and her friends.

"Where are you going?" Fiadh asked.

Djumo shrugged. *"North."*

He would say no more. Fiadh told herself he could not yet trust her. Even if her intentions were good, she might be captured.

Djumo introduced his son, Taukan. Fiadh thought Djumo to be forty years old. Taukan was the spitting image of his father, twenty years younger.

The conversation turned to the gunmen. Djumo knew they were not illegal loggers or minors. Rather, they were *"men from the north"* who came to the Selva two years ago and built a camp well upriver.

A month ago, those men began killing Arqueiros.

That was the provocation Fiadh had come to prove. Now she had to learn about the men and their motives.

Djumo did not know who the men were. He knew nothing about their motives. He only knew they had occupied Portao da Dor. They were transporting goods from their camp to the outpost.

The men were killing Arqueiros and other white men in the Selva.

The Arqueiros were at war.

FIADH AWOKE to find the Arqueiros breaking camp. She was used to the day and night sounds of the Selva. Her first weeks in the jungle, she learned to sleep through the madhouse of jungle noise. More importantly, she learned to detect subtle differences in the sounds. Silence woke her.

The more time she spent in the Selva, the more knowledgeable Fiadh became. She marveled at the depth of the Arqueiros' knowledge.

The Arqueiros passed a stream.

"Bring us food," Djumo said to Taukan.

The war chief's son hastened to the stream.

"Go with him," Djumo told Fiadh. *"You will learn something."*

Fiadh liked the way Djumo tapped the side of his head with one finger. It was a gesture easy to comprehend in any language. She hurried to catch up with Taukan.

Taukan showed her a plant. Took a makeshift mortar and pestle from his haversack and crushed its leaves.

"Watch," he said, and dripped the juice into a stream. Fish swam through the cloud, then floated belly-up. Taukan picked up the best fish and the Arqueiros cooked them for a meal.

What surprised Fiadh was that the remaining fish woke up a few minutes later. Swam away unharmed. The plant produced a powerful narcotic.

With his hands, Taukan made stabbing motions. *"If one is wounded, this medicine removes pain."*

"How much should you use?" Fiadh asked.

"One must have experience to know."

The jungle provided thousands of ways to kill a man, but it produced just as many ways to save him. Fiadh made notes and took photographs of the plants. It was possible doctors and pharmacologists were already aware of these drugs. It was equally possible she was being shown undiscovered marvels.

Fiadh moved further up the Arqueiro column. She

learned that for many maneuvers, the column would split in
two. One group would be led by Djumo, the other by Taukan.
Djumo was their war chief, Taukan his second-in-command.
As such, the two men rarely walked close together. Rather,
they walked apart, ready to lead their separate groups when
necessary. Fiadh walked with Djumo whenever she could. At
other times, she walked with Taukan.

THE ARQUEIROS SPENT NEARLY a week in the north of the
Selva da Morte. Fiadh did not know what they were doing,
and Djumo would not tell her. For the better part of a day,
they would hide in the brush, watching and listening. Then
they would prowl the forest, searching trails and streams for
tracks.

It was clear the Indians were on the hunt. Fiadh did not
know if they were hunting animals or men.

One morning, Djumo raised his hand and signaled the
column to stop.

Fiadh crouched behind him. Watched as he signaled
Taukan to take his men and spread out through the brush.
When he was satisfied with the dispositions of his band,
Djumo got to his feet. Took an arrow from his quiver and
nocked it.

Djumo motioned for Fiadh to wait. Advanced slowly with
several men.

Minutes passed.

Fiadh heard a bird call. A signal from Djumo, and the
Arqueiros advanced. Fiadh screwed up her courage and
followed them.

The trail opened into a small clearing.

During her time in the Selva, Fiadh had seen horrors.
Examples of what miners and loggers did to Indians. What
she saw in the clearing was terrible, but not the worst.

Four men had been hung from a stout branch of a low tree.

The men were Indians. They did not wear the distinctive war paint of the Arqueiros. They had been hung by their necks, with their hands bound behind their backs. Their toes barely touched the ground, so they strangled slowly, their legs free to kick. They had been gutted and their entrails left to hang for animals to forage. The animals had not been able to reach all the way up their bodies. Remains were scattered everywhere. Insects covered the hanging corpses in dense clouds.

Fiadh turned away. If God was merciful, blood loss had caused the men to lose consciousness.

Djumo turned to her. *"Gurojas,"* he said.

The Gurojas were a small tribe occupying the north of the Selva. There were only two hundred of them, and now there were four less. They were peaceful people who lived near the riverbanks of the Amazon and its tributary, the Rio Preto.

"Who did this?" Fiadh asked.

Djumo circled the carrion. Studied it with a critical eye.

"Not the men who attacked you," he said. *"These have not been shot with guns."*

He was right. The Gurojas had not been shot. They had been taken captive. Then they were strung up and gutted. There was no purpose to the killing. The murderers had killed for pleasure.

Fiadh was consumed by a cold rage.

Looking about herself, she saw the Arqueiros felt the same. Djumo's face was black as night behind the white war stripes. Gurojas were a peaceful tribe, subsisting on fish from the rivers. They coexisted with the Arqueiros.

Taukan stepped into the clearing. *"We have found their trail,"* he said.

Djumo nodded. Taukan turned and led the Arqueiros into the jungle.

Every man in the war party was bent on justice.

Fiadh squeezed her eyes shut. Reminded herself that vengeance was reserved for God.

But she wanted it anyway.

29

DAY SIX

Selva da Morte – The Logging Camp

Taukan led the war party directly west. It was plain they were heading for the shore of the Rio Preto. Djumo deployed men to the left and right of the column. They would provide warning of any trouble in the forest.

"How many?" Fiadh asked.

Djumo held up six fingers. Shrugged his shoulders. Held up ten.

Six or ten men. All they could tell from the tracks in the clearing.

Night fell, and they made camp. Djumo set twice the number of sentries. Every man slept with his weapons close to hand. Fiadh had only her machete. She took it into her hammock, slept with it across her chest.

When morning came, they continued their journey.

THE ROAR of chainsaws guided them to the logging camp.

Djumo, Taukan, Fiadh, and two other Arqueiros advanced ahead of the main party. Fiadh never asked for permission. She followed Djumo or Taukan, waited for them to shoo her off. They never did. Sometimes, they motioned for her to stay back, or follow last.

They crept to the edge of the forest and looked out on the clearing.

It was on the shore of the Rio Preto. A hundred yards of riverbank, forty yards deep. The loggers had felled dozens of trees. They were using chainsaws to strip them of branches and prepare them for shipment.

The loggers had lit cooking fires on the bank, and pitched tents for sleeping. The tents were quality designs. They were equipped with screened flaps to provide ventilation. Nets to prevent the entry of snakes and centipedes. The shelters would also protect inhabitants from vampire bats and insects.

There were eight loggers in the clearing. Two men stood at either end of the camp. Both carried M16 rifles. The other six sweated in the heat. Their weapons were stacked outside the tents. Branches and leaves, hacked and sawn from the fallen trees, formed an untidy pile at the jungle's edge.

Sweat cools the body by virtue of its wicking effect. As a breeze blows over the liquid, body heat is conducted into the air and whisked away as sweat evaporates. In the Selva, the wind didn't blow and sweat didn't evaporate. It sat on a man's skin, absorbed the heat, and baked him alive.

Stretching a quarter of a mile to the opposite bank, the Rio Preto flowed languidly north. Carried the greenish-brown lifeblood of Amazonas. Rank, brackish weeds floated like rafts on its surface. Caimans sunned themselves on the shores, slid like gruesome pirogues into the water.

The jungle was not noisy in the sweltering heat. But it spoke continuously, in a flat voice, audible above the roar of the chainsaws.

The loggers must have found the Gurojas fishing. Followed them into the jungle and took them prisoner.

Djumo whispered to Taukan. The younger man crawled back into the jungle to gather his men.

Fiadh studied the loggers. Tried to divine from their features the kind of evil that led them to do what they did to the Gurojas. She could not tell. The men looked ordinary in every respect. They were young men. Healthy and energetic. They looked like anyone you might pass on the street.

A sharp bird call pierced the air.

Taukan.

The men ignored the sound, kept working.

Djumo cupped his hands and responded with a call of his own.

Instantly, four arrows whipped through the air and drilled the sentries. Two arrows each, piercing their chests and emerging from their backs. The two men stared in stupefaction at the shafts embedded in their flesh. Then they collapsed on the shore.

It took the other men a second to realize what was happening. One of them shouted a warning. They dropped their tools and ran for the rifles stacked outside their tents.

They never made it. With cries, Taukan's men intercepted them. The Arqueiros carried spears, knives and hatchets. They captured the loggers and immobilized them.

Djumo rose and strode into the camp.

"Bind them," he snapped. Then he gave his men instructions.

Djumo's Arqueiros provided security by standing guard at the edge of the jungle. Taukan's group bound the six loggers, hand and foot. Sat them in a circle, backs to each other, next to one of the cooking fires.

Taukan's Arqueiros went to work with axes, hatchets, and other tools the loggers kept at the camp. They worked from the logs their captives had already made. Cut sixteen posts, each twelve feet high. Then they cut notches in the flat tops of the posts.

The Arqueiros dug holes in the shore, eight feet apart and two feet deep. They sank the posts in the holes, then fashioned cross-pieces from thinner poles.

When the loggers realized what would be done to them, they began to cry and beg. The Arqueiros ignored them.

Djumo turned to Fiadh. He spoke and signed with his hands. *"You do not want to watch this."*

Fiadh's throat was dry. She had an idea what was going to happen. She could have turned away, but she felt a compulsion to prove to Djumo that she could bear whatever he could. Djumo was not an animal, nor was Taukan. They were men, doing what needed to be done. A message to loggers to stay away.

"No." She shook her head. *"I must see."*

Djumo turned to his men. *"Hang them by their heels."*

One by one, the loggers were hung upside-down from the cross-pieces. Their clothes were cut from them. The two dead ones first, then the six live ones.

Djumo nodded to his men to proceed.

First, they gutted the dead men so the live ones would know the fate that awaited them. Screams and pleas for mercy filled the air. Arqueiros proceeded down the line. A firepit was dug and widened on the shore and the scraps were burned.

Fiadh had seen enough. She turned away from the sight and stared at the river. The sounds of what was being done behind her were enough.

A kind of humid mist rose from the carpets of weed that drifted on the surface. A milky white cloud, above a carpet of black and green, floated on the brown river. Above it, the verdant green wall of the far shore.

Like a mirage, a structure approached. A square house on the water. Gray sides and a white structure on top. The vision nosed around the bend in the river and came closer.

Djumo called out. The Arqueiros ran into the jungle. Sought cover behind the tree line. Fiadh stared at the river long enough to assure herself that the vision was a ship... a Navy gunboat. Then she turned and followed the others back to the shelter of the trees.

The Arqueiros hadn't finished their work. Fiadh saw that seven of the men were dead. The eighth remained alive. The arrival of the gunboat had saved him. She searched up and down the line of Arqueiros... they knew her by now. She found Djumo and threw herself to the ground next to him.

Nevoa steamed up the middle of the river and stopped offshore. Fiadh knew it hadn't come to a complete stop, because it was still fighting the current. The current that vomited South America's guts into the Atlantic.

Tiny stick figures moved on the decks. She wished she had binoculars. She did not see many men in white. The figures she saw wore camouflage uniforms. Marines. Ten days in the Selva and she had been reduced to a jungle animal. At the sight of Nevoa, she clawed her way back to the twenty-first century.

The Marines lowered a Zodiac and men climbed into it. A second Zodiac with more men joined them from the other side of the gunboat. Together, the two rigid inflatable boats approached the shore.

Arrows whizzed in high arcs toward the boats.

Fiadh's heart jumped in her chest. This wasn't supposed to happen. Her newfound friends, men who had saved her life, were trying to kill her people.

A Marine was hit.

Machine guns on the navigation deck and poop hammered. Heavy-caliber bullets cracked, splintered the trees above. The gunboat was firing over their heads. Warning shots.

Fiadh grabbed Djumo's arm.

"Stop shooting," she said. Words she knew in dialect. Then she signed him, *"They are only trying to frighten you. Please stop."*

For a long moment, Djumo stared at Fiadh. He was deciding whether to trust her. Finally, he cupped his hands and gave out two sharp bird calls.

The flights of arrows ceased as quickly as they had begun.

The machine guns on Nevoa fell silent.

Fiadh squeezed Djumo's arm. *"Thank you."*

Men piled out of the Zodiacs. They tended the wounded Marine, sent him back to the ship.

Two of the men wore civilian clothes. Fiadh's stomach clenched when she recognized Eurico Vargas. That meant Sales, the Minister of the Interior, was aboard the gunboat. How she loathed those men.

The other man in civilian clothes looked rather ordinary. Six feet tall, he was strong and fit, but not outrageously muscled. He had dark hair and walked with a quiet economy.

One of the Marines stumbled to the river's edge and vomited. Vargas looked at him with contempt. Went to the man who was still alive. Questioned him in Portuguese.

The man refused to answer.

Vargas went to a pile of logging equipment and picked up a chainsaw.

30

DAY SIX

Selva da Morte – Garden of Eden

"You watched the Arqueiros massacre those loggers."

"Yes," Fiadh says. "Don't look at me that way, Breed. I told you what they did to the Indians. Those men had it coming."

I'm not about to tell Fiadh no one has *that* coming. I know what men are capable of. In the Selva, such an atrocity is business as usual.

"Your Marines were right to fire over our heads," Fiadh says. "They know FUNAI policy is to never kill Indians. Marine policy is to kill only as a last resort. Djumo saw that. He knew you meant no harm."

I say nothing. The silence grows thick between us.

"I watched you fight Vargas," Fiadh says at last.

"How much did you see?"

"I saw *everything*."

Again, we fall silent. This time, it feels like we are enveloped in a warm bath of shared experience. We've seen things that can't be unseen. Images that haunt our dreams and torture our sleep. We've tilted with men like Vargas. We know good does not always triumph.

Djumo walks toward us, raises his hand. "Fiadh Arqueiro," he says.

Fiadh looks up. They exchange words. Satisfied, Djumo walks away.

"Why did he call you that?" I ask.

"Among the indigenous, one's last name is the name of one's tribe." Fiadh smiles. "They've adopted me."

"What did he want?"

"Taukan's force will join us at dawn. Together, we'll head south."

DJUMO POSTS SENTRIES, and the rest of us string up our hammocks. Warily, I peer into the shadows above me. Don't want to bed down under a sleeping anaconda. Satisfied, I arrange my mosquito net. My ruck and rifle lie against the tree by my head. It's a rule, never violated. Your rifle must never lie out of reach.

The Arqueiros arrange mosquito netting around their hammocks.

"Mosquitoes don't seem to bother them," I say. "Why the nets at night?"

"They're not for mosquitoes," Fiadh says. She crawls under her own net.

"What then?"

"Vampire bats. Those things will suck you dry."

I take off my boots and roll them up in a plastic bag. I don't want snakes, centipedes and spiders to crawl into them overnight.

The SIG joins me in the hammock. I'd started with nine rounds in Manaus. There are only four left. I lie in the hammock and close my eyes. I hold the pistol in my right hand.

Djumo wants to attack the FARC base camp. I want to see the secrets it holds. Sales and Vargas are shepherding a secret cargo along the Rio Preto. A piece of the puzzle is missing, and I have a hunch I'll find it at the FARC base.

Fiadh is another problem. Cuchulain wants her back, but she won't go. As the operator in the field, how should I interpret my mission? I wanted to find Fiadh. Now I want her safe.

I fall asleep.

Night in the Selva da Morte is black and noisy. Creatures dormant during the heat of the day are active at night. The figure that steps to the side of my hammock makes no noise. It is a sixth sense that wakes me. My eyelids flutter open, and I slip the safety off the SIG.

Fiadh lifts the mosquito net and steps into my space.

I slip the pistol's safety back on. She leans over me, places her palm flat on my chest. My heart hammers. I'm certain she can feel it. I look over her shoulder, use my peripheral vision to bring her figure into focus. It's a sniper's trick. The rod cells in the periphery of your retina are more sensitive to dim light.

She's wearing nothing but her shirt.

Both of her palms flat on my chest, she pushes down. Her weight adds tension to the hammock, keeps it from swaying. She knows I'm awake and aware. As though mounting a horse, she swings her leg over. She straddles me and climbs in.

Fiadh can't sit back or she'll tip us over. Hands on my chest, she leans forward and kisses me softly.

This was going to come. Sitting across from her was like making love without touching.

My hands cup her heels, the soles of her feet. Slowly, I

stroke up her ankles and calves. I suck a breath of surprise...
of course she hasn't shaved her legs in two weeks. The sensation of running my hands over the fine, soft fur excites me.

She reaches with one hand and pulls me out. No
fumbling. Every movement is efficient and perfectly
executed. Like she's rehearsed it all in her mind, she pulls me
into her heated core. It feels like I'm home.

We lie motionless. She stretches out, settles on my body.
We feel the sensation of two human beings joined as one.
Our hearts beat together. I feel her tears on my face. Realize
they are mingling with mine.

31

DAY SEVEN

Selva da Morte – The Chase

B ird cries echo through the forest.
Djumo lifts his face, cups his hands about his lips, and responds with a sharp bird call of his own. The Arqueiros get to their feet.

A group of Indians step from the shadows and approach. I count nineteen men, all armed and wearing war paint. Together with our companions, Arqueiro strength numbers thirty-five. One of the newcomers goes to Djumo and embraces him briefly.

"That's Taukan," Fiadh says.

"Tough-looking bunch."

"They didn't lose anyone," Fiadh observes. "Djumo is smart. As soon as he saw you running for the waterfall, he split his force. Set up the ambush."

"He's got a tactical brain."

"Yes. Djumo has been attacking small groups of FARC. He wants to wear them down before he attacks their camp."

"Where is the FARC camp?"

"Six miles southeast of Portao da Dor," Fiadh says. "The Arqueiros have known about it for two years, but left it alone. FARC has a lot of guns. No one is going to take on that camp unless they have to."

"How many men does FARC have?"

"Djumo says sixty. Less the twelve he killed yesterday. With another twenty or so around Vila de Deus, that leaves twenty-eight at the camp."

The sophistication of Djumo's strategy is impressive. "That's why he traveled north," I say. "He wanted to draw off FARC's strength."

"Exactly. Now he's doubling back to attack a reduced force."

We set off with the Arqueiros. Djumo changes the order of march. His lieutenant leads the file, while the war chief travels in the middle with me and Fiadh.

Seventeen men ahead of us, and seventeen behind.

"Djumo looks like he expects trouble," I tell Fiadh.

"He does."

"Care to tell me about it?"

"We killed all the FARCs who followed you into the cave, but they weren't alone."

"No, I avoided another group, on the river trail. When I left them, they were headed for Arvore de Ouro to join their point element."

Fiadh replies without taking her attention from the trail. "They heard the shooting and doubled back. Taukan's men spotted them from the falls."

"And they let us sleep overnight?"

"Djumo and Taukan both posted lookouts. No one travels at night in the Selva."

It was the same during the Vietnam war. Only recently did we develop Night Optical Devices—NODs. Night vision is restricted to military and law enforcement personnel.

"This is the last significant FARC unit loose in the Selva," Fiadh says. "If Djumo can destroy it, we'll face equal numbers when we reach their base camp."

"There were a dozen men, all armed with automatic weapons. More, if they were joined by those at Arvore."

Fiadh looks back and smiles. "Djumo says there are eighteen of them. We're used to those odds. Djumo figures he has a secret weapon now."

"Oh yeah?"

"You." Fiadh winks. "You impressed him with your shooting."

"I have twenty-seven rounds left. They won't win any small wars."

"They've been fighting with bows and spears for a month. In your hands, twenty-seven rounds is a huge advantage."

She's right. In the right position, I can inflict terrible damage on an enemy force. There is no deadlier weapon than a Delta sniper and his rifle.

I hope that's not the only reason Djumo is keeping me alive.

THE SELVA DA Morte surprises me with the variety of its terrain. Near the rivers, the vegetation is dense and virtually impenetrable. Deep inside, vast stretches of forest are screened from light by the triple-canopy jungle. There, the trees are widely spaced, and shrubbery does not grow. The earth can be remarkably dry. There are fewer gnats and mosquitoes. Over such stretches, we hike unimpeded.

Streams and creeks are ubiquitous, and we ford the occasional river as we hurry south. Djumo seems singularly careless about leaving tracks. He makes no effort to cover our trail. With luck, the FARCs following us assume we are unaware of their presence.

After hiking for two hours, the jungle vegetation thickens. We break through to a narrow riverbank. The riverbed itself is a hundred and fifty yards wide, with a broad sandbar meandering up the middle. The sandbar is more mud than sand. Dark red in color, thick in some places, narrow in others. The river flows around it. It's easy to imagine the sandbar shifting with the current and the depth of the river.

Djumo signals the column with a bird call. The point man splashes into the river and hikes upstream in shin-deep water. We wade in after him. This is the first effort the war chief has made to cover our tracks, and it won't be effective. Anyone with rudimentary tracking skills will be able to see where we stepped into the river. They'll see we didn't come out the other side.

I sweep the river and the surrounding terrain. The jungle crowds our shoulders. The riverbanks are nonexistent. No sign of falls. The terrain is flat, except for a slight rise from the riverbed to the sandbar and tree lines.

Fiadh and I sheath our machetes. My skin crawls at the thought of maneuvering, exposed, in the middle of the river. I don't like the thought of men with rifles in the tree line. I unsling the M16 and carry it, high-ready.

"I hope Djumo knows what he's doing," I tell Fiadh.

At the mention of his name, Djumo turns to me and grins. His teeth flash white against that dark, painted face. I doubt he understands what I said, but he knows what I'm thinking. Soldiers are students of terrain. A good soldier is a good soldier, no matter which army he fights for.

"Trust him," Fiadh says. "He's done pretty well these last few weeks."

My head is on a swivel. In a team, each man would cover a slice of the three-hundred-sixty degree arc around the patrol. In three dimensions. Alone, I try to cover all quadrants myself.

Ahead, the trees rise from the river. They form an impenetrable fence on three sides. I blink sweat out of my eyes. In the middle of the river, we are exposed to the unforgiving punishment of the sun. Horizontal waves of mirage ripple from the surface. They distort the image of the green wall two hundred yards ahead of us.

Every fifteen yards, Djumo signals his men. Two at a time, they deploy to the tree line on either side of the riverbed. One man left, one man right. The black-and-white skeleton figures take up their positions with the precision of a military unit.

We're approaching a river bend. That's why the triple-canopy towers ahead of us. The river's course is turning sharply to the left, east into the Selva. I see what Djumo is doing. When we reach the bend in the river, he leads us straight up the narrow bank and into the trees. Djumo has twelve men on each riverbank and ten with us at the bend.

"I can't believe it," I tell Fiadh. "He's set up an X-ambush. I wouldn't try it if his men were armed with rifles—too risky. But with bows, and the elevation of the riverbanks, it can work."

Fiadh crouches behind a tree. "You see? He knows what he's doing."

Yes, he does. I would have set up an L-ambush in exactly this location. Men on the leg of the L, parallel to the river. More men at the bend. With his low-powered weapons, he's able to occupy both sides of the leg, setting up a hybrid X and L ambush.

The risk is that his quarry withdraws downstream, out of range of his bows.

That's where his secret weapon comes in.

With a high-powered rifle, positioned at the bend, I can cover the length of the river for four hundred yards.

We crouch in a line, under cover of trees and vegetation.

Fiadh is on my left, Djumo on my right. He lays his hand on my shoulder, grins, and points first at my rifle, then the river. The long river, the black-red sandbar, baking in the sun.

A four-hundred-yard kill zone.

I nod in acknowledgement. Djumo pats my shoulder again. We settle down to wait. I shrug off my pack, lie prone, and use it to support the rifle. A spare shirt, balled up, goes under the toe of the M16's stock.

The ranges involved are perfect for the M16's battle-sight zero. I validated it yesterday at the waterfall. The enemy won't come inside twenty-five yards. Most of the engagement will occur between forty yards and three hundred. I will either hit high or on-sight. Beyond three hundred, I'll hit low. Either way, I can compensate for holdover without adjusting my sights.

I scan little puddles of water sitting on the sandbank. Red mud and smears of black. Not a ripple. I check the leaves on either side. The air is still. Humid and stifling. Not a hint of a breeze. The hot film of sweat covering my face tells me the same thing.

Zero windage.

Fiadh glances at me. Her green eyes shine bright behind her face net. Her cheeks are sunburned and freckled. I think of our slow lovemaking.

Get a grip, Breed.

I turn my attention back to the kill zone.

The first FARCs emerge from the tree line six hundred yards downriver. They look at the mud on the riverbank, stare upstream. Confer.

I force myself to think about what can go wrong rather than what can go right. Right takes care of itself. Wrong needs to be dealt with.

Djumo's men could fire too soon. My optimum range is between twenty-five and three hundred yards. The Arqueiros are deployed for two hundred yards on either side. Their bows have an effective range of sixty to seventy-five yards. It is highly unlikely they will shoot before FARC is inside my optimum.

FARC should assault the ambush. Take advantage of their superior firepower. The X-ambush makes that a difficult proposition.

FARC can withdraw. That means I have to adjust my fire, and pretty damn quick. I'll go from hitting high this side of three hundred to hitting low on the far side. On the far side, the enemy will present smaller targets. Harder to hit with iron sights. The front sight post could obscure the target.

I lick sweat from my lips.

They're coming. Wading into the river, turning upstream, rifles at high port. Nervous, they scan the tree line on both sides of the river.

I flick off the safety, rest my trigger finger on the lower receiver. Raise my face net. Screw the mosquitoes. I want a good look at what I'm shooting at.

How many? Eighteen men in the river. Ten yards separation.

Eighteen men, a column of one hundred and eighty yards. If we wait till they are all in the kill zone, the closest will be twenty-five yards away when we engage. At that range, I will hit on-zero.

They're still coming.

"Lie down," I tell Fiadh. "Flat. Put your face on the ground and *don't* lift your head."

The point man is at eighty yards. Still, the Arqueiros refuse to shoot. They're waiting for Djumo's signal. I have no idea what it will be.

Seventy yards. Mentally, I adjust my holdover.

Sixty yards. Djumo is one cool customer. He's waiting for the targets to be inside the effective range of *all* his bows.

Fifty yards.

Thirty.

I slide my finger to the trigger. Ready to tickle.

Djumo cups his hands and issues a bird call.

Thirty arrows fly simultaneously. I break my shot.

The point man goes down, a crimson flower blooming across his chest. Arrows thud into his belly and arms.

FARCs in the middle are hit by arrows.

I fire a second time. The last man in the column jerks. He was hit by two arrows. My round blows his head off.

The FARCs turn in both directions and open fire on full automatic. Rake the tree lines. Several men have been wounded by arrow strikes. They dive into the shallow water and continue firing. The current breaks over the cowering men. Half-submerged, they make challenging targets for the archers.

Djumo points, says something in his dialect.

"Shoot at the sandbar!" Fiadh cries. "Those dark patches."

Bullets snap through the air around us. "I told you to keep your head down."

I put two bullets into the sandbar. Djumo yells at me.

"More," Fiadh urges. "Shoot some more."

I don't get it. As far as I'm concerned, it's a waste of precious ammunition. I fire five more times. Watch the rounds smack into the bar, kick up black and red clots of mud.

The surface of the sandbar comes alive. Dozens of huge snakes, bodies as thick as my thigh, uncoil. The anacondas had been lying still, half covered in mud. One after another, they rouse themselves. A black tide, the snakes ripple across the sandbar.

With the speed of lightning bolts, the snakes launch themselves into the water. They thrash among the FARCs crouching in the current. I doubt the snakes are venomous, but they snap at the men and lash them with their coils.

I lay my sight picture on one guerrilla. Open-mouthed, he stares. A snake uncoils, stares back. The anaconda rears up and hurls itself full-length through the air. A lance, flat black, ribbed belly the color of pewter. It buries its fangs in the FARC's face. Three hundred pounds of animal, all fifteen feet of it, drags the man under.

The guerrillas shriek. Get to their feet and run back the way they came. Problem is, the snakes are swimming downstream with them. The surface of the river boils with the thrashing of men and snakes.

More FARCs are hit by arrows.

Crack!

Another man pitches facedown in the water, shot in the back. The water goes red, then pink. His blood is washed downstream.

Two men run downriver as fast as they can. A hundred and sixty yards out, they pass the corpse of the second man I shot. I adjust my holdover and fire.

Hit.

One man drops, shot between the shoulder blades.

I fire again. The second man jerks in mid-stride. Shot in the left shoulder, he twists in mid-air and crashes into the water. He struggles to his knees, raises his M16, and fires it one-handed.

Who does he think he'll hit shooting like that? I lay the sight on him and squeeze the trigger.

The man's face explodes into a red mask. A halo blossoms behind his head and dissolves into a pink mist. He drops the rifle and falls onto his back. The rushing water courses over his corpse.

The colony of anacondas thrash downriver, a black shadow forty feet long.

Wounded, arrows protruding from his body, a FARC raises himself on his hands and knees. I shoot him in the chest, through the right armpit. He collapses and lies still.

It's over. Eighteen FARCs lie dead or dying in the water.

Thirteen rounds left.

Djumo gets to his feet, issues another bird call. Taukan steps from the tree line, a hundred yards downriver. Triumphant, he waves his bow, turns and leads his men to the river. Taukan's men go to work, finishing off the wounded with hatchets.

Pleased, Djumo squeezes my shoulders with both hands.

"Can't believe we walked right past those snakes and didn't see them," I say.

Fiadh gets to her feet. "That's how God made them, Breed. Everything alive here lives its way for a reason."

"Except man."

"No, we're God's creatures too. We behave as He made *us*."

32

DAY SEVEN

Selva da Morte – The Murderers

The river runs straight north-south, parallel to the Rio Preto. We can make good time hiking along its narrow banks. But Djumo is careful. The closer we get to the FARC camp, the more likely we are to encounter FARC patrols.

Djumo is unwilling to take that risk. He leads us south, hiking inside the tree line. We are likely to spot FARC or other hostiles before they spot us. I walk with the rifle slung across my back, Golok in hand.

"Tell me about the murdered men," Fiadh says.

"Gaspar the first officer, and Morais the radio operator," I say. "I don't know much about Gaspar's death. I think he was knocked unconscious and slipped over the side. The current carried him away in the dark. No one on watch saw the body disappear behind the Nevoa."

"Why was he killed?"

"That, I know for certain. The Nevoa had a close call with

another ship when we left Tieves. Gaspar thought the cargo might have shifted. Said he would check on it."

"He found the missiles."

"Either he found the missiles, or he was killed to *prevent* him from finding the missiles. Which scenario doesn't matter. The last time he was seen alive was half an hour before dinner. All the senior passengers were together at the meal. That leaves thirty minutes before, and five hours after, when anyone could have killed him.

"If they killed him before dinner, they needed a place to hide his body. The killer could have dined with the rest of us and pretended to go to bed. Later, he could have returned and disposed of the corpse."

"Where could the body have been hidden?"

"That," I tell her, "is an excellent question. The answer leads us to potential suspects."

"Explain."

"Gaspar was going to check the cargo right away, so it made sense for him to be killed right away. They had to hide his body. There's a lot of traffic along the main decks of the ship. I think the body was hidden on the engine deck."

"The engine deck."

"Yes. The Nevoa has a shallow draft, only three to five feet. The engine deck is used for the engines, fuel tanks, fresh water stores, and the magazine. Only two people bunk on the engine deck and use it regularly. The first engineer, Elvir Collor, and the second engineer, Delfin Dutra. I think they are the murderers."

"Did both have opportunity?"

"Collor was at the helm when Gaspar told me and Captain Silva he was going to check the cargo. I think Collor gave his partner... either Dutra, or another of Sales's henchmen... a heads-up. The killer then murdered Gaspar and hid the body on the engine deck. One of them returned later and got rid of the corpse."

"Alright. What about the radio operator?"

"We were at dinner when he took a dive off the bridge deck. He landed right outside the wardroom, in a heavy rainstorm."

"Was he dead before he fell?"

"Yes. Somebody let him have it across the side of his head. The weapon was a heavy steel wrench. The kind engineers are likely to have stuffed in their hip pockets. The wound was perfectly horizontal above his ear. Like somebody took careful aim and tried to knock his head off. I think he was sitting at the radio and the killer was standing behind him."

"Whoever killed him had to be soaked."

"Exactly. That narrows down the list of suspects. The major players were all at dinner when his body hit the deck. I climbed up to the widow's walk right away. In seconds, I was soaked. I searched the cabins, then went into the bridge. Collor was at the helm, dry as a bone."

"He couldn't have done it."

"No. And he was alone on the bridge. Now, there are only two ways *off* the bridge deck. Down the ladder I had just climbed, or down one of the companionways to the fo'c'sle. I think Collor's partner, Second Engineer Dutra, killed Morais and got soaked. He then went down the companionways while I was climbing the ladder. There is a hatch on the fo'c'sle behind the 40mm Bofors mount. It leads to the magazine on the engine deck. I think the killer ducked down the hatch, closed it behind himself, then went back to his quarters. Changed into dry clothes."

"That simple?"

"That simple." I stop, close my eyes for a moment, feel the sweat ooze out of every pore on my skin. Ahead of me, Fiadh is soaked. I grit my teeth and follow her. Refuse to show weakness to the Arqueiros behind me. "Everything becomes simple when you accept the existence of more than one killer. With free access to the engine deck. The engine deck runs the length of the ship, with access to the fo'c'sle and quarterdeck. Then the third murder makes sense, too."

"I thought you said there were two murders."

"Two murders and one *attempted* murder. They tried to kill *me*."

"Outside the radio room."

"Yes. I *think* the captain was asleep in his cabin, but I can't be sure. I know I heard one of the conspirators in the radio room. He was communicating with Portao da Dor. That was why they killed Morais. With Morais gone, they had free access to the radio. Somebody hit me from behind. A steel wrench, the same weapon used on Morais. I dodged at the last second. A glancing blow. Not enough to render me unconscious, but enough to incapacitate me.

"They didn't expect me up there. Unlike with Gaspar and Morais, they had to improvise. The man who was using the radio made tracks right away. I think he escaped through the bridge and down the companionways. From the fo'c'sle, he could have either gone down to the magazine or back into the forward superstructure. So it could have been anyone. But— Collor was at the helm. So it couldn't have been Collor. But he saw who did, as the man made his escape. This proves Collor is involved, one way or another."

"That was the man using the radio," Fiadh says. "What about the man who hit you?"

"I saw a dark, blurry shape. He hauled me out to the widow's walk to pitch me over the side. Captain Silva interrupted him. I think he ran around the widow's walk and down the companionways. Again, Collor would have seen him. That cements Collor's guilt."

"Could it have been Captain Silva?"

"By his own admission, Captain Silva is the only other member of the crew who has a working knowledge of the radio. I assumed he was asleep in his cabin, but he could have been in the radio room. After they attacked me, he could have easily slipped back into his cabin. In spite of all that, I don't think he's involved."

"Why not?"

"A logical contradiction. If he were involved, the killer wouldn't have been frightened away. The two of them would have pitched me over the side."

"That means the gang includes Minister Sales, Vargas, the two engineers, and others."

"Yes. Doctor Fonseca is involved, but I don't know how or why. I can't rule out the other two petty officers, Lieutenant Quadros, and one or two Marine sergeants."

"Why the Marines?"

"Sales is going to trade those weapons for whatever FARC is transporting to Portao da Dor. There are forty armed Marines aboard Nevoa. That means they have to either be killed or fooled when the time comes. The best way to fool anyone in the military is to suborn their commanding officers. That makes Lieutenant Quadros a prime target for corruption."

"Otherwise?"

"Cash and dead men tell no tales."

33

DAY SEVEN

Selva da Morte – The Base Camp

The FARC camp looks deserted.

Fiadh and I crouch with Djumo and Taukan at the jungle's edge. Survey the collection of thatched huts. There are ten of them, set in two parallel rows of five, separated by twenty feet of open space. The open space looks like a road. A main street for the little village. The structures have been built under the triple-canopy. Indigenous tribes look for clear areas, for light and ventilation. FARC selected their location for concealment.

The jungle crowds the huts. We can't be more than fifteen feet from the nearest one. The camp was designed to be invisible from the air.

"Where have they gone?" Fiadh asks.

"Portao da Dor," I say. "To meet the Nevoa."

"Wasted trip?"

I shake my head, sling the rifle across my back. "They wouldn't leave the camp unguarded," I say. "Not if they're coming back."

"Maybe they're *not* coming back. Maybe they plan to relocate after exchanging their goods for the weapons."

It's possible. The FARCs might intend to hide the weapons at another location. Strike north and maneuver toward the Colombian border.

I don't like it. The guerrillas occupied this camp for two years. They would be reluctant to give it up. On the other hand, it made sense for them to store the weapons in a cache at a secret location.

"Stay here." I draw the SIG, hold it two-handed, high-ready. "Tell Djumo to let me clear the place before he shows himself."

Carefully, I step from the trees. Approach the first hut, pistol extended.

Go to the entrance. No door, just a woven blanket hanging across the opening. I retract the weapon, hold it close to my chest. Indigenous huts are circular. These huts are boxy. They reflect the preferences of their modern owners.

I hate these blankets. It's easy to get tangled in them. Wherever you go, the principles of close quarters combat are the same. I push through, check first one cut, then the other. Clear.

It's a barracks. Wooden racks, woven straw mattresses, cotton pillows. The size of the interior surprises me. The hut has space for eight men.

Empty.

I cross to the opposite hut. The open space between the rows of buildings has been rutted by the wheels of handcarts.

The entrance to this hut is wider than the first, but the arrangement of the doorway is similar. I repeat the clearing maneuver.

This hut has been built for work and storage.

Scraps of splintered wood litter the floor. Cardboard boxes filled with hammers and nails sit in one corner. The earth on the floor has been scarred by heavy objects dragged across it. Rough planks are piled on the floor next to a pair of sawhorses. The hut was used to make crates and load them.

Load them with what?

Step outside, go to the next hut.

Push the curtain aside. Cover the left cut, then the right. Clear.

This is another workshop. Crude wooden shelves line one wall. They are loaded with iron pots and pans. The place is like a kitchen. I cast my eyes to the ceiling, discover a four-foot-square section open to the jungle air. A wood-framed thatch cover has been built to cover the opening in foul weather.

Beneath the chimney, a square fire pit has been dug. It's four-by-four feet, rimmed with stones to keep the fire where it belongs. The pit is full of charcoal and blackened firewood. On either side are iron supports for cross-pieces. All designed to hang pots over the flames.

Against one wall stands a row of stainless steel flasks. I bend to pick one up. Damn thing weighs a hundred pounds. Far out of proportion to its size. Cement isn't this heavy. I squeeze the SIG into my hip pocket. Examine the flask.

Never seen anything like this. The cover *screws* on and off, like a thermos bottle. I twist the top, find it easy to open. When the lid is free, I set it on the floor, look inside.

The flask is filled with a thick, silver liquid. I tip the flask carefully, pour a small amount into my hand. It slides around, assumes different shapes as it molds itself to the mounts and valleys of my palm. It's amoebic... alive.

Mercury.

In a flash, the realization strikes me. My questions have been answered. I know why Sales is shipping weapons to Portao da Dor. Why Gaspar and Morais were murdered. Why the loggers are hunted and killed. Why Pedro and Anna were shot.

My thoughts are interrupted by the violent blast of an automatic weapon. No comparison to the high-pitched crack of M16s. This is the murderous fury of heavy machine gun fire. A crew-served weapon... an M240 or PKM.

Then—the terrible screams of mortally wounded men.

I RUSH TO THE DOORWAY, throw myself flat. Cheek to the earth, I peer around the corner.

Two rows of huts. The rutted road in between. From the jungle, at the far end of the road, the blinding muzzle flash of a tripod-mounted machine gun. It's slinging 7.62mm rounds straight down the middle.

Arqueiros entered the camp. Through Fiadh, I'd warned them to wait until I'd cleared it. Something had been lost in the translation. Men have been cut in half, lie dead or rolling around in the dirt.

Where's Fiadh?

No sign of her. The Arqueiros entered the camp between the two rows of huts. The FARCs waited until a good number of them were in the kill zone, then opened fire. They killed or maimed half a dozen with the first burst. A similar number of Arqueiros scattered to the huts on both sides of the road. They're hiding behind the structures, loosing arrows at the muzzle flashes.

Djumo is on the ground, clutching his belly.

With implacable brutality, the machine gun blasts the huts. Bullets shred the thatched structures and cut the Arqueiros to pieces.

I switch to a Weaver grip, fire the SIG at the muzzle flashes.

"Fiadh!"

"Breed!"

Thank God, she's alive.

"Tell Taukan to go around. Around!"

Does she get it? Is Taukan alive?

I empty the SIG at the machine gun. Crawl back inside the hut and eat dirt. The FARCs turn the weapon on me. It's an M240. Belgian design, made in the USA. Supplied by the USA. Captured from government troops or sold on the black market. It is slaughtering us.

Trust universal principles. I unsling the M16. If I can provide a base of fire, Taukan can attack the machine gun from the jungle. Fall on the FARCs from the side, or behind. What kind of a base of fire can I provide with thirteen rounds of five-five-six? Against a weapon that spits seven hundred and fifty rounds a minute?

Machine gun bullets shred the walls of the hut around me. I crawl back to the doorway, fire once at the flashes, scramble back inside.

The machine gun leaves me, sweeps the other huts. There are more cries as bullets connect with Arqueiros trying to bring bows and arrows to bear.

I crawl to the back of the hut. Unlimber the Golok, attack the thatched wall. Hack at it until a patch is loose enough to knock out with the butt of the M16. Thank goodness the jungle's edge is so close. I crawl out of the hut on my belly, glance in the direction of the M240.

As I expected, my view is blocked by other huts. I have a clear run to the tree line. I get to my feet, duck into the vegetation.

Game on.

I scramble inside the tree line, look for a view of the machine gun nest. Ideally, a clear angle between two of the huts in the camp. I find one, search the shadows behind the flickering muzzle flash.

Three men. Gunner, loader, and team leader.

God, they're only twenty-five yards away.

It was an intimate ambush. They had several opportunities to kill me. They waited until the Arqueiros came, then executed them at point-blank range.

I lay my sight picture on the gunner's face. At twenty-five yards, there is zero holdover. I squeeze the trigger.

The gunner's brains splatter the team leader. The dead man drops and the team leader reels with shock. I turn the rifle on the loader, fire a second time. The bullet hits him in the throat. His hands go up to cover the hole—he's choking. I fire again, and he disappears from view.

A black-and-white skeleton falls upon the team leader. An Arqueiro hatchet flashes in the gloom.

Silence falls over the camp.

I walk to the machine gun nest. Taukan stands, the bloody hatchet in his hand. I bend over the man he killed. Lift a bandolier of M16 magazines from the corpse. I sling the ammo over one shoulder and across my chest.

Taukan walks into the camp and I follow him. The remaining Arqueiros are arranging their dead in a row. Bandaging wounded with leaves, and applying poultices made from mud and crushed vegetation.

Fiadh is on one knee, holding Djumo's hand. The war chief is dead. She murmurs a few words, closes his eyes.

"I'm sorry, Taukan." He doesn't understand my words, but he knows my meaning.

Fourteen dead and wounded. That's a high price to pay for a mistake.

The FARCs played this one perfectly. They left one machine gun crew in hiding, sucked us into the trap. Djumo should have waited for me. We might have minimized the casualties.

But I might have been killed in the first burst.

"I know what it's all about," I tell Fiadh.

Fiadh gets to her feet. Stares at me like a lost child. "Alright. What?"

"Gold. They've been collecting and refining gold here for two years."

"How do you know?"

"There are flasks of Mercury in that hut. It's used in the extraction and processing of gold."

I check the remaining huts. All are empty barracks and mess shacks.

"They must have moved all the gold to Portao da Dor," Fiadh says.

"Yes. That was the deal. Sales would ship the weapons up the Rio Preto on the Nevoa. Unload the weapons at Portao da Dor and float the gold out in crates. Off-load them somewhere along the way. Cash out at his convenience."

"What should we do now?"

"We have to go to Portao da Dor and stop them. Can you explain this to Taukan?"

"I'll try."

Fiadh turns to Taukan, speaks to him in dialect. Uses sign language. The young Arqueiro responds, shakes his head. That means *no* in any language. He's a strong man, but he's lost his father. He's in shock, dealing with grief.

"He says there are too many guns at Portao da Dor. He has lost his father and half the men."

"Tell him we can win because there are men on the boat who will help us."

"You mean the Marines?"

"Yes. They can't all be in on it. I bet most, if not all of them, are clean. That's why Sales couldn't tip his hand until Nevoa got to Portao. Not everyone aboard was in on it."

Fiadh tries again. This time, she speaks with an imploring

tone. Taukan shakes his head. Uses the name "Fiadh Arqueiro." His tone is apologetic.

"It's no use," Fiadh says. "He has a responsibility to his people. Now that his father is gone, it's up to him to take care of the Arqueiros."

"Tell him we understand. His father would want him to take care of his people." I check my watch. "Can we make Portao before dark?"

Fiadh shakes her head. "No. We can make it most of the way, but we'll have to pitch camp for the night."

"That won't work," I tell her. "There's a good chance Sales plans to leave Portao with his gold by dawn tomorrow. We'll get there late and have to face FARC. It'll be a wasted trip."

"Then we'll have to travel at night. It could take us eight hours to do the last mile."

"That's how it has to be."

"Alright."

Fiadh and I shoulder our packs, say goodbye to Taukan and the Arqueiros. She checks her GPS and leads the way into the brush.

"Do we have a chance?" Fiadh asks.

"Not without the Marines. I'm going to gamble that Lieutenant Quadros is clean. If he is, Sales is going to lie about the weapons and the gold. He'll probably stick to his original cover story."

"How will he explain the gold?"

"No one knows anything about any gold. Once the weapons are off-loaded, he'll make up any old story and Quadros will have to accept it."

"What kind of story?"

"Something about expired supplies that have to be disposed of. It doesn't matter. Sales is a powerful political figure. Neither Silva nor Quadros would challenge him."

"You'll speak to Quadros."

"Yes."

"What if he's in on it?"

I shrug. "If Quadros is in on it, I'll kill him. You and I will make for Vila de Deus on foot. Let the chips fall where they may."

"Breed," Fiadh says, "these are lousy odds."

I smile. Playfully, I poke her shoulder.

"Don't you believe in miracles?"

34

DAY EIGHT

Portao da Dor – The Warehouse

F iadh was wrong.

It took us *ten* hours to do the last mile in the dark. For a while, I thought we wouldn't make it. Fiadh gave me her GPS and I led the way, hacking with the Golok until my arm was numb with fatigue. Every step, I worried about snakes and quicksand. I worried more when we had to get on our hands and knees to negotiate the most tangled obstacles.

Our eyes were as night-adapted as they would ever get, and the Selva remained pitch black. Our world was reduced to grappling with unseen demons. They materialized as dark shadows, only to disappear once more into blackness.

Around us, the never-ending cacophony of the Selva. I wanted to scream for silence. Parrots screeched, monkeys bawled, and mosquitoes whined. The midges were louder than Vargas's chainsaw. Thick, unseen bodies crashed through the vegetation on either side. The thought of running into a caiman or jaguar was horrible enough. The idea of disturbing a viper while on my hands and knees didn't bear thinking about.

I blundered into Portao at 0400 hours. Half delirious with exhaustion, I blinked at the sight of a pinprick of light. I stopped, gloved hand on the trunk of a tree. Fiadh stumbled into my back. Holding onto my shoulders, she slumped against me.

The light came into focus.

One of three lamps on the Nevoa's boat deck. We'd made it.

Then, on top of all the jungle noise, came the distinct crackle of gunfire. I dragged Fiadh to the ground. We collapsed against each other. Listened to the shooting, gathered our strength. It was half an hour before we sat up and stared at the outpost.

Portao da Dor is tiny.

In my mind, I always pictured a small town. In fact, the outpost is a dock and four wooden buildings arranged in an inverted "U". The dock forms the crosspiece of the "U", and runs several hundred feet along the Rio Preto. A warehouse-like structure stretches along the right-hand bar of the "U". Three smaller buildings in a row form the left-hand bar.

One of the three small buildings stands apart. Sixty feet separate it from the others. That must be the generator shed and fuel store. One of the other two buildings in that row will be the barracks. The other will be a workspace and office. It will house the desk-mounted HF radio, the ManPack, and a store of spare batteries.

The outpost has no security whatsoever.

Like Vila de Deus, and other settlements we've passed,

the jungle crowds the buildings. The Selva is anxious to reclaim land man has torn from its breast.

There, alongside the dock, sits Nevoa. Long, low and dark. Dim lamps light the boat deck. A warm orange glow emanates from sodium lights on the bridge. Figures move around inside. Sales, Captain Silva, others. They are casual and unhurried.

Shoulder-high, a pile of crates sits on the dock. Large wooden handcarts are parked to one side. Imagine lugging all that gold six miles through the Selva. We know what the trails are like.

One of the Zodiacs is tied up at the stern. It looks like they are going to use it to transport single crates of gold to the starboard side for loading. Two guerrillas are mounting an outboard motor on the Zodiac. A low growl comes from the warehouse.

FARC guerrillas file out of the warehouse and gather on the dock. A few walk up the gangplank. They examine the cargo we took on at Tieves. The missiles. To check the goods, they pry open one of the crates. Lift one of the black cases and set it on the deck. It's a large plastic cylinder. Built-in square supports at each end prevent it from rolling around. Preserve its orientation inside the packing crate and on the deck. Within the case lies the olive drab missile tube.

The guerrillas assemble the Javelin. Attach the Command Launch Unit—the CLU—to its disposable launch tube. One of the men powers up the CLU. He hands the fifty-pound weapon to one of the others and flashes a thumbs-up.

Those missiles could win the war for FARC. All they have to do is get one of those Javelins within a mile of the president. The anniversary of the peace deal. A missile lock on his vehicle as it leaves the presidential residence. An open-air speech. Any number of possibilities.

A figure in white speaks with the FARC. I recognize that

mustache. It's Collor, the first engineer. Together, they start up Nevoa's cargo cranes. They must unload the cargo of weapons before taking on the gold.

I turn to Fiadh.

"I'm going to try and find Quadros," I tell her. "Whatever happens, stay here."

"Think he's in that warehouse?"

"I don't know." I reach into my pocket and take out her cross. Fasten it about her neck. "I forgot to give this back to you."

Fiadh leans forward and kisses me softly.

I thrust the rifle into her hands. "If things go against us, make for Vila de Deus. Stay off the trails."

"You need this."

"There'll be a lot lying around," I say. Hand her the bandolier of five-five-six magazines.

I counted twenty FARCs. I still don't know how many of the crew are part of Sales's gang. Fonseca and the two engineers. The two petty officers are unknown quantities.

Where are Quadros and the Marines? I didn't like the sound of the shooting we heard.

I follow the edge of the jungle, walk around the back of the warehouse. There are no windows. The whole structure is dark. The muffled growl gets louder.

There's a door. I turn the handle, push it open slowly. Left cut clear. The right is cluttered with stacks of crates.

A large room. Not vast, by any means, but large. Supplies have been piled the length of the far wall. Bare tungsten bulbs hang from beams that stretch across the low ceiling. A veil of smoke hangs in the air. Like exhaust fumes or cigarette smoke, it diffuses the hot tungsten light.

My stomach turns. In long rows, dead Marines are piled on top of each other. Forty of them. Quadros's platoon, executed with their hands bound behind their backs. Two of the dead men wear the white uniforms of sailors. The petty officers from Nevoa. The air in the warehouse is thick with the copper smell of blood.

The floor at my feet is littered with brass. Spent shell casings. The back rank of bodies lie slumped against the stacked supplies. A second rank lie at their feet. A third rank has collapsed over the legs of those in the second rank. Without mercy, the FARCs mowed them down.

To my right is a straight-backed chair. Quadros sits in the chair, arms bound behind his back. His head is tilted at an unnatural angle, sightless eyes staring at the ceiling. His throat has been opened with a knife.

The point of the knife was thrust into the left side of Quadros's neck, blade facing the killer. The point emerged from the opposite side, and the killer ripped everything out the front. Veins, arteries, trachea... all the tubing of life has been severed and hangs free. Great gouts of arterial spray soaked the floor and the front of Quadros's uniform.

The killer must have been drenched. He made the lieutenant watch the execution of his troops. Killed him last.

I'm sorry to have doubted the Marine officer.

Behind Quadros is the source of the growl and smoke. A rubber boat has been propped against the back wall. Next to it is a rack hung with three outboard engines. A fourth is running in a steel drum of water. There is a Zodiac tied up at the Nevoa's stern. They must have replaced its outboard. This one is burning oil. Smoke rises from the barrel and drifts through the interior.

A bolt of pain shoots through my body. There's a splintering crack, a jarring impact, and I'm thrown onto my face. I fall against corpses in the first row. I hear the rattle of wood tossed onto the cement floor.

I force myself to move, roll over.

Vargas stands over me. He hit me across the back with a

two-by-four. The plank cracked with the impact, and he discarded the pieces. He must have heard me open the door. Hid behind the crates, the club in his hands.

"I thought you might come, Breed." Vargas draws a foot-long knife from his belt. The one he used on Quadros. "I am going to gut you like a fish. Stem to stern, the sailors say. I shall enjoy it."

The pain is blinding. I can move my legs, so he didn't break my back. Vargas flips the knife in the air, catches it blade-up. A thrill of fear shoots through me. He knows what he's doing.

Vargas steps forward, bends to seize me by the front of my shirt. He holds the knife at his hip. He's looking for a thrust into my belly, then a long, tearing slice to my throat. I hook one instep behind his left ankle. With all my strength, I kick him in the knee.

With a grunt, Vargas falls over. Lands on his back.

I get to my feet. Vargas scrambles back to his. Thrusts the knife at my stomach. With a circular sweep of my left hand, I strike the inside of his wrist. Knock the weapon aside. I grab his wrist and step into him. Seize his shirt with my right hand, try to draw him over my hip.

He's seen that move before. Grabs my right shoulder with his left hand and throws his weight against me.

It's all about balance. I step back with my right foot before he can throw me over. Let go of his shirt, punch him in the gut. He grunts. Butts me in the side of the head. There's a boom in my ears and I see stars. I fight to keep hold of his knife hand. As he snaps his head forward, I whip my own. With my crown, I catch him on the edge of the jaw.

There's a solid crack. Vargas reels. I feel his knife hand relax. Close-in, I punch him in the throat with the claw of my hand. The space between the inside of my thumb and index finger. Grab him by the throat and drive him against the warehouse wall. Slam his knife hand against it.

We're nose-to-nose. Gasping, sweating. I slam his wrist against the wall a second time. I'm rewarded with a clang as he drops the knife on the cement floor. He punches me in the right side and I lose my grip on his throat. He tries to bite my face and I throw my head back. Punch *him* in the face. He brings his knee into my groin. I twist my body. The knee goes into my thigh. Dull pain. No tearing, though—the muscle is intact.

"*Cuneo.*" Vargas's spittle flecks my face.

"Fucker."

I pin him against the wall. Claw him in the throat again. With my right foot, I stamp on his right instep. Use the ankle lock as a pivot. I grip his throat with such force my thumb and fingertips meet behind his trachea. With a grunt, I wheel him over the pivot. Slam him onto his back.

Tough guy. The breath explodes from his body, but he manages to grab the knife with his left hand. I drop my left knee on his chest with all my weight. His ribs snap like matchsticks. I straighten his knife arm and break it over my other knee. His elbow cracks. The knife falls to the floor.

I stand up, look down on Vargas. Think of Quadros and all the other men this monster has butchered.

Vargas stares up at me. Flails like a roach on its back.

I lift the outboard motor from the barrel. Free of the water, the propeller's growl rises to a whine. I grasp the machine, one hand on the tiller, the other on its mounting bracket.

"No, Breed!"

Vargas sees what I'm going to do. Scrabbles for the knife with his broken arm. His fingers scratch at the rough cement. He manages to reach the haft, but I step on his bicep. He cries out.

The outboard is heavy in my hands. The heady smell of hot metal, fuel and smoking grease fills the air.

Vargas shouts over the scream of the propeller.

"No, Breed! Please—No!"

The propeller bites into Vargas's chest and I lean on the outboard. Feel his sternum give way. He shrieks like an animal. Blood, tissue, and bits of shattered bone spew from his chest.

I lift the outboard an inch to check my progress. The noises coming from the hole of Vargas's mouth change in pitch. I plunge the machine into his chest cavity until the skeg bumps his spine. Lean to my left, then my right. Vargas squeals like a butchered pig until the prop blades shred his heart and lungs.

Outside the warehouse, the sound of shouts and rifle fire.

The cries of Arqueiros.

Taukan's come through for us.

I discard the outboard, draw the back of my hand across my forehead. It comes away smeared pink.

"Breed."

Fiadh stands at the door, holding the rifle, gold cross at her throat. She looks at the gutted cockroach that used to be Vargas. Stares at me.

She'd better *not* give me shit. "What?" I snap.

"I guess he had it coming."

Smart girl.

"Come inside," I tell her.

My eyes sweep the back of the warehouse, the end that faces the river. The loading bay doors are shut, but there's a side door. I step past Quadros's butchered body. I hope wherever the lieutenant's soul has gone, it feels better.

I open the door a crack, peer out. FARCs have retreated behind the crates of gold. Several of them have been hit by arrows. Two lie dead or dying. Another is crawling for cover, an arrow embedded in his back. Taukan's Arqueiros have fanned out. They are shooting from the tree line. From behind the generator shack and garrison's quarters.

The stars to the east are fading.

If the FARCs heard Vargas's slaughterhouse screams, they're pinned down and unable to come after me. More likely, they think Vargas was having fun with Quadros. Torturing him to death.

Fiadh joins me at the door.

"I'm going to sneak onto the Nevoa," I say. "Will it do any good to tell you to stay here?"

"I'll cover you." Fiadh takes a knee, raises the rifle, and braces herself against the doorjamb. A solid firing stance.

"Don't shoot unless they see me."

"I've got your back," she says. "Do what you have to do."

I will.

35

DAY EIGHT

Portao da Dor – Close Quarters Battle

The sky is lightening over the rim of the high trees. Good thing it's only thirty feet from the warehouse to the river. From behind the crates, the FARCs fire at Taukan's men. Arqueiros shoot arrows the other way. It looks like a stalemate, but at least the guerrillas' attention is drawn away from me.

I run to the water's edge. A thick line of Manila hemp fastens the Nevoa's stern to the dock. A short distance below, a thinner line ties the Zodiac to the gunboat.

Without hesitation, I grasp the rope with both hands and roll off the dock. I cross my ankles and hold the rope with my feet. Hanging upside-down, I pull myself hand-over-hand. Bend my knees, hook the rope under my boots and push. In no time, I reach the Nevoa, haul myself over the fantail.

I crouch low, check for lookouts. There are none. Forward on the boat deck, the first engineer and FARCs are firing on the Arqueiros. I go to the nearest companionway and climb to the after-superstructure on the poop. It's deserted.

Behind their sandbags, the two Browning .50 caliber machine guns sit on their pintles. I go to the one overlooking the dock and pull the canvas condom from its muzzle. Open the top cover and check the belt is properly seated. Close the cover and rack the charging handle. Twice.

The sandbags stink of mold. Soaked by the rain and still damp, the burlap sacks are covered with fungus.

I set the weapon on full auto and grip the spade handles. Lay my thumbs on the butterfly triggers, swing the muzzle to cover the FARCs.

They've got Taukan's men outnumbered two-to-one. Still, the guerrillas cower behind the crates. None of them want to risk a poisoned arrow.

I suck a breath, fire a short burst. The muzzle flash is blinding. Spent shell casings and links from the disintegrating belt fly from the breach. The recoil is so violent I can't keep the sights on target. I'm shooting FARCs in the back. The heavy-caliber rounds slam into them, blow through their bodies, splinter the crates.

From within the broken crates, a yellow metal gleams.

The shock of the first burst wears off and I fire again. And again. I'm squeezing off five and ten-second bursts, killing two or three FARCs at a time. They're screaming, turning their rifles on me. Muzzle flashes flare on the dock. High-velocity bullets blow through the metal sides of the poop. Whack into the sandbag barricade.

Hell with it. I clamp down on the butterfly triggers and let fly. The pintle mount is bolted to the Nevoa's superstructure, but the recoil is so violent, the gun is barely controllable. The heavy-barreled M2 is a macho weapon. You get carried away, forget it's the hits that count. I force myself to hold the gun on target.

Footsteps pound on the deck. FARCs scramble up a

companionway and open fire on me with M16s. I throw myself left, shoulder against the sandbags, and turn the Browning's muzzle onto them. The big .50's muzzle flash half-obscures the charging figures. They are so close I can't miss. Spent brass showers the deck.

I hold the butterflies down, watch thumb-sized bullets cut the FARCs in half.

With a cry, Arqueiros surge forward. At range, they fight with bows and arrows. Close-in, they attack with spears, hatchets, and machetes.

One of the Arqueiros leads the charge. He's wearing the top half of a jaguar's skull over his face. The upper canines are curved like scimitars and the size of my thumbs. The white bone has been painted with black and red circles about the eyes.

It must be Taukan. The FARCs are caught between his warriors and my .50 caliber.

The Arqueiros swarm over the dock. They mingle with the FARCs, so as to make the guerrillas' rifles ineffective. The damage hatchets and machetes do to human flesh is shocking.

I can't use the .50 caliber anymore without hitting Arqueiros. I leave the machine gun and go to one of the FARCs lying dead on the poop. Pick up his M16 and discard its magazine. I pull a fresh magazine from his webbing, lock and load. Take two more magazines, squeeze them into my hip pockets.

Time to clean 'em up.

Down the companionway, leading with the M16. Three dead FARCs. No sign of Collor. Where is he? Where's his partner, Dutra?

Of course, both ship's engineers are in on it. They bunk together below decks. They were double-teaming, covering for each other the whole time. Both are qualified to run the engines and man the helm. With those two on his payroll, Sales was confident of bringing the Nevoa home. With or without Captain Silva.

I step forward onto the boat deck. The Zodiac bay is empty. The rubber boat is floating at the stern. The crates of weapons sit on the deck, loose of their lashings. One of the crates is open. There's the Javelin they assembled, lying next to its cylindrical plastic case. The CLU, still attached, is good to go.

Collor steps from behind the crate closest to the forward superstructure. Hook nose, droopy mustache. He lunges for the hatch that opens from the boat deck to the waist super-structure.

He's making for the engine space. Once down there, he'll have an advantage. I've never been below deck. It's a warren of machinery, fuel tanks, magazines, and bilges. He knows it like the back of his hand. He can barricade himself and keep me from coming down. Alternatively, he can run forward and climb up to the fo'c'sle.

Off-hand, I open fire. My rounds hit the hatch cover, strike sparks, and ricochet. Collor leaps away from the hatch. He looses a long burst at me. It's a circus act. You can't hit anything on full auto like that. He misses by a mile. Turns and runs for the hatch leading to the wardroom.

That's panic. He's a deliberate killer, but he's not used to making decisions under fire.

I raise my rifle and fire twice. A double-tap between his shoulder blades. He drops his rifle and crashes to the deck, short of the hatch. I step forward, shoot him once in the back of the head.

The hatch is heavy. Holding the rifle in one hand, I jerk it open. I cover the opening, kick the hatch's prop into place.

No left cut to worry about. Shift the stock to my left shoulder, cover the right cut. The wardroom is empty. I stoop, grab Collor by the back of his shirt. Drag his body over the knee-knocker and use it to block the door to the galley. He leaves a slug trail of gore on the floor.

Corridors are a bitch. I open the door leading to the cabins. Kick in the first door on my left.

Fonseca flinches against his desk, hands raised.

"I am not involved," he cries. "Breed, I am not involved."

Poor, gutless son of a bitch.

"Don't leave this room," I tell him. "Step outside and I'll kill you."

I kick in the opposite door. Laura faces me, her hands flat on her desktop. She says nothing.

"Stay here," I tell her. Lean in, pull the door shut.

The rest of the cabins are clear. I check the sickbay and dental surgery. Empty.

Through the forward hatch, I step onto the fo'c'sle. The deck and Bofors mount are clear. I do a body count in my head. Marines all dead. Quadros dead. Two petty officers murdered. Collor dead. Fonseca out of action, Laura in her cabin.

Apart from any remaining FARCs, there should only be three people aboard. Sales, Dutra, and Captain Silva.

I shut the hatch leading to the Bofors magazine. If Dutra is down there, I don't want him coming up behind me.

There's no sunrise. The jungle canopy to the east is so high it blocks the rays. But the sky overhead has turned pale blue. I carry the M16 with my right hand on the pistol grip. Climb the portside companionway to the bridge deck.

From this angle, the front windows of the bridge reflect blue sky. Can't see who's in there. The bridge is a fortress, an elevated position that can only be accessed from forward and aft. Two men can defend it. Sales should have Dutra cover one end of the widow's walk while he covers the other.

Sales doesn't have a tactical brain.

Carrying a rifle, Dutra steps from the bridge. He raises the weapon and points it at me. I fire twice. The first round hits him in the weapon and he drops the rifle. The second round drills him low in the throat and he falls from view.

I reach the top of the companionway. Scan the bridge windows. I glimpse Sales and Silva inside. Turn to Dutra. He's lying on his back, blood bubbling from the hole in his throat. I raise the rifle to my shoulder and shoot him once in the face. His head splits around the entry wound like a melon.

Step onto the bridge, rifle raised.

Sales stands behind the captain, holds a pistol to the side of Silva's head. "Put it down, Breed. I'll kill—"

Crack!

Before Sales can get the last word out, I shoot him in the face. The bullet hits him on the bridge of the nose. Blows his brains out the back of his head. The minister drops the pistol and crumples to the deck.

Slack-jawed, Silva stares at me.

I turn to the door leading to the bridge deck cabins. "Anyone else up here?"

Silva shakes his head.

"What about the navigation deck?"

"There is no one."

I push the door open, clear the cabins. They are deserted.

"Can you handle the Nevoa alone?" I ask.

"Difficult, but possible."

"Check out the radio, raise Tieves. We need to call for help."

I allow myself to breathe. Step to the widow's walk, look out over the dock. The Arqueiros are mopping up.

The Arqueiro wearing the mask stands on the dock and turns to face me. His eyes meet mine through the orbits of the jaguar's dead skull. Scraps of desiccated flesh remain attached to the bone. Strips of cured leather have been used to bind the jaguar to the man.

Taukan lifts his hatchet to me and waves. The handle of the hatchet is wet. Crudely textured to prevent it from slipping after heavy use. The FARCs killed his father and half their men. I would not like to be a FARC captive.

I raise my rifle over my head and return Taukan's wave.

Time to take care of unfinished business. I climb down the companionway and back into the superstructure. The engines have been running to provide electric power. Thank God for Nevoa's lights and air conditioning. I close the fo'c'sle hatch behind me to keep the cool air in. Walk toward the wardroom.

I push open Laura's door. She stands where I left her, hands behind her back, leaning against the desk. Her soft hair cascades about her shoulders and falls to her breasts. Her work shirt, open at the collar, shows off the tan on her face, the elegant hollow of her throat. The thin V of skin above her breasts is pale.

Where Fiadh still seems an energetic girl next door, Laura comes across as a beautiful woman. I realize it must have always have been so, from the first time they met. Fiadh, struggling with her faith, yet driven to engage with the world. Laura, certain of her nature, confident in her beauty.

"It's over," I say.

"Is it?"

"Yes. Sales, Vargas and their people are dead. Collor and Dutra. The engineers were the murderers. The missiles and the gold aren't going anywhere."

"Missiles and gold?"

"We picked up the missiles in Tieves. Sales was going to trade them to the FARCs in exchange for gold."

"You have it all figured out."

"No, not everything."

"What's left?"

I've almost figured it out. But there are still missing pieces. Laura can fill in the blanks.

"Why did you try to kill Fiadh?"

36

DAY EIGHT

Portao da Dor – Laura's Story

"**W**hy did you try to kill Fiadh?"

Laura looks away. She's trying to decide whether to deny the charge. She meets my stare with defiance. "I did everything I could to persuade her not to go. Everything."

It's a gambit, to find out how much I know. Of course, I don't have to prove anything. Not out here in the Selva da Morte.

"When she decided to go anyway, you told Sales her intended route. He passed it on to FARC. It was no accident FARC was on that trail."

A switch flips in Laura's head. She, too, knows I don't need to prove anything. Besides, there's an arrogance in those beautiful, intelligent features.

"No, it wasn't," she says. "It is not my fault they are incompetent. I told them to wait for her at Arvore de Ouro. Instead, they went to meet her on the trail. They thought they would have no difficulty disposing of three unarmed young people. They did not expect the Arqueiros to become involved."

"Why are FARC killing everyone in the Selva?"

"Not everyone," Laura says, offended. "You know the reason."

Laura is on a roll. Let's keep her rolling. "I want to hear it from you."

"Alright. Loggers and miners have always engaged in skirmishes with Arqueiros. There is nothing unusual about white men killing Indians in the Selva. But FARC was never active in the Selva before. They killed anyone who could convince authorities that Colombian guerrillas were in the Selva."

"You wanted the attacks blamed on Arqueiros, so Sales would have a reason to take the Nevoa to Portao da Dor."

"Of course. FARC killed the FUNAI workers and Marines at Portao. Killed any loggers they found. If those loggers were arrested, they would tell stories about Colombian guerrillas. The loggers had to die. Fiadh wanted to learn who was responsible for the attacks. She was very capable of doing so. So she had to be stopped."

"But FARC screwed up, and the Arqueiros saved her."

"Sales was afraid Pedro told Father Camos about FARC."

"What if he had?"

"Depending on who else Father Camos told, it could have been a disaster. Fortunately, neither Fiadh nor any of the others knew who was shooting at them. Sales wanted to wipe out Vila de Deus. Kill everyone, dispose of the bodies, burn the mission down. I convinced him to leave well enough alone."

"I suspected as much. What I want to know is why *you* threw in with Sales."

Laura smiles, and I shiver.

"Oh, Breed. You are so naïve and romantic. Can't you see the whole business was *my* idea? Sales was a corrupt politician and Vargas was a thug. Sales couldn't think past his penis. He thought he seduced me, but I allowed him to do so. I won favors for my father and enjoyed the company of a powerful man. I teased Vargas all the time, gave him nothing.

"I *allowed* Sales to get me pregnant. Then I made him take care of it. He paid Fonseca, his private doctor, to perform the procedure. In Brazil, the punishment is four years in prison. Our laws are terribly outdated. I made Sales hold the crime over Fonseca's head, turned him into our slave. We tortured him with threats. Turned the weakling into an alcoholic."

"While *you* held the same crime over Sales."

Laura laughs. "I didn't need to. Sales could be controlled with sex. He was so unimaginative, I did not have to work hard to impress him."

"You told Fiadh he forced you to get rid of the baby."

"Of course. Fiadh's heart went out to me. People are brought closer by the secrets they share. Fiadh tortures herself over questions to which the answers are obvious."

I suck a breath, recoil from Laura's contempt for her friend.

"But Vargas couldn't stop hitting on you. He made advances in your cabin as soon as we boarded."

"The fool never got it through his head that I would never let him fuck me. That made the game so much more enjoyable. Fonseca was next door, cowering with his whiskey. Don't you see the beauty in the situation?"

Laura is a reptile. To think I slept with her.

"Where did FARC get the gold?"

"FARC consolidated control over illegal mining. In Peru and the White Triangle. There was only one problem. Two years ago, Peru discovered a discrepancy between the amount of gold mined and the amount of gold exported. They cracked down on the export of illegal gold. This prevented

FARC from monetizing its gold stores. It also prevented them from buying the weapons they needed.

"FARC approached Sales with a proposal. FARC gold for weapons procured on the black market. Missiles that could be used to assassinate the president of Colombia from two miles away. Sales didn't want to do it. Vargas had the connections to obtain the weapons. Sales could think of no way to transport them to the Selva and bring back the gold."

Laura's eyes gleam like those of a conspirator about to share a secret.

"It was *my* plan," she says. "All of it. Sales is a coward. Happy to trade favors for scraps from the tables of rich men. He was given an opportunity for his own wealth. Can you imagine him refusing the offer? A profit of fifty million dollars.

"I showed him how to do it. All we had to do was create conditions under which we could kill everyone on Nevoa. Come home and leave the gold at a spot near a railroad. Blame the Arqueiros for the deaths. Nobody would ever know."

"The Navy would send another expedition to learn the truth."

"What truth? The river and the jungle swallow bodies whole. We didn't need to kill all the Arqueiros, because they resist contact."

"Did you plan our first meeting in Manaus?"

"No," Laura says. "I improvised. Sales had Vargas hire those men to kill you. Vargas wanted to do it himself. Why is it men like you and Vargas always want to kill each other?"

I say nothing.

Laura continues. "I hadn't met you at the time. Vargas is a professional killer, but I had no confidence in the men he hired. I was right to be concerned. When it became obvious they were out of their depth, I stepped in. Won you over."

"I fell for your act."

"Don't feel bad, Breed. I've been working on my act for years. That night you slept in your hotel, I slept with Sales. I told him I was going to come aboard with you. I would keep you close and learn what I could. At some point, we would dispose of you. Like we disposed of the radio operator, and that diligent first officer. We didn't think Fiadh was alive. When you broke out on your own at Arvore de Ouro, Sales had FARC send out patrols to kill you."

"Who operated the radio?"

"Vargas. Like yourself, he is ruthless and resourceful. Unfortunately, he is unable to control his more violent tendencies. A killer devoid of inhibition. There are not many men like him."

"More than you think. Now there is one less."

Laura lifts an eyebrow. "I would have put money on you. Vargas was always too much of an animal."

"How did Sales get the Marines to surrender?"

Again, I can guess. This time, I hope I'm wrong.

"Sales held a pistol to my head." Laura smiles at the memory. "He told Lieutenant Quadros he would shoot me if the Marines did not lay down their weapons. The gallant officer gave the order. Men are so predictable."

I take her by the arm. "Come on."

There is a movement, a glint of steel in the corner of my eye. Laura's hands come from behind her back. One hand goes to my shoulder, the other lunges with a six-inch stiletto. I twist sharply, feel the point enter my side. The blade slides into me like a heated lance. I cry out, drop the rifle. She holds the knife steady, and I feel it slide out as I fall onto her bunk.

"I'm sorry, Breed." Laura looks at me with pity. "This hasn't worked out for any of us."

She bolts through the doorway and runs to the wardroom.

The blade missed vital organs, but blood is coursing from the hole. I've seen similar wounds caused by spike bayonets. Thank God, this isn't one of the triangular bastards... They make it impossible to stitch up the wound.

I stuff my shirttail into the hole. Get to my feet, pick up the rifle.

Doctor Fonseca steps into the corridor. Aghast, he stares at the wound in my side. The healer in him struggles to surface from a lake of booze. He lurches forward, throws his arm around my shoulders.

"Breed," he says, "let me help you."

I don't think I'll kill him for disobeying my instructions. A doctor's house call would be nice, but I have things to do.

"Not now, Doctor. I have to see about something."

Dazed from exhaustion and blood loss, I push his arm off. Turn him around and guide him back into his cabin. Slam the door. No idea why I'm taking the time to be so helpful. I stagger through the wardroom and onto the boat deck. There's no sign of Laura.

Fiadh runs up the gangplank. She looks toward the stern, then at me. "What's going on?"

She must have seen Laura running aft along the quarterdeck. There's a roar as an outboard explodes into life.

"You're hurt." Fiadh throws an arm around my shoulder. Sucks a breath at the bloodstain spreading over the front of my shirt.

I look aft along the side of the ship. Laura has climbed into the Zodiac and started the outboard. She cuts the mooring line, leans on the tiller, and roars north along the Rio Preto.

"Where's *she* going?" Fiadh asks.

"She's in on it," I tell her. "I'll explain later."

Laura wasn't just in on it. By her own admission, she

planned Sales's operation and all those deaths. She planned to kill Fiadh.

The outboard thrashes the turbid green water. Already, the Zodiac is two hundred yards downstream. A thousand yards away, the Rio Preto curves sharply. Laura will soon be gone from view.

Four hundred yards is a tough shot with iron sights. Especially at a target sitting on a bouncing Zodiac. Laura is gaining ground with every second.

I lurch to the open packing crate and pick up the Javelin. Batteries included, the weapon is live. The guerrillas left the CLU on. The display is bright, the built-in cooling unit operational. I take the caps off the round, expose the infrared seeker.

Agonizing pain shoots through me. I lower myself to the deck on the dock side of the packing crate. I take a sitting position, brace myself against a stanchion. "Sit next to me," I tell Fiadh. "Don't stand behind the tube."

The Javelin's two-stage launch system reduces the weapon's backblast, but it's still a good idea to stand clear.

Fiadh remains silent. She crouches on the deck. Watches Laura draw further and further downriver. I have to achieve missile lock before she rounds the bend.

The Top Attack mode indicator is lit. The Javelin is designed to lock onto an enemy tank with an infrared seeker. The missile flies one or two hundred yards into the air, then plunges onto the target. It has an effective range of a mile and a quarter. The specifications are conservative. In Afghanistan, I personally took out targets at a range of two miles.

Dawn has broken. Although the jungle is hot, the flowing waters of the Rio Preto are cooler than the Zodiac's outboard motor. The CLU display provides good differentiation. I lay the crosshairs on the outboard motor and press the lock-on trigger.

Laura's locked. The Zodiac is almost to the bend, but it doesn't matter anymore. From an altitude of a hundred yards, the missile's seeker will find her. I fire the weapon.

Orange flame flickers from the front and back ends of the tube. The launch motor catapults the round fifteen feet before the flight rocket ignites. The Javelin climbs into the sky, a softly glowing ball of fire.

I lower the launcher to the deck. Slump against the stanchion. Fiadh puts one arm around my shoulder, takes my hand in hers.

Higher and higher, the Javelin rises. Flight time should be five seconds. The missile reaches its apogee, noses over, and falls toward the river. Laura races for the bend. Then she stiffens and lifts her face to the sky. Looks straight up. Does she see the molten spear plunging toward her?

The Zodiac disappears in a blaze of light. From the flash spits a red-and-black ball of flame. Twisted metal, a torso, and other human remains vault skyward. Debris pelts the surface of the river over a twenty-yard radius.

Seconds later, a boom echoes across the water.

Fish food.

37

DAY EIGHT

Rio Preto – Daylight

"I cannot raise Tieves," Captain Silva says.

"What's wrong?"

"I told you, HF communications this deep in the Selva are more art than science. Petty Officer Morais had the touch. I am competent, but I am not an artist."

I'm staring up at him from the sickbay's surgery table. Doctor Fonseca is probing my stab wound with steel instruments of torture. Forehead knit with anxiety, Fiadh sits on the opposite side of the table.

"You're a lucky man, Breed." Fonseca takes a swig of Scotch. "She didn't puncture your peritoneum. Missed important organs."

"Aren't they all important? Give me some of that."

The doctor hands me the bottle. I take a swig.

"Of course. The point is, I can stitch you up until we get to Tieves. They should be able to fly you to Manaus from there."

"We have to get to Tieves first," I say. "Captain, let me try to raise them."

"You are not going anywhere," Fonseca says.

"Get started, Doctor. How long will it take to stitch up that little hole?"

"It is not that simple. I have to debride some tissue. Clean the wound. Then I can suture it."

"I doubt you can climb to the bridge deck," Silva says.

"Then bring me the ManPack," I tell him. "It's got a range of three hundred miles. Enough to reach Tieves."

Fonseca prepares an injection.

"What is that?" I ask.

"Anesthetic," he says. "This is going to hurt."

"No anesthetic. I need to be awake to help with the radio. Captain, please get going. Bring the ManPack."

Silva leaves the sickbay.

Fonseca bends to his work. The pain is excruciating. It goes on and on. I do not know which of us is sweating more.

The captain returns with the olive drab ManPack.

"Open it on the floor," I tell him. "Take out the antennae."

The 40 Watt ManPack is a HF communications *system*. That means the pack includes the radio set, power supply, and HF antennae. There are different antennae, suitable for different combat, geographical and meteorological conditions. There's a five-foot folding whip, a portable dipole, and a long coil that we use to wire up trees. In our current situation, there is only one choice—the long coil.

"Hook one end up to the set." I groan in pain as Fonseca cuts and removes a bloody piece of tissue from the wound. "God, I hope I don't need that."

"You're a hard man, Breed." Fonseca hands me the bottle. "Have some more."

I turn to Fiadh. "Take the long coil. Run it out the door, through the hatch, and up the companionway to the bridge. Go aft... the back of the bridge... climb to the navigation deck.

String the free end of the coil as far up Nevoa's mast as you can manage."

Fiadh takes the coil and I squeeze my eyes shut.

"What now?" Silva asks.

"Do you know the Tieves frequencies by heart? If you don't, go to the radio room and find Morais's notes. We'll try as soon as Fiadh strings up the antenna."

When Fiadh and the captain return, we fire up the ManPack. Silva tries the Tieves frequencies. First the commercial, then the Navy. In both cases, there is nothing but a hiss of static.

"Okay," I say. "Try this for the Navy frequency."

I give Silva a frequency with an offset to the one he tried. He looks at me skeptically. "This is different, Breed."

"Yes. HF is often dependent on the ionosphere. An offset can get you better reception. Look around you at how close the canopy is on the Rio Preto. The Amazon is much wider. On the Rio Preto, you only have so much sky above you. On the Amazon, you have much more."

More hissing. Silva looks worried.

Fonseca does something that makes me cry out sharply. "Butcher."

"Stop whining, Breed."

"Jiggle it a bit," I tell Silva. "Try a bit above and a bit below."

Silva twists the dial. The hiss turns to a crackle. The sound of a broken voice comes through.

"There," I say. "You've got something. Bracket until it's clear."

"Tieves, this is Nevoa. Come in, please."

Garbled chatter. Silva turns the dial. "Tieves, this is Nevoa. Come in."

A strong voice issues from the speaker. "Nevoa, this is Tieves. Go ahead."

Silva opens communications with Tieves. I motion Fiadh over.

"What is it, Breed?"

"We have to get Nevoa going. Even if the captain summons help, we are better to meet them on the river than wait here."

"Why?"

"We don't know what else is out there in the Selva. The sooner we leave, the better."

That's only half the reason. Father Camos warned us wounds sustained in the Selva da Morte go green overnight. I remember his story of maggots debriding Pedro Bernardes's wound. Fonseca may have done a good job, and I may be shot full of antibiotics, but I'm taking no chances.

"As soon as the captain and I finish with Tieves, you and he have to load the gold."

"All two of us?"

"Of course not. You need to translate for him. Speak with Taukan, get the Arqueiros to help. Not the least, you have to warn Taukan to get his men out of Portao before the Navy and Marines arrive. Carry away their wounded and dead. Leave the rest."

"Okay, I'll try."

"It won't be easy. You'll have to work with the captain. He has to make sure Nevoa doesn't bottom out."

In fifteen minutes, Silva has the Navy dispatching fast patrol boats to Portao da Dor. One, carrying a replacement crew, will meet Nevoa on the Rio Preto.

I tell Silva and Fiadh what I want them to do about the cargo. When they have left the sickbay, I take one last swig of Fonseca's whiskey and slump on the table.

.   .   .

FONSECA FINISHES SEWING ME UP. He's as exhausted as I am. Removes his latex gloves and mops his face. "I can do no more. It is a good job. They may redo it when you reach Manaus, but frankly, they do not have to. They can monitor you. Provided you do not develop an infection, you will be fine."

"Help me to my cabin," I say. "I want to rest."

I throw my arm around Fonseca and he helps me to my feet. We shuffle to my cabin and I lie on my bunk.

The doctor sits on the chair next to me.

"Will you tell anyone about me and Laura?" Fonseca asks. I lie back.

"It wasn't just Laura, was it?"

"No." The doctor looks miserable. The cabin is cool, but his red face glistens with sweat. "Sales and Laura held it over me. Whenever he got a girl in trouble, they made me bail him out. Laura was terrible. She brought him girls, many of them very young. No more than thirteen or fourteen. You can imagine the rest."

"Why did they bring you on this trip?"

"They were sick, Breed. Sales and Laura enjoyed toying with people. They brought me along to play more games. I suppose with me as ship's doctor, there was one less person they would have to kill."

"I won't go out of my way to tell the authorities," I say, "but I won't lie. To be honest, you'll be the least of their concerns."

"Thank you, Breed."

I crane my neck, glance at the bottle of Bourbon on my desk. Exactly where I left it before I set off with Laura for Arvore de Ouro.

. . .

FIVE HOURS LATER, Nevoa is steaming north on the Rio Preto. Captain Silva is at the helm. Fiadh joins me and Doctor Fonseca in my cabin.

"How did the cargo loading go?" I ask Fiadh.

CONTACT ESTABLISHED, Fiadh and Silva turned to the cargo. Taukan and his men helped load the gold onto Nevoa's boat deck. It was a crude job, but Silva was a competent captain. I doubt there was any piece of equipment on the Nevoa he could not operate, including the cranes. After four hours of sweaty work, the gold joined the weapons on the boat deck.

The captain frequently went to the waterline to check Nevoa's draft. He took the remaining Zodiac around to the starboard side. By measuring the draft, port and starboard, he maintained an even keel and kept the Nevoa off the bottom.

We were lucky. Nevoa's draft, five feet with the weapons, extended to six feet with the gold. The melting snows of the Andes helped. Nevoa could navigate the Rio Preto while carrying both cargoes.

"IT WAS HARD WORK," Fiadh says, "but it went well. Taukan and the Arqueiros will clean up at Portao and leave. When the Marines arrive, they'll find a lot of dead guerrillas. Evidence to prove this was all a conspiracy between FARC and Minister Sales."

Fonseca gets to his feet. "I'll be in the wardroom."

"Doctor."

Hand on the door, Fonseca looks back at me.

"You're free of Sales and Laura," I tell him. "It might be a good time to think about starting over."

The doctor shuts the door behind him.

I look out the porthole of my cabin. We're still in the

narrow waterway of the Selva da Morte. The atmosphere is gloomy, but I feel relieved. Knowing the Nevoa is on its way to the brighter Amazon lifts my spirits.

Fiadh sits closer, holds my hand. "It's hard to believe Laura tried to kill me."

"I suspected when you told me your story. It was different from the story everyone else told."

"How so?"

"When Pedro told Father Camos what happened, a lot got lost in translation. Chinese Whispers. The story was, your team blundered into a fight between gunmen and Arqueiros. That's not what happened. FARC encountered *you* on the trail and tried to kill you. It was a meeting engagement. The Arqueiros heard the shooting. They found you."

"Yes, that *is* what happened."

"Which means FARC knew which trail you would use. Laura told them to set an ambush for you at Arvore de Ouro. Instead, they went right into the bush to kill you. Either Sales transmitted the wrong instructions, or the FARCs were over-confident. They would have killed you all, if the Arqueiros didn't intervene."

"I thought Laura and I were friends. The lies she told me about the baby. Sales and Fonseca. She twisted the truth, so it came out different. I was in pain for her."

"That's how the best lies work," I tell her. "They tell the truth in such a way the effect is different."

"She was evil." Fiadh shudders. "Thinking back, nothing she said or did came from an honest place."

"If you believe in good, is it so hard to accept the existence of evil? We can't know anyone perfectly, but Laura and Vargas were as close to pure evil as I can imagine. Sales was corrupt. A different kind of evil."

"And Doctor Fonseca?"

"Fonseca's weak. He made a mistake, Laura and Sales exploited him. I don't think he's beyond redemption."

"Redemption," Fiadh says. "The Selva is what Eden must have been like. Out there, good and evil get so mixed up. But when you boil everything down to motives, it all becomes clear."

I say nothing.

Fiadh leans forward, lays her cheek against my shoulder. "What about us?"

"We're human. We try to do the right thing. It's not always easy."

"That's not what I mean."

"No?"

"I love you, Breed."

How many women have told me that? Girlfriends in high school. We were too young to know what we were talking about. I went into the Army right after graduation. To hear those words from this girl, who seems my mirror, is astonishing.

I squeeze her hand and she squeezes back. Compared to mine, her skin feels smooth. I let go and stroke her fingers. Palm-to-palm, we caress each other.

"You know I won't stay long in Chicago," she says. "I belong here in Brazil."

"I know that."

Can two people love each other and want different things? I don't think I can stay in Brazil because I love Fiadh.

She understands.

"Will you stay with me while I'm in Chicago?" Fiadh asks. "We can be together awhile."

"As long you want, Fiadh Arqueiro."

38

EIGHTEEN MONTHS LATER

Manaus

F ather Andrew, I hope you enjoyed the photos and videos of little Peter. Remember, I told you once I would never go unprotected until I met the man for me. When Breed and I visited you and Dad in Chicago, you probably saw right away we were in love. You've always been able to look into the hearts of men, so this should not be a surprise for you.

I love Breed and our little boy. I want to tell Breed and Dad, but don't know how. Maybe you can help? I need your advice.

The Selva still draws me, though I haven't been to visit since Peter's birth. I am spending most of my time in Manaus, working with Manuel Barros and FUNAI. I've given up my work with the Mission of Our Lady of Hope.

You know I don't like Father Aguiar, so I decided to stop taking his money. I work with volunteers, and fund them myself, or through FUNAI. We work with Father Camos at Vila de Deus. I've often said if I could feel closer to God while standing on my head, that is what I would do. I feel closer to God working with Father Camos.

Father Camos says his people still find evidence of Arqueiros in the Selva. Taukan and his people carry on, as they have for hundreds of years. I know that if I return, they will welcome me. My biggest fear was that the contact last year would bring them disease. That has not happened, and I breathe easier every day.

My sleep is still disturbed by terrible dreams, the movie in my mind. But the dreams fade quickly in the light of day, when I go to Peter.

Peter and I are happy, Father Andrew. I think we'll be happier when I tell Breed and Dad, though I don't know when that will be. As ever, I don't want to leave Brazil, and Breed is his own free spirit.

Bearing Peter without his father present was difficult. As was bearing him without the sacrament of marriage. But God will forgive me this too, I think. Especially since he knows, as you and I do, that this has been my choice, and Peter's father is a good man.

Please, Father Andrew, would you baptize Peter? You know I'm going to raise him with God's teachings.

I have to go for now. Never fear, you are all in my thoughts.

Love always, Fiadh

Pater,
Quaeso auxilium mihi quieti in beatitudinem,
Ut a risus ut morari in labiis meis,
Habitare intra admirabile memoria,
Ambulare retro per solem.
Amen

Father,
Please help me to rest in your happiness,
To allow a smile to linger on my lips,
To dwell within a wonderful memory,
To walk back through the sunshine.
Amen

The End

ACKNOWLEDGMENTS

This novel would not have been possible without the support, encouragement, and guidance of my agent, Ivan Mulcahy, of MMB Creative. At his urging, I made an effort to provide a more nuanced picture of Breed's inner life.

I would also like to thank my publishers, Brian Lynch and Garret Ryan of Inkubator Books for supporting the series. Thanks also go to Jodi Compton for her editorial efforts, Claire Milto for her artistic efforts, and Stephen Ryan for his support in the novel's launch.

Not the least, I wish to thank members of my writing group and beta readers. In particular, Sarah Moraghan, who helped me make Fiadh's life in Dublin real.

If you could spend a moment to write an honest review on Amazon, no matter how short, I would be extremely grateful. They really do help readers discover my books.

Feel free to contact me at cameron.curtis545@gmail.com. I'd love to hear from you.

ALSO BY CAMERON CURTIS

Breed Thrillers Box Set (Books 1 - 4)

Made in the USA
Middletown, DE
05 April 2025